BARDO BY THE SEA

Borne Back Books
West Egg, New York

First Borne Back Books trade paperback edition May 2022

Cover Design: Damonza.com
Author Photo: Selfie

Manufactured in the United States of America

Publisher's Cataloging-in-Publication Data
provided by Five Rainbows Cataloging Services

Names: Gibbs, Chad Alan, author.
Title: Bardo by the sea / Chad Alan Gibbs.
Description: Auburn, AL : Borne Back Books, 2022. | Summary: Sixteen-year-old Izzy Brown attempts to solve a murder while battling anxiety and opioid addiction. | Audience: Grades 9 & up.
Identifiers: LCCN 2021925071 (print) | ISBN 978-0-9857165-8-5 (paperback) | ISBN 978-0-9857165-9-2 (ebook)
Subjects: LCSH: Young adult fiction. | CYAC: Teenagers--Fiction. | Coming of age--Fiction. | Murder--Fiction. | Drug addiction--Fiction. | Mystery fiction. | BISAC: YOUNG ADULT FICTION / Mysteries & Detective Stories. | YOUNG ADULT FICTION / Coming of Age. | YOUNG ADULT FICTION / Social Themes / Drugs, Alcohol, Substance Abuse. | YOUNG ADULT FICTION / Neurodiversity.
Classification: LCC PZ7.1.G4991 Bar 2022 (print) | LCC PZ7.1.G4991 (ebook) | DDC [Fic]--dc23.

BARDO BY THE SEA

a novel

CHAD ALAN GIBBS

Once more
for Tricia

*"I didn't like the story I was given,
so I wrote a new one."*
—Nellie Bly

BARDO BY THE SEA

1983

Ricky Lee was freezing.

He was eleven the last time snow fell on the Florida Panhandle, and he wondered if he'd see it again tonight. The wind was calm, but the dark December clouds hung low and heavy over the rolling Gulf of Mexico.

"Looks like snow," the man behind the register at the 7-Eleven said when Ricky tried to pay for his six-pack of Budweiser.

The man didn't charge Ricky.

Didn't card him either.

The perks of being the star quarterback.

Stopping to flip over the cassette in his Walkman, Ricky cursed when Talking Heads' *Speaking in Tongues* fell from his numb fingers into the sand. It was no colder tonight than the night before when Ricky led Bardo Academy to a last-second victory in the state semi-finals. Still, he couldn't stop his teeth from chattering. He'd give any-thing for the warmth of his letterman's jacket, but it was hanging in his locker.

Ricky snatched the cassette, blew off the sand, and popped it back into his Walkman. He smiled when "Burning Down the House" filled his ears, and David Byrne's guitar intro quickened his pace.

The note said to park at the public beach access, and Ricky obeyed because the note was everything. He'd already gone a mile, past the last beach house, and onto the unspoiled sands of Topsail Hill. Ricky hated the feeling of walking on sand in tennis shoes, but it was too cold to go barefoot. He soldiered on.

Was it one hundred yards from here or two hundred? Ricky reached for the note in his back pocket but remembered he'd left it at school. He tried to read it in his mind, but the details were foggy. Only the closing stood out. *Yours forever, with love.*

The note was signed with love.

This was an escalation.

A terrifying but most welcome escalation.

One hundred paces and no sign of whatever it was Ricky was supposed to look for, but up ahead, someone had beached a small daysailer. Ricky's pulse quickened. They'd always been so careful. Way more careful than this. What if someone saw them?

This was a public beach.

This was a risk.

A huge risk.

Two hundred paces and nothing. Ricky took off his headphones and listened to the crashing waves. He wished he had a flashlight, but he only had beer, so he opened one and took a long swig.

A whistle from the dunes caught his ear.

Ricky smiled and followed the call to find a blanket in the beach-grass, a flickering candle in a jar, and another note. He set the beer down, realizing the blanket was a roof tarp. Not quite as romantic, but it was the thought that counted.

"This is nice," Ricky said to the night sky, but when no reply came, he grabbed the note and read it in the candlelight.

"Only for you," Ricky said with a laugh. Following the instructions, he retrieved the blindfold from underneath the candle and tied it around his head. "And we're putting it on you next," he added as the footsteps approached from behind.

A hand fell soft on his cheek, sliding back through his hair.

From his knees, Ricky looked up and smiled, anticipating a kiss.

Not the sharp blade.

Not the vicious slash.

Not the end of all things.

Blood sprayed the tarp, but Ricky never saw it. He was unconscious before he could wrestle the blindfold off, dead a minute later, and within the hour, wrapped in the tarp and dumped in the Gulf.

Ricky's body wouldn't wash up for another week. A retired couple made the grisly discovery searching for shells. And while the murder was all anyone on 30A could talk about, the *Walton Observer* buried the story on page two.

And what was the front-page headline in declaration-of-war size font?

"Bardo Academy Wins First State Title"

Some things are more important than life or death.

CHAPTER ONE

I'm bad with dates, but January 2nd, 2008, is hard to forget. Our sad little three-foot Christmas tree still sat in the corner, the box of ornaments we never bothered to hang up underneath it. Leftover fireworks from New Year's Eve were piled high on our kitchen table, next to an empty bottle of five-dollar champagne. And one of the richest men in Florida stopped by and changed our lives forever.

Of course, it was all set in motion decades ago when a Category 3 hurricane called Eloise made landfall near Panama City Beach, Florida, causing over $150 million in property damage. Included in that figure were two dozen acres of timberland in Washington County owned by Dalton Wolfe. The loss of a few acres did not affect Dalton Wolfe in any tangible way. He owned over 97,000 acres of timberland spread across the Panhandle, along with hundreds of properties on the coast. What bothered Dalton Wolfe was those ten acres, once full of longleaf pines, now sat barren, not earning him a dime. The idea to cover the recently cleared land with one hundred mobile homes was

Dalton's. His wife, Ella Kay, came up with the name Pineview Villas. Pineview, get it? Because the trailers were surrounded by—yeah, screw you, Ella Kay.

My name is Izzy Brown, and I grew up in one of Dalton Wolfe's trailers with my mom and twin brother, Axl. We lived on the outskirts of Dandridge, Florida, a town you've likely driven through on your way to the beach, though I doubt you stopped. It wasn't exactly a Norman Rockwell childhood, but having that many neighbors in such close proximity did mean an abundance of kids to play with. The problem was, Dalton Wolfe didn't waste an inch of land, so there wasn't anywhere for us to play. Neighborhood games of tag took place on the gravel roads running between rows of trailers, which wasn't ideal because our redneck neighbors took the absence of speed limit signs as an invitation to race their Camaros. And frolicking in the surrounding pine forests, full of diamondback rattlesnakes, was not an option.

Neither Axl nor I had ever heard of Dalton Wolfe until he showed up on our porch that cold January day. I suppose Mom was vaguely aware of the man since she wrote rent checks each month to D. C. Wolfe Properties, but naively, I'd always assumed we owned our trailer. Turns out, we didn't even own our microwave.

The four of us sat in the den—Mom, Axl, and me on the couch, Dalton Wolfe in the recliner across the room. I remember being mesmerized by his shoes. They were brown and shinier than Mom's car after she made us wash it. And though I knew next to nothing about anything, I knew shoes with that much fancy stitching likely cost more than everything the three of us owned combined.

Dalton Wolfe scooted to the edge of the recliner, concealed a belch with his fist, and said to my brother, "Helluva season, son. Helluv-a season."

"Thank you … sir," Axl said, the word "sir" added hastily and sounding like he'd just remembered Mom spent the better part of the morning lecturing him to call Mr. Wolfe, sir—because she had.

"Helluva season," he repeated for the third time, nodding his head in apparent agreement with himself. Dalton Wolfe was the largest man I'd ever seen in person. Tall as the door frame and fat from excess, it seemed, not McPoverty like so many of our neighbors. Axl was six-foot-four and full of muscle, but even he looked like a child compared to this giant who reeked of cigar smoke and aftershave. I glimpsed a ring not much smaller than my fist on one of Mr. Wolfe's bratwurst-sized fingers, and he caught me staring.

"Looking at my ring, hon?" he barked.

"Yeah, I lost one just like it," I said, because my mouth was usually several steps ahead of my brain. "Where'd you find it?"

"Izzy," Mom said, with a hush-your-mouth glare, but Dalton Wolfe laughed and, with considerable effort, pried his ring off and tossed it across the room to me.

"The 1993 National Champions," he said, while I turned the vulgar thing over in my palm, marveling at more diamonds and rubies than I knew existed on Earth, much less in one ring.

"Were you on the team?" I asked, realizing how stupid the question was as it left my mouth, but with no way to pull it back in.

Dalton Wolfe belly laughed, and I blushed. "Yeah, hon, I was on the team. Forty years ago. I send a lot of checks to Tallahassee, though, so when we finally won it all, Bobby made sure I got a ring too."

I wasn't sure who Bobby was, but Dalton Wolfe said this like he was one of our mutual friends, so I said, "Good old Bobby" and walked the ring back across the room to him.

Working the ring over his giant knuckle, he said to Axl, "I know Bobby has his eye on you, son."

Axl smiled. As a freshman, he'd led the Dandridge Manatees to the state championship game for the first time in school history, setting all sorts of passing records along the way. Mom kept an ever-growing stack of his newspaper clippings on our coffee table, and from time to time, I picked one at random and tossed it in the trash.

"But from what I hear," Dalton Wolfe continued, "you won't go anywhere with your test scores."

Axl's smile vanished.

My brother was—how do I put this delicately—a moron. Okay, not a moron, but lazy. Well, not exactly lazy. He worked harder at football than most people ever work at anything. Axl just lacked academic motivation, I guess. But when a secret cabal of educators and coaches conspired to maintain his eligibility at any cost, I'm sure algebra homework never felt like a priority. He knew in middle school that football was his way out of Pineview Villas. Still, Dalton Wolfe had revealed the fatal flaw in my brother's strategy, namely that big-time college football would require at least some classroom effort. So far, Axl had put forth none.

"One of Axl's teachers told me about a tutor in town that could help him get his test scores up," Mom interjected, putting an arm around her only son, "but Mr. Wolfe, times are hard, and I ain't got the money to—"

"Times are hard, Brandi," Dalton Wolfe said, cutting Mom off by raising his fat hand, the sunlight reflecting off his Rolex and making me squint. "I understand. But Axl's got a gift, and I'd hate to see him throw it away."

I thought Dalton Wolfe was about to offer to pay for Axl's tutor. I assumed that was why he was sitting in our trailer, drinking coffee out of Mom's favorite mug. Just by mentioning it, Mom all but asked him to, though her pride would never allow her to make the request outright. But Dalton Wolfe wanted more than for my brother to squeak out the minimum score on his ACT. Dalton Wolfe wanted Axl to play quarterback for his Florida State Seminoles. To assure that, Dalton Wolfe needed Axl in his debt. Deep in his debt.

"I suppose you all have heard of Bardo Academy?" Dalton Wolfe asked.

Of course, we had. Bardo, formally known as Bardo by the Sea, was a laboratory-developed beach community in Walton County that seemingly materialized out of nothing one night in the mid-seventies. Its narrow, redbrick roads were lined with idyllic pastel bungalows that initially went for a hundred grand but now sold frequently for thirty times that, and on its white sands sat a row of Gatsby-esque mansions that can likely be seen from space. The rumor was producers of *The Truman Show* chose to shoot in neighboring Seaside because Bardo by the Sea was a little too perfect.

Bardo Academy, which Dalton Wolfe spoke of, was a private K–12 academy boasting annual tuition fees in the ballpark of a certified pre-owned Mercedes. Thanks to its ability to cherry-pick star players from surrounding public schools, it was also a football powerhouse.

"Well," Dalton Wolfe said, cracking his knuckles like bubble wrap, "I just so happen to be on the board of trustees there, and Axl, I'm here to offer you a full scholarship."

I couldn't breathe. I hated my brother the way only a sister can, but I loved him too, and the thought of him leaving me alone in Dandridge had me gasping for air. Axl and Mom were crying, and Mr. Wolfe was touting Bardo Academy's unparalleled academic reputation in a canned speech, but his words were garbled like the trailer had suddenly filled up with water and only I had noticed.

Typically my anxiety built slowly over weeks, culminating in a tearful breakdown and a week's worth of headaches; however, this attack struck at horrifying speed, paralyzing me in the process. But then an emotion even stronger than fear took control of the situation—unbridled rage.

"Bullshit," I said through a cough.

"Izzy Brown, you watch your damn mouth," Mom barked.

"Ain't you happy for your brother, little lady?" Dalton Wolfe asked.

No, I wasn't. Dandridge High School was okay. Some of our teachers rocked. Others were ten years past caring. But unlike Axl, I'd worked my ass off there because no one was going to pluck me out of Pineview Villas. I'd have to dig my way out. My grades were solid, and I'd undoubtedly earn a partial scholarship somewhere, likely Pensacola Junior College. A four-year school wasn't out of the question if I could improve my own ACT score, but so far, I'd only managed three consecutive twenty-fives while hyperventilating through parts of the math and science sections.

Bardo Academy, though, existed on a wholly different academic plane. It had an absurdly intimate student-teacher ratio. Most of those teachers even had their doctorates. And every fall, Bardo graduates set off for Cambridge, or New Haven, or West Point.

"Oh sure," I said, "I'm thrilled my semi-literate brother's ability to read a Cover 2 defense earned him a scholarship to the best academic school in the state."

"Izzy," Mom snapped, but I didn't look her way.

"Now, don't be angry," Dalton said as I stood and headed toward my bedroom.

"I'm not angry," I said. "This all aligns nicely with my expectations of life's fairness. Now, if you'll excuse me, I need to study for the ACT, so I don't end up living in one of your shitty trailers the rest of my life."

As I reached the door, I heard my mother ask, "Mr. Wolfe, what about Izzy?" I stopped and turned back to see Dalton Wolfe looking me over, perhaps to see if I had the body of an All-American linebacker, and he'd somehow missed it. But seeing my skinny-girl self, he coughed and said, "Well, Brandi, from what they tell me, Izzy is doing fine at Dandridge, and I—"

"I ain't splitting up my kids, Mr. Wolfe," Mom said, and I loved her for it, even if she was about to cost Axl his chance to play for Bobby, whoever that was. Dalton Wolfe took a deep breath and, with great effort, climbed to his feet. He was about to tell Mom to forget it, and Axl would hate me forever, but instead, he raised a meaty finger and said, "Y'all give me a minute."

Dalton Wolfe stepped onto our little porch, and Axl stared daggers through me while I watched an ant crawl across our cloudy linoleum floor. Minutes passed like years, pine trees grew and fell, and finally, Mr. Wolfe burst back in and said, "Izzy, you can start at Bardo in the fall. Axl, you start next week. That's the best I can do, kids. We got us a deal?"

I squealed and ran across the room, ignoring Dalton Wolfe's outstretched hand as I wrapped my arms around him and squeezed. Axl soon joined me, both of us now crying.

If we'd only known what the next year would hold, we'd have cried for a whole other reason.

CHAPTER TWO

In January, Dalton Wolfe arranged for Axl to move into his Bardo Beach mansion. From what I gathered, listening to Mom's side of her nightly phone calls with my brother, he struggled mightily that first semester. Under immense pressure from folks like Dalton Wolfe, Bardo Academy teachers were not about to let Axl fail. But they weren't going to let him coast either, and their insistence he try a little in the classroom was almost too much for the poor boy.

"Son, I ain't letting you quit," I heard my mother say at least five times that winter. But by spring, Axl had seemingly adjusted to life with a minimum of academic responsibilities, and his requests to return to Pineview Villas ceased.

Socially, his transition was much easier, because, well, because he was the starting quarterback. It's a chicken or the egg dilemma, I suppose, quarterbacks and their alpha social status. Is the precise blend of confidence and attitude necessary to achieve maximum high school popularity their reward for throwing perfect spirals? Or are they merely the beneficiaries of an unequal share of self-assurance and arm strength doled out at birth by an inattentive creator? Either way, the minute Axl stepped foot in Bardo Academy, he was the big man on campus, and the hopes and fears of the state playoffs rested on his broad shoulders. By March, he was dating Sophie Wolfe, Dalton's granddaughter, and the most popular girl at school. Come April, he was sneaking through her bedroom window nightly.

Mom and I moved south in late August. Dalton Wolfe initially found us a place in Vermillion, a boomtown across the Choctawhatchee Bay. But the morning of our move, he called to say, "I bought a place from my boy, Junior, that's nearer the beach." Turns out, we'd live only a few hundred yards from where Ricky Lee's body washed up a quarter of a century ago.

I used to think Dalton Wolfe was a mobster. He wasn't, I'm almost sure, but he did have men, and he was always saying he'd have one of these men do this or that. When the catalytic converter in Mom's car went bad, Dalton Wolfe sent one of his men to replace it, and when a tropical storm blew a palm tree over in our driveway, one of Dalton Wolfe's men appeared with a chainsaw. The day of our move, one of Mr. Wolfe's men drove the tiny U-Haul, which, though it contained all our worldly possessions, wasn't even half full. We followed the moving van through Bardo by the Sea, past one-percenters walking their designer mutts or getting in their morning run before the midday sun punished their latitudinal transgressions, and kept going east for a half-mile to Rosemary Beach, close to where 30A and Highway 98 join together as if they're afraid to go into Panama City Beach alone.

"I guess we're stopping at Mr. Wolfe's house first," Mom said, as we followed the van through the gates of Tartarus Shores, a neighborhood consisting of a single brick road leading toward an ornate fountain in a circle and the shimmering sea beyond. For sale signs dotted the empty lots between 30A and the Gulf of Mexico, and on the left, just past the entrance, stood the only house on the street, a tall, robin's-egg blue Craftsman with white trim and shutters. Dalton Wolfe and my brother waited on the front porch swing.

"Now, Brandi," Mr. Wolfe said, meeting us on the street with bear hugs, "I know you remember when we whooped those Nebraska Cornhuskers back in '93."

Mom did not, so Dalton Wolfe reminded her. "18-16, in the Orange Bowl. Now don't forget that score. It's the code to get you through that gate over yonder."

I think we both assumed Mr. Wolfe told us this so we could access his share of the Emerald Coast from time to time. But instead, he turned, and waving a meaty hand toward the house behind him, said, "Welcome home."

The Germans probably have a word for the sick feeling you get when you know a perceived blessing will only encourage someone's flawed worldview. My mother used to buy scratch-off lottery tickets the way a sensible person would contribute to their 401(k). She laid the firstfruits of her biweekly paycheck on the goddess of fortune's altar, even though doing so kept our utility bills perpetually past due. As early as fourth grade, I tried staging an economic intervention, but she wasn't having it. She thought—no, she believed—financial freedom hid behind those pink flamingos, and one day she'd scratch our way to riches. My stomach turned whenever I'd hear her shout from the next room after winning twenty or even a hundred bucks, because I knew it would only reinforce her flawed monetary policy. At least she didn't blow money on cigarettes too.

My mother stopped buying lottery tickets several years ago, though. Not because she realized they were just a tax on people who were bad at math, but because Axl threw six touchdowns in his first start for the Dandridge Junior Varsity team. After the game, his coach told Mom, "Brandi, that boy of yours is gonna make millions one day."

From that day forward, Axl, not a flamboyance of scrape-off flamingos, was our path to prosperity, and money she would have given to the Florida Lottery now went toward new cleats and football camps.

"You do know Axl is more likely to be struck by lightning than make the NFL," I'd say whenever I'd catch her cutting out magazine photos of the mansions famous athletes bought their mothers.

"What are plans if not wishful thinking?" she'd always reply.

And after Dalton Wolfe helped Mom back to her feet, for she collapsed in tears after realizing this was our new home, she turned to me and flashed the smug smile of the rewarded faithful.

Admittedly, after living my entire life in a decades-old mobile home, I was impressed by any home without wheels. But the house Dalton Wolfe rented us was amazing by any standard. I looked it up the other day and saw it was for sale again, over a decade later. Here's the listing. The asking price is $4.4 million if you're interested.

Gorgeous 3-story home located on desirable 30A. Wraparound porches on every level with three huge bedrooms. Spacious open concept living, with ample natural light and plenty of outdoor living space. 3rd-floor tower room with deck and breathtaking Gulf views. Massive master suite with jacuzzi bath, double shower, and a sunset porch for enjoying Gulf breezes. Recently updated stainless steel appliances, marble countertops, and hardwood floors throughout. Numerous restaurants and shops less than a five-minute walk away, or listen to live music on your private deck. Move-in or rental ready.

Dalton Wolfe gave us the tour. The living room was soft blue, with a plank ceiling and inviting white sofas and chairs I knew we'd ruin with stains within the week. The chef's kitchen came fully stocked with all manner of food and culinary gadgetry and flowed into the dining room, which featured a long table that didn't look like it would collapse if you dropped your books on it after school. Upstairs, the bedrooms all had en suite bathrooms with showers large enough to hold a beached whale, working televisions, and, get this, actual beds, not twin mattresses tossed on the floor. And sure, I felt a twinge of guilt over benefiting from my mother's misplaced faith in my brother's right arm, but my room had a private balcony with Gulf views, so I got over it.

"Mr. Wolfe, this is all too much," Mom said as we sat on the front porch, sipping lemonade, while Dalton's men unloaded our belongings.

"Nonsense," Dalton Wolfe barked. "I did Junior a favor taking this place off his hands. It sat empty for over a year."

Axl's iPhone rang, and I realized my brother now owned an iPhone. "It's Sophie," he said, walking inside to take her call. Dalton Wolfe stood to leave, and Mother thanked him one last time.

"You ain't gotta thank me, Brandi," he said with a wink. "Thank that boy of yours. Long as he keeps tossing touchdowns, y'all ain't got nothing to worry about."

The damn enabler.

CHAPTER THREE

"Were you never going to mention the car?"

Even though Mom's old Toyota Camry had a Kelly Blue Book value of about six bucks, I'm still not sure how she could afford it. So, it came as no surprise there was no car waiting for me outside our trailer when I turned sixteen in early August. However, my brother and I were currently in his brand-new garnet red Dodge Charger, cruising west on 30A toward Bardo. Axl was having dinner at Sophie Wolfe's, and late that afternoon, he remembered to tell me, "Sophie said you should come too." I'd hastily showered and agonized over an outfit, not exactly sure what to wear to dine with a family Axl claimed was "richer than shit," whatever that meant. But when Axl showed no intentions of changing from his gym shorts and sweat-stained Bardo football tee, I settled on a pair of khaki shorts and a black tank without fear of arriving underdressed.

"Nothing to mention," Axl said, his sunburnt arm hanging out the window, fingers tapping a beat on the door while his mop of brown hair blew in the breeze. He'd always resembled a Ken doll, with his washboard abs and big, beautiful quarterback head, but even more so in this Barbie dream car. "I needed a car to get around and go to workouts and stuff, so Mr. Wolfe helped me out."

"Aren't there rules against giving football players cars?" I asked, turning down Flo Rida because I was sick of hearing about Apple Bottom jeans and boots with the fur (with the fur.)

"I don't know," Axl said, cranking the volume back up. "In college, maybe. Besides, he didn't give me the car. He's just letting me borrow it."

Dalton Wolfe, who, as you know, had several men capable of completing any odd job in a matter of minutes, routinely ignored complaints from the residents of Pineview Villas for months on end until most gave up and hired a plumber or electrician with money they couldn't spare. So I wasn't exactly buying this portrait Axl was selling of Dalton Wolfe, the philanthropic car-disbursing tycoon. The car, the house, the scholarship, they all had strings attached.

"Can I borrow it sometime?" I asked.

"No," Axl said.

I huffed and snatched his phone off the center console. "So, this is an iPhone?"

"Yep," he said, snatching it back before I could even figure out how to turn it on. "I'm getting the 3G next month. You can probably have this one unless Mr. Wolfe wants it back."

Try as I may, I couldn't hide my smile, and I hated myself a little for it. But I was also getting an iPhone, so whatever.

"Clyde, my man."

We stopped at the pearly gates of a beachfront Bardo neighborhood called Eden Shores, and Clyde, the two-hundred-year-old man in the gatehouse, scribbled down my brother's driver's license and tag number on his little notepad while we waited.

"Mr. Axl, how's your ankle?" Clyde asked while he wrote.

"Good as new," Axl said. He'd suffered a grade 2 ankle sprain in March and missed most of spring practice, but the whole of Bardo breathed a sigh of relief when the X-rays came back negative.

"That's what I want to hear," Clyde said, handing my brother his license back with a toothy grin before opening the gates to Eden Shores with the press of a button, and waving us through to its mansions beyond mansions.

"I never knew people were this rich," I thought aloud while catching glimpses of the sugar-white sand and emerald-green sea between the ten-thousand-square-foot palaces.

"Crazy thing is," Axl said, stopping at the security gate of the last house on the street, "some of these are just vacation homes. The people who own them are only here a couple of weeks a year. The rest of the time, they sit empty since Bardo has a no rental policy."

"No rental policy?"

"Yeah, some 30A neighborhoods have a no rental policy, but here it's the entire town. Sophie told me if you can't afford a home in Bardo without rental income, you can't afford a home in Bardo."

I tried to process this information, but the fact this family lived inside a gated house inside a gated community had overheated my brain. Who were they trying to keep out? Were gangs of pastel-shorted thugs wandering the streets of Bardo, roughing up people for wearing the wrong brand of boat shoes? I was about to ask Axl when a girl's raspy voice crackled through the speaker on the gate.

"It's me," Axl said.

"Come on up, babe," the sexy voice replied. "We're on the middle deck."

We parked outside the green stucco Death Star, between a chromed-out Humvee laughing in the face of four-dollar unleaded and a sporty European number laughing in the face of any car with doors that didn't open like butterfly wings. And while I stood watching the security gate close behind us, Axl walked through the front door like he owned the place. I hurried to catch up but didn't make it past the foyer, where a spiral staircase with an impossibly ornate railing climbed toward the heavens. I stared through the corkscrew at a crystal chandelier that, like Everest, had undoubtedly claimed the lives of dozens of men who'd attempted to scale its peak to change the light bulbs.

"Izzy," Axl said from ahead, and tentatively I kept moving into the house, my footsteps echoing on the porcelain floor. My footsteps echoed because the room I'd just entered—and I hesitate to call it a living room because I can't imagine people living in it—was roughly the size of the New Orleans Superdome. Actual paintings, not framed art posters from Target, hung from every wall, and a gleaming white grand piano sat in front of an enormous picture window looking out on the Gulf of Mexico. Axl kept walking, but again I hesitated, overwhelmed by the mass assemblage of marble, mahogany, and crystal. Running my fingers across the back of an antique sofa that I doubt came from Rooms To Go, I said to myself, "This place looks like the set of *Gossip Girl*."

Axl huffed, and when I looked his way, he pleaded, "Izzy, try and be cool. Okay?"

"Yeah, sure, okay," I said and followed him through the Louvre out onto the middle deck—the word "middle" implying there were at least three decks, maybe five. Near the railing, reclined in a beach chair, lay a blonde girl in a white bikini top and little blue running shorts, soaking up the terminal rays of the setting sun while sipping something pink from a champagne flute. At a long table in the shade sat a dark-haired boy with bushy eyebrows wearing a blinding white polo shirt and playing a game on his phone while tapping his foot to "Viva La Vida," a song I heard an estimated six million times that summer.

"Hey, hey," Axl said, strolling onto the deck like he'd spent his entire life, not just the last six months, living in a beachside mansion. The girl in the bikini stood, spilling some drink on her hand and sipping it off before sauntering toward us. She slung her free arm around my brother's neck and kissed him for so long I began to wonder if I was on a practical joke show.

"Sophie," Axl said, when the make-out session mercifully ended, "this is my sister, Izzy."

We all like to believe we're not the type of person who judges books and/or people by their covers. Still, when Sophie Wolfe squealed and hugged my neck like she'd waited to meet me her entire life, I concluded with minimal deliberation that she was every bit as fake as her boobs, which I wanted to stop staring at, but they were apparently filled with a magnetic silicone that attracted every iris in a forty-foot radius.

"Whatcha drinkin'?" Sophie asked, raising her glass and dropping her g's, and Axl pointed toward the boy at the table's bottle and asked, "Do you have more Corona?"

"Hell yeah," Sophie said, before asking the boy at the table, "Another Corona for you too?"

"Sure," he said, without looking up from his phone, "Dad is out of town."

"Izzy?" Sophie asked, turning to me?

"I'll take some cobra wine if you have it."

Sophie opened her mouth to reply but couldn't, and Axl shot me a look.

"Or water, I guess. Water is fine. Are your parents not home?"

"No, they're here," she said, blinking at me like I'd asked her to explain the theory of relativity. Walking over toward an intercom on the wall, she added, "Mom is upstairs, taking one of her rosé and Xanax baths. And Dad is in his office, bending over for the bank."

"Where are the twins?" Axl asked about Sophie's nine-year-old brothers whose names I'd never learn.

"Probably in the playroom," Sophie said, "killing hookers on *Grand Theft Auto*." She pressed the intercom button and said, "Rosalia, we need two Coronas, another pink lady, and a ..." She looked back to me for confirmation.

"Water," I said.

"... and a bottle of water. We'll take the food now too."

The three of us joined the boy with the eyebrows at the table, and Sophie threw a coaster at him and said, "You're being rude, Blaine. Are you not even going to say hello to Izzy?"

"Sorry," the boy mumbled, tapping several more buttons on his phone, "a hurricane struck my SimCity, and I have to restore electricity before my citizens revolt."

Sophie rolled her eyes, and when the boy finally set his phone down and looked at me, his mouth fell open ever so slightly. I'm not sure what he expected me to look like, maybe Axl in a dress, but the look on his face said he was pleasantly surprised.

He flashed a smile time has undoubtedly exaggerated in my memory, but it warmed me, and swaddled me like a newborn, and whispered, "Everything's gonna be alright." Even today, after everything that happened, when I think about Blaine's smile, I'm reminded of a snug blanket on a chilly morning, or a cool drink on a scorching afternoon, or twenty milligrams of oxycodone hitting my bloodstream.

And before you go picturing some perfect male model, know that Blaine was cute despite an odd assortment of facial features. His ears were too big, and his mouth was a little too small, but his face as a whole was somehow greater than the sum of its parts. He was a little chubby too. Too chubby for his slim-fit polo shirt, at least. But he wore it with rich kid confidence, and I smiled back at him until I blushed.

"I'm Blaine Park," he said, pointing toward a Mediterranean-style fortress. "We live down the beach."

"In that giant blue house?" I asked.

"The beige one next to it," Blaine said. "The blue one is Mustang's."

"Mustang's?" I asked, laughing.

"Terrance Jones. Terrance 'Mustang' Jones," Axl said. "You know, the old NFL running back who invented that fat-reducing grill."

I shrugged and said to Blaine, "Your house is beautiful," even though it looked like the set of a drug lord film.

"Thanks," he said.

"Blaine's mom, like, runs our school, and his dad works at a bank or something," Sophie said.

I looked to Blaine for confirmation, and he shook his head. "Dad is the president of WalCo Bank. Sophie makes it sound like he's a drive-thru teller."

I laughed too hard at this, and while Blaine smiled at me, Axl asked, "Wasn't Mustang a scholarship kid at Bardo Academy?"

"Yeah," Blaine said, "probably around the time that kid got murdered."

"Wait, what?" I asked.

"Back in the eighties, some Bardo kid on a football scholarship was stabbed twenty times and dumped in the Gulf. Police said it was a drug deal gone bad."

"Didn't people think some crazed rival fan did it because the kid committed to Florida State?" Axl asked.

"I've heard that one and that his old high school teammates wanted to rough him up but accidentally went too far," Blaine said.

"Y'all, stop talking about it," Sophie said. "Dad knew that kid, and he hates when people talk about it."

"Sorry," Blaine and Axl mumbled in apology.

Sophie forgave them, then barked, "Where's the fucking food?" before storming inside to check.

"We hitting up Nowhere next weekend?" Blaine asked my brother after a moment, and Axl said, "Yeah, I'm in."

"You should come," Blaine said to me, but before I could ask what they were talking about, Sophie returned holding drinks, followed closely behind by Rosalia, an old Hispanic woman carrying a tray of plates and looking like she was strongly considering quitting her job and walking straight into the ocean.

"Go where?" Sophie asked.

"To Nowhere next weekend," Blaine said.

"Don't call it that. You know I hate it when you guys call it that."

"Sorry," Blaine and my brother apologized again.

Rosalia set our dinner on the table, which consisted of red snapper covered in a spicy crawfish and sausage concoction, okra fried until it begged for mercy, garlic whipped potatoes, and rolls served with this creamy honey butter I still dream about. It was the best meal I'd ever eaten, but here it was just something thrown together for some teenagers to eat on the deck.

"Are you going with us though?" Blaine asked Sophie.

"Maybe," Sophie said, and noticing Rosalia still standing by the table, she fluttered her fingers at the old woman and said, "Okay, we're good here. Go clean the kitchen or something. God."

"Straight through those doors, down the hall, third or fourth door on the right," Sophie said after dinner when I inquired about the closest restroom.

I tiptoed back through the Louvre, where I could hear Rosalia mumbling Spanish swears in the adjacent kitchen, and continued down the hallway to the restroom, which contained nothing more than a toilet and sink, yet was the size of my childhood bedroom. Leaving, I heard a man's agitated voice coming from further down the hall, and because I'm nosey to a fault, I stopped and listened.

"Tommy, I told you my father bought the spec house on Tartarus Shores, so I'm a little more liquid now—No, nowhere near the asking price, but I had to move it, and—No, I'm not asking him for money. You know we're not close. He lowballed the hell out of me on the spec house, but what could I—You know I can't rent this house, I spoke to the city council, but—No, Tommy, I'm not putting our house on the market. Why do you think? Because it would bring half of what it's worth right now and—No, I'm not selling the boat either, it's—Okay, yeah, I should sell the Hummer. Gas prices are killing me. But listen, Tommy, I'm just asking for some time here, I—No, I appreciate all you've done through the years, and I know you've been patient. But you've also been around long enough to know these things never last more than a year or two. People who panic during these little dips get hammered, and I'm not about to—Yes, I have plenty of life insurance, and I resent the implication, asshole. Listen, Tommy—"

The man, whom I gathered was Sophie's dad, Junior Wolfe, stepped into the darkened hallway and saw me standing there, then quickly retreated into his office before slamming the door behind him.

The rest of the evening stretched deep into tomorrow. Several pink ladies and Coronas later, our party relocated to the beach, where we played with sparklers, and Sophie loudly presented her plans to hook me up with Blaine. Axl protested, citing River Lewis, a sweet Dandridge boy who'd taken me to Applebee's and prom. But I'd extinguished that small flame before the move and reassured Blaine of my availability by repeatedly brushing my hand against his. It was so flirtatiously out of character that I laughed every time I did it, but they were all drunk, and by morning I'd be the only one who remembered anything that happened after dessert.

Around two, I drove us home in Axl's new car and escorted my stumbling brother to his new bedroom, where he collapsed and slept for the next twelve hours. Then I lay in my soft new bed, but sleep and I could not find one another in the dark, so I stepped onto my balcony and sat in an Adirondack chair and pondered the absurdity of my new life. A sliver of yellow moon drifted across the sky, and I breathed in deep the salty air while listening to the waves batter the shore a few hundred yards away, erasing the day's labor of children who thought their sandcastles would stand forever. A shadow darting across the empty lot next door caught my eye, and I watched until it reached the streetlamp, revealing itself to be a stray tabby. And as I considered fetching it a bowl of milk from the kitchen, the cat's eyes glowed bright, and it scampered back into the tall grass to escape the sports car rumbling past our house.

A man emerged from the vehicle after parking near the fountain at the end of our street, and he walked down the dune toward the sea. I had so many questions about why this person was here at three in the morning. One being how'd he get through the gate unless old Florida State scores were easy codes to guess. Half an hour later, when my curiosity piqued, I put on my shoes to investigate, but as I did, the man returned. His engine revved, and he throttled back down our road and out the gate onto 30A, leaving me and my unanswered questions alone with the waxing crescent.

CHAPTER FOUR

Bardo Academy wasn't technically in Bardo. The land there was far too valuable to use for a school. Instead, it sat north of Highway 98 on some unincorporated Walton County timberland generously donated by you-know-who.

Axl drove us on the first day of class, me so anxious I could puke, him singing along loudly with Katy Perry about kissing a girl and liking it, and after he parked his I'm-a-big-time-football-recruit car, I followed him toward the twin towers of the school, a large brick structure built to resemble Florida State's Westcott Building. The campus was nice, don't get me wrong. But I'd read so many novels where girls went to Hogwarts-looking private schools in Connecticut that my first glimpse of Bardo Academy was a letdown. It just looked like, I don't know, a school. Walking on the brick sidewalk, I did notice the grounds were perfectly manicured like so many Bardo Labradoodles, a marked improvement over the weedy lawn of Dandridge High School. And the football stadium across the parking lot was ridiculous, complete with million-dollar fake turf and a high definition video scoreboard.

No, Bardo Academy had money public schools could only dream of. Still, the staircases didn't move, and magic candles didn't light the lunchroom, and my first impression was forever tainted in meh.

"They'll have your schedule at the front desk," Axl said when we reached the doors to the main building before taking off to catch up with some friends.

I stared at the entrance to Bardo Academy and froze. Inside was the answer to a prayer, a life-changing opportunity, a gift that asked only to be received. But my feet disobeyed direct orders and refused to budge, giving that grating little voice in my head ample time to flood my mind with all the what-ifs I'd fretted over since January. What if all my classmates hated me? What if my classes were too hard and I failed miserably? What if the halls were infested with alligators and I was eaten before homeroom? And sure, that last one was unlikely, but sometimes my anxiety had all the subtlety of a hurricane.

"Wait, Axl," I called after my brother.

He spun around.

I wanted him walk me into the office but didn't want to ask. "Nothing," I said, and he left without a word.

"So, you're our new quarterback's little sister," Principal Baugh said as I stood in front of her desk, feeling stupid in my school uniform, a checked skirt and blue polo shirt.

"Twin sister," I corrected, and when she looked at me like I was an idiot, I added, "Identical twin sister."

I'd hoped for a laugh but only got an eye roll, and I cursed myself for already annoying the person at Bardo Academy best positioned to make my life hell.

"Right," she said, tapping her nails on her desk, "well, despite our rigorous academic standards, it appears you are now enrolled here, so I do hope you'll make the most of your opportunity and take advantage of our tutoring services, which I suspect you'll sorely require."

"Thank you," I muttered.

Principal Baugh stared at me, daring me to make another smart-ass comment, but I bit my tongue to the point of blood and flashed my fakest smile while speculating on her monthly Botox budget.

"Now, let's see," Principal Baugh said, turning to my schedule on her desk, "AP English, precalculus, chemistry, American government, and French. Young lady, this is a considerable course load. I fear you will not be up to the task."

"It's the same classes I'd have taken at Dandridge," I said with a shrug.

Principal Baugh flashed something like a smile and said, "I suspect you'll find our academic standards are a step above what you're used to."

"You let my brother in, so I suspect I won't," I said, immediately regretting it.

Principal Baugh cleared her throat. "Unfortunately, Miss Brown, I have little say concerning who is and who isn't admitted to Bardo Academy. Otherwise, we would not be having this conversation. But, you are here, so we will try to make the best of the situation. Here is your schedule. We've recruited a classmate of yours, Elton Jones-Davies, to escort you around your first day. Please, wait for him in the lobby."

And just like that, my meeting with Principal Baugh was over. I showed myself out of her office and, as instructed, sat in the lobby, next to a massive glass case bursting at the seams with trophies. In the middle, next to the 1983 State Championship plaque, sat a framed photograph of a cute blond-haired boy with a letterman's jacket folded underneath. I wondered if Axl's jacket would one day be on display too when a tall, beautiful woman wearing glasses and a charcoal skirt suit entered the room. "Isabelle?" she asked. I nodded, even though that wasn't exactly my name, and the woman smiled and said, "Come with me, please."

I followed the woman into her office and sank into a chair across from her giant mahogany desk. "Isabelle, I'm Katherine Park, and I wanted to be the first person to officially welcome you to Bardo Academy. However, I believe you've already met Principal Baugh and my son, Blaine."

"Yes, ma'am," I said, and Katherine Park smiled and pushed her glasses up the bridge of her nose. With her blonde hair pulled back tight and a strand of pearls hanging from her neck, she looked like the villain in a movie about housemaids. Still, her smile seemed genuine, and she immediately put me at ease.

"Well, welcome to Bardo all the same."

"Thank you. Are you the vice-principal?" I guessed.

"Heavens no," Katherine Park said with a laugh. "I don't think I could stomach working under Selena Baugh. I'm president of the Bardo Academy Foundation."

"Oh," I said, not having any idea what that meant.

"It's a volunteer position," she said with a smile. "Just my way of giving back to this community. I raise money for the school to pay for scholarships and keep the lights on."

"Oh, well, thank you," I said. "Axl and I are both on scholarship."

"Actually, Dalton Wolfe handles all athletic scholarships personally. The Foundation provides academic scholarships for deserving students. Speaking of academics, may I see your schedule?" I watched her look it over while biting her lower lip.

"Now, is it Isabelle, or—"

"Just Izzy."

"Just Izzy," she repeated, and I reached for the little sailboat on her desk because I struggle with boundaries.

"Do you sail, Izzy?" she asked.

Our trailer park had a yacht club, but I stuck to playing polo, I thought. "No," I said.

"I began sailing solo when I was thirteen," she said, "and my husband started even younger." When I offered nothing to this conversation, Katherine Park turned back to my schedule. "This should keep you busy," she said, "but good for you for challenging yourself."

"Thank you," I said. "Principal Baugh seems to think I've bitten off more than I can chew."

"Yes, well, Principal Baugh also injects toxins into her forehead every Tuesday," Mrs. Park said, flashing a conspiratorial smile.

I laughed, then confided, "I got the impression she doesn't want me here."

"Probably not," Mrs. Park said matter-of-factly. "Her family was against scholarships twenty-five years ago, and she still has a hang-up with them today. But that's her loss. In my experience, our scholarship kids are some of the best and brightest Bardo has to offer. Speaking of, tell me about your interests outside of class."

"I've signed up to work on the school newspaper," I told her.

I'd written for Dandridge's school newspaper, and freshman year,

I'd caused a minor sensation by exposing a school board member's scheme to sell expired lunchroom food to a local strip club, who in turn served it in the grossest all-you-can-eat buffet in human history.

"So, you enjoy writing?" Mrs. Park asked.

"Sort of," I said, "but I really like busting powerful people doing sketchy things."

Mrs. Park smiled. "Sounds like I'm looking at the next Nellie Bly."

"Was he a pirate?" I asked.

Mrs. Park shook her head and laughed. "She was the first investigative journalist, and she's famous for feigning insanity to report on the brutality and neglect at a women's asylum in New York City."

"Badass," I said, then covered my mouth when I remembered I was talking to an adult. However, Mrs. Park just smiled and said, "She was rather badass."

"Investigative journalist," I said. "I like the sound of that."

"Me too," Mrs. Park said with a smile. "*The Bardo Breeze* is lucky to have you on staff, and I know you'll flourish there. Our extracurriculars often give Bardo Academy graduates that extra something college admissions boards look for." She looked over my shoulder into the lobby and said, "Ah, I see your guide has arrived." She stood, so I stood too, and with a hand on my back, she ushered me to the door. "Again, welcome to Bardo Academy, Izzy. I cannot wait to see what you accomplish this year."

Outside, the tallest kid I'd ever seen in person stood waiting in uniform pants that struggled to reach his bony ankles.

"Hey, I'm Izzy," I said, offering a fist bump he didn't know what to do with.

"Elton Jones-Davies," he replied, louder than I thought necessary.

"Do you play basketball, Elton Jones-Davies?" I asked, and the receptionist stifled a laugh.

"Are you asking because I am Black?"

"No, because you're like six-foot-eight, you donkey."

Elton bit his lip in thought and stared at me for a long moment. "Your eyes are disproportionately large."

"Thanks," I said, feeling more confused than self-conscious.

"And they are brown," he noted. "Red hair and brown eyes is the third rarest color combination for human beings, occurring in only .79 percent of the population."

When I didn't reply to this, Elton turned on his heel and left the office, and I followed him through the main building, down the hallway toward the chemistry labs. "My mother is British," he offered out of nowhere. "The British are fond of double-barreled last names. It is confusing because not everyone hyphenates. Helena Bonham Carter does not hyphenate. I do."

"Gotcha. Well, my mother is from the eighties, and she's fond of—"

"Guns N' Roses," Elton said.

I laughed. "How'd you know?"

"I spend a great deal of my spare time reading and editing Wikipedia," he said. "It is an open-collaborative online encyclopedia that—"

"Yeah, I know what Wikipedia is."

"Well, that is where the vast majority of my knowledge of hair bands comes from, though the fact you and your brother were named after Axl Rose and Izzy Stradlin would be obvious to anyone with an affinity for the 1980s."

"And you have an affinity for the 1980s?"

"Among other things," Elton said, opening the door to the chemistry lab for me.

"That's cool, I guess," I said. "We should watch *The Breakfast Club* one day."

"I am not allowed to date," Elton said.

"Not what I meant, Elton."

"Forgive the misunderstanding," he said with an awkward bow. "I have Asperger syndrome. It is a form of autism. I should have told you upon our introduction. My therapist said casually working the information into conversations will help manage others' expectations."

"Well, I have smart ass syndrome," I said, "so I suspect we'll be peas in a pod."

He squinted at me before admitting, "I struggle with idioms."

"Sorry, I only use them once in a blue moon."

Elton stared at me for a long time before laughing way too loudly and walking away without another word.

My first day at Bardo Academy was fine. Blaine was in a couple of my classes, and that was nice, considering the rest of my classmates either ignored me or only talked to me because they wanted to know if Axl's ankle had healed. Extras were last period, and at the end of the day, I found myself in the *Bardo Breeze* newsroom, which was an exercise in extravagance. Two rows of cubicles ran the length of the room, each equipped with sparkling new iMacs loaded down with the finest publishing software available, and against the window sat the industrial-sized printers used to produce the weekly rag most Bardo students tossed in the trash upon receiving.

I was sitting in a back cubicle with Elton Jones-Davies when the editor-in-chief, Denham Frost, a girl who looked every bit as rich as her name, approached and said, "We don't have room for you on staff."

"But I'm tiny," I said, and Denham glared.

"Principal Baugh insisted I find something for you to do, though, since your brother is the almighty football god. So, you can either help Elton with his assignment, or you can sit in the corner and stay out of everyone's way."

"What's your assignment?" I asked Elton after Denham mercifully left.

He opened a folder of newspaper clippings. "This year marks the 25th anniversary of Bardo Academy's first state championship. I am writing a story about the team for a special homecoming game edition of the *Breeze*. I have worked on it all summer."

I took the folder from him and began flipping through the clippings.

"Those are in chronological order, please do not—"

"Calm down. I'm not getting them out of order."

Elton sat back but continued to make little pained noises every time I flipped over a page.

"Whoa, my brother band his friends were talking about this the other night," I said, showing him an article with the headline, "Bardo P. D. Says Slain QB Victim of Drug Deal Gone Bad."

"Ricky Lee," Elton said, taking the clippings away from me and putting them back in order. "Number twelve. Quarterback. Fifty-three touchdowns, six interceptions, 4,190 yards passing. Murdered by drug dealers. His letterman jacket is on permanent display in the school office."

"I saw it this morning," I said, thinking back to the photograph of the cute boy in the trophy case. "Do you really think he was killed by drug dealers?"

"The police said so," Elton said, showing me the article I'd just showed him.

"And the police never lie?" I asked.

It took Elton a moment to catch my sarcasm, and when he did, I could tell he didn't like it.

While Elton continued to re-sort his pile of newspaper clippings, I recalled something Mrs. Park said that morning. *Sounds like I'm looking at the next Nellie Bly.* I'd never thought of my natural inclination to stick my nose where it didn't belong as a possible career path, but why not? Snooping around the back of a nasty Dandridge strip club to bust a school board member was about the most exciting thing I'd done in my life, and I felt listless and empty for weeks after my investigation ended, wishing I had another lead to follow. Maybe my work for the *Bardo Breeze* would catch the eye of a college admissions board, even if I couldn't pull up my ACT. Maybe this was my path out of Pineview Villas. But helping Elton write stories about washed-up jocks wouldn't cut it. I needed to do something spectacular. Something no one else had done.

Back at Dandridge, there was a kid in my grade named Garrison James, who, like Elton, had Aspergers, a diagnosis that was folded into the umbrella of autism spectrum disorder years later. We found Garrison sitting at his desk several times after fire drills because no teacher had explicitly given him permission to leave the room. Elton gave off that rule-following vibe, and though I'm not exactly proud of what I did next, it wouldn't make the top ten list of worse things I've done.

"I'm going to help you with your football story," I told Elton.

"Thank you," he said, visibly uncomfortable, "but I do not need your—"

"It's my pleasure," I said, cutting him off, "but Principal Baugh asked you to help me with my special project in return."

"Principal Baugh?" Elton asked with wide eyes, and I nodded gravely.

"What special project?" he asked.

I leaned in close and whispered, "We're going to find out who really murdered Ricky Lee."

1983

Ricky Lee hated Bardo.

This wasn't what he'd signed up for because, technically, he hadn't signed up for anything. Dalton Wolfe approached Ricky's shady uncle, who approached Ricky's father, who said yes to a Bardo Academy scholarship and an implied commitment to Florida State with zero input from Ricky.

It's the opportunity of a lifetime, he said.

You'll make new friends, he said.

Because I'm your father and I said so, he said.

The Lee family moved south from Cowden in late July. Dalton Wolfe put them up in a modest house in Freeport, where Reagan-Bush decals adorned every bumper. When two-a-days started in August, Ricky practiced with the first team from day one. This did not surprise Ricky. He'd led Cowden High School to consecutive state championships, earning all-state recognition both years. Bardo Academy didn't bring him in to play backup. However, this was a surprise to Junior Wolfe.

Junior was the starting quarterback.

Junior was the big man on campus.

Junior dated the head cheerleader.

But not for long.

Junior knew his father dreamed of funneling star recruits through Bardo Academy to Tallahassee. But until now, the board of trustees had always balked at athletic scholarships. But money is convincing, and Dalton Wolfe had a lot of it. In June, Dalton offered Bardo Academy's first athletic scholarship to a running back from Pensacola, who'd double as the private school's first Black student. The parents lost their shit, but Dalton didn't care. Junior didn't mind the idea of having a stud running back to hand the ball to. Bardo might even make the playoffs this year, and besides, as the starting quarterback, he'd still receive most of the glory. Junior wouldn't learn about Ricky Lee until the first day of practice.

"Hey, Coach, what the hell?" Junior asked Coach Evans, his offensive coordinator, the first time Ricky stepped under center. "You're just giving him my job?"

"Your daddy gave him your job, Junior," Coach Evans whispered back. "If you want it back, take it from him."

"Hey dick slap," Junior yelled across the practice field to Ricky, "so you know, this is my team, and I'm QB1."

Ricky and Junior locked eyes, their hatred raising the temperature of the already sweltering practice field by several degrees.

A teammate hadn't insulted Ricky in so long he'd forgotten what it felt like. At Cowden, he'd commanded the fear and respect of a five-star general. He'd have to earn that here, either on the field or by breaking this whiny asshole's face in front of God and everyone. Ricky chose the former if only to keep from injuring his throwing hand on Junior's big nose.

"You've got to be shitting me," Junior muttered after Ricky threw his first pass of the practice, a twenty-yard out route that audibly whistled as it cut through the thick Florida air. Junior glanced at Coach Evans, who returned a sympathetic shrug. The job was Ricky's.

"Start dropping his passes or consider yourself permanently disinvited to my parties," Junior told Mason Driscoll, the team's best wide receiver, during the first water break.

Mason obliged, letting a pair of perfectly thrown fly routes slip through his gloved fingers.

"One more drop, Driscoll, and you'll find yourself on the second team with Junior," Head Coach Wallace called from his watchtower through a megaphone.

"Sorry, dude," Mason said to Junior as he jogged past. He didn't drop another pass the rest of the season.

When classes began, Junior reclaimed his crown as king of Bardo Academy, if only for a week. At his command, classmates treated Ricky Lee like a leper. The shunning was so thorough, Ricky began to doubt his own existence until someone wrote "Go home trailer trash" on his locker in permanent marker. The bullying was never physical. Ricky stood six-foot-six and could whip any two guys at Bardo Academy at the same time. Still, the week took its toll.

Ricky Lee hated Bardo, and he wanted to go home.

CHAPTER FIVE

Before our zip code improvement initiative, I spent fifteen hours a week frothing milk and pulling espresso shots at Stanton's Cafe in East Dandridge. It would be wrong to suggest my mother forced me to spend my weekends in the employment of Tripp Stanton, the proprietor of Stanton's and the biggest pervert west of the Suwannee River. However, she strongly suggested the quality of my wardrobe would be roughly equal to my struggle for legal tender. So, for every hour I spent serving coffee and warming stale muffins in the microwave, I earned $5.85 and the assurance I would not go to school wearing the latest in homeless chic.

That my brother was never forced into labor to subsidize his attire was not lost on me. Sure, he spent hours each day running and training under the murderous Florida sun, but he also took a lot of naps, and he never had to worry about Tripp Stanton checking out his ass whenever he bent down to retrieve the caramel syrup.

"If Axl ever wakes up, I'm going to see if he'll drive me to Seaside," I told my mother over breakfast on Saturday morning following my first week at Bardo Academy. "I want to apply for a weekend job at Amavida Coffee."

"Don't you bother him with that," Mom said, pushing her scrambled eggs around her plate with a fork. She'd just finished her first week as the personal assistant to someone else's personal assistants at one of Dalton Wolfe's property management companies. She always worked weekends at Dandridge Waffle King, and I got the feeling she didn't know what to do with her Saturday off.

"Well, I'm not walking to Seaside," I snapped, misunderstanding her reply as an admonishment for my intentions to inconvenience the football star for a lift around town.

My tone got her attention, but the words didn't register because she stared blankly at me across our breakfast table—for we now had a breakfast table and a dinner table—and after a moment, I clarified, "I'm not walking to Seaside to look for a job."

"Oh," Mom said, an understanding dawning as she sipped the last of her black coffee, "I meant you don't need to bother looking for a job."

"Okay, but—wait, really?"

"Really," Mom said with a smile and a pat on my hand. "I hear your new school is tough, so you'll need the time to study. And have a little fun."

I have no idea how much Dalton Wolfe compensated my mother for whatever it was she did during her brief time in his employ. Still, it was the first extended period of my life that money, specifically a lack thereof, was not the foremost stress of my day-to-day existence.

After breakfast, I walked to the beach, for the first time noticing that the two dozen for sale signs marking the empty lots between our house and the Gulf all featured the smiling face of Dalton Wolfe's son,

Junior. His twenty tailored suits and swoops of blond hair and sets of big, perfect teeth had faded from too many days spent for sale under the relentless Emerald Coast sun, and I wondered if these unsold properties were the nexus of the tense phone call I'd overheard the week before.

After walking down the beach a ways, I lay on my blanket and watched a family of five struggle past, the mom wrangling three small children, the dad pulling what appeared to be all their worldly possessions in a big-wheeled wagon. For several minutes, the dad struggled to corkscrew a rainbow umbrella into the sand, while the mom applied an impenetrable layer of SPF 100 to her squirming children. Then the kids began splashing in the shallow surf while the parents leaned back in their beach chairs, looking more relaxed by the minute.

Watching them, their coconut-scented sunscreen filling the air, I too felt the onset of a peculiar condition that presented symptoms of easy breathing and relaxed shoulders. My anxiety, which I'd lived with like a conjoined twin for as long as I could remember, had vanished. Realizing this, I was momentarily worried about not feeling anxious. But this was fleeting, and lying there on the warm sand, soaking up the morning sun and watching dolphins frolic in the Gulf, I savored the carefree existence I figured everyone else enjoyed all the time.

The feeling is hard to explain, but it is not dissimilar to those three or four glorious seconds immediately after waking when I've momentarily forgotten whatever it was that kept me up the night before. Upon rising, my whole being feels lighter somehow, like if I pulled back the sheets, I could float into the kitchen for breakfast. But then my traitorous subconscious realizes something isn't right, and it floods my mind with the worry du jour. Usually, it was school. I made straight

As, but what if I slipped? What if I screwed up the numbers on a multiple-choice final and missed every single question? It had happened before, I'd heard. And there were classes like English Literature that are entirely subjective. If Mrs. Porter—who hated me and sent me to the office three times for a dress code violation even though Vice-Principal Clayton measured and said my shorts were acceptable each time—if Mrs. Porter didn't like my interpretation of Gatsby's green light or Dr. Eckleburg's eyes, she could fail me, no questions asked. She had that power. Then I'd be done. No scholarship, no future, no escape from Pineview Villas.

Of course, there were boys and all the typical teenage anxieties brought on by the Y chromosome. I dated a couple of guys from Dandridge, but never for long because I didn't particularly care to have them pick me up or drop me off and see where we lived. Boys were interested. That wasn't necessarily a problem. But Mom told me once I was pretty in all the wrong ways, and though I'm still not exactly sure what she meant, it left me slightly apprehensive of any boy who was into me. When a guy tells you that you have pretty eyes, the natural reaction is not to try and figure out what the hell is wrong with him, but here we are.

I was healthy, apart from my migraines, which felt like a tiny jackhammer convention in my skull. I mean, I threw up more than I'd like to, but only because of my headaches, and sometimes I freaked out and got so scared I couldn't breathe, but that usually passed after I vomited or broke down and cried for half an hour. And now, on second thought, maybe I wasn't that healthy after all.

Then there were the million or so random worries that had, at one time or another, lived rent-free in my mind. Things like nuclear war, shark attacks, killer asteroids, carbon monoxide poisoning, brain tumors, the second coming of Jesus Christ, bird flu, flying (not that we were ever going to fly anywhere), Al-Qaeda, hurricanes, and the one time I took too many Tylenol in a six-hour window, and after a Google search feared for several weeks I needed a liver transplant. I'd fixate on these things for weeks at a time, usually culminating in a series of migraines, followed by a couple days of feeling blah. When my worries proved unfounded, I'd curse myself for getting worked up over something so trivial in the first place, only to repeat the process again weeks later.

But even my baseline sense of dread was gone that morning on the beach, which leads me, the amateur psychiatrist that I am, to conclude that my mother, and specifically her ability to provide for us, was the root of all my mental anguish. Makes sense, because in my experience, parents who should love and care for you, i.e., my father, can up and leave without so much as a goodbye kiss.

But that morning, I was wrapped in the embrace of my new carefree actuality, and with the sunshine warm on my skin, I spent several lovely hours in the company of my own untroubled mind until a giant shadow blocked out the sun.

"Weekend greetings," Elton said when I opened my eyes.

He looked ridiculous, in his school uniform, on Saturday, on the beach.

"Hey, Elton," I said, squinting up at him and covering myself with a towel because his formal dress made me feel half-naked in a bikini. "What are you doing here?"

He held up a thick folder. "I have come to solve a murder."

CHAPTER SIX

"Ricky Lee's parents reported him missing on Sunday night, December 9, 1983," Elton said across our breakfast table.

I took the *Walton Observer* clipping from him and read it. "Wait, he didn't come home at all on Saturday, and his parents didn't bother to call the police until the next night? That's weird, right?"

"Ricky's father told police he did that every Saturday, but he usually showed up around lunch on Sunday hungover and hungry."

"So Ricky was wild as a buck, and his parents looked the other way. That sounds familiar."

Axl, hungover himself, stumbled into the kitchen in his boxer shorts and belched loudly. "What sounds familiar?" he asked.

"Nothing," I said, hoping he'd go away.

Axl opened a cabinet and poured a giant bowl of Cap'n Crunch. "Are you not going to introduce me to your boyfriend, Izzy?"

"I am not allowed to date," Elton said, and Axl looked at me confused. "We are at work on an assignment."

"School work on Saturday? Nerds."

"This assignment is of the utmost importance," Elton said, and not catching my please-shut-the-hell-up expression, he added, "Izzy and I are solving Ricky Lee's murder."

"You're what?" Axl said with a laugh and flopped down at the table with us, spilling milk on several of Elton's newspaper clippings. "They solved that murder. It was drug dealers, right?"

"No one was arrested," I said.

Axl crunched loudly on a spoonful of nautically themed cereal and asked, "Okay, if it wasn't drug dealers, who did it?"

"We started our investigation ten minutes ago, you dummy," I said. "We'll need at least half an hour to solve a twenty-five-year-old unsolved murder."

Axl rolled his eyes, and I asked, "But wait, maybe you can help us. You're the starting quarterback for Bardo Academy. Who would be most likely to murder you? Sister excluded since Ricky Lee was an only child."

Axl extended his middle finger in my direction and thought for a moment. "A jealous backup quarterback, or maybe a jealous backup girlfriend."

"Jerk," I said, and my brother shrugged.

"All the guys from Dandridge were happy for me when I got a scholarship here, but maybe Ricky Lee's old teammates were pissed. Or maybe some guys on the team Bardo was set to play in the finals wanted to scare him but went too far?"

"What about the jealous fan theory?" I asked.

"Sure," Axl said. "He was the top recruit in the country, so a lot of teams were jealous when he committed to FSU."

"The United States Department of Justice estimates 82 percent of murder victims know their killer," Elton said, and Axl and I both looked across the table at him.

"Does he always talk that way?" Axl asked, but I ignored him.

"Okay," I said, "so we can't rule out a stranger, but odds are Ricky knew his killer. Do we know who his friends were at school? Girlfriend? Who did he hang out with on Saturday night before he ended up in the Gulf with his throat slit?"

"I have read that somewhere," Elton said and began furiously flipping through his folder of clippings.

"Seriously, though, why are you doing this?" Axl asked me.

"Because I'm going to be the next Nellie Bly."

"Who?"

"Nellie Bly, you know, the first—actually, you wouldn't know. I'm doing this because I want more out of life than Pineview Villas. I'm going to be an investigative journalist, and that starts with a scholarship to a decent college, and solving this murder would turn the heads of any admissions board."

"You're wasting your time," Axl said and slurped the last of his milk. He tossed his bowl in the sink and threw a touchdown pass to an imaginary receiver, celebrating with the victory pose Usain Bolt had made famous that summer in the Beijing Olympics. "Peyton Manning made twelve million dollars last year, and he didn't even start as a high school freshman. I did, and I broke the state record for touchdowns. We're gonna be crazy rich, Izzy. Stop worrying so much."

"You'll have to excuse me if I don't share your faith in your right arm."

Axl shrugged and gestured to the house around him. "My right arm brought us this far."

I opened my mouth to argue, but he was technically right, and while I struggled to think of a comeback, Elton said, "I have located it." He handed me the clipping and said, "Most articles about the murder only say Ricky spent Saturday evening with friends, but this one identifies them."

Axl sat back down as I read the article aloud.

"Ricky Lee's classmates are still reeling from the loss, even as they celebrate their school's first state championship. 'It's just not right,' said Bardo Academy senior and backup quarterback Junior Wolfe while wiping back tears. 'Ricky had such a big future ahead of him. I loved him, man. We all loved him.' Wolfe said he and Bardo teammate Mason Driscoll spent most of Saturday evening celebrating with Lee on the beach—"

"Mason Driscoll?" Axl asked. "Why do I know that name?"

Elton cleared his throat. "State Representative J. Mason Driscoll. Bardo Academy Class of 1984. Number eighty-eight, wide receiver, 1,298 yards receiving and seventeen touchdowns his senior season."

"The politician, that's it," Axl said, snapping his fingers. "His picture is hanging up at school."

I skimmed the rest of the article and said, "Okay, so Junior Wolfe claimed he and Ricky and Mason were on the beach all day. Several classmates popped in and out, but late that night, it was just the three of them again. They called it a night around eleven, only Ricky never made it home." I turned to Elton. "Junior Wolfe and Mason Driscoll were the last people to see Ricky Lee alive. We need to talk to them."

"Whoa, whoa, whoa, Sherlock," Axl said, standing up. "Look, this little investigation is cute and all, but you heard Sophie. Her dad doesn't like talking about Ricky Lee."

"Maybe because he murdered him," I said, and Axl glared at me.

"Or maybe because people don't enjoy talking about their murdered friends. Please, Izzy, the Wolfe family is the only reason we're living in this house and going to Bardo Academy. Let's try not to piss them off. And while you're at it, don't annoy Mason Driscoll either.

"So you're saying you don't care if Ricky Lee's killer gets away with murder so long as you get to live in this big house and drive your fancy new car and talk on your stupid new iPhone?"

"That's exactly what I'm saying," Axl said, heading back upstairs to his room. "Remember, Izzy, if you piss off the wrong people, we'll be right back in that Dandridge trailer park. So promise me you'll drop this shit."

"I promise," I lied.

CHAPTER SEVEN

Imagine that through reprehensible means, you could procure a large fortune for yourself. However, in doing so, you'd also trigger the collapse of the global economy. The good news is you will never be held responsible for this, no one will even know your name, and though billions of people around the globe will suffer for a decade or more, you will remain filthy rich. The bad news is at night, when your mansion is quiet, and you're lying on your $40,000 mattress, you won't be able to sleep because your conscience, or what's left of it, will be loudly reminding you that you're an asshole.

This isn't purely hypothetical. People had this opportunity in the early years of the millennium, and did they ever take it. My freshman health class at Dandridge only provided two days of personal finance instruction, so I'm no economist here. Still, from what I understand, bankers can bundle together several mortgages into a bond, and investors then buy those bonds betting homeowners will pay their mortgages.

This worked fine for a long time because homeowners did pay

their mortgages. They paid them because banks, understandably, used to be selective about who they'd lend hundreds of thousands of dollars to. But then the banks realized they could make more money if there were more mortgages to bundle into bonds, so they began lending hundreds of thousands of dollars not only to people who were likely to repay it but to anyone who walked into their bank, even if they were only looking for the restroom. Investors kept betting because the rating agencies, which should have said, "Yeah, these bonds suck," were instead like, "These bonds are cool. Triple-A or whatever." A few years later, when graffiti artists and panhandlers began defaulting on their half-million-dollar mortgages, the world economy went to shit.

Of course, we hardly noticed this in Pineview Villas, where the local economy was already well below the shit line. On the coast, new home building had slowed. Our mostly empty street was evidence of this. Still, we wouldn't see the repercussions of the financial meltdown in Bardo until the end of September, when banks and the stock market fell like Icarus. To me, everyone seemed rich and happy. But beneath the facade of carefree wealth, there were people in Bardo acutely experiencing the effects of the crisis. Axl and I were on our way to see one of them.

"You know, Junior Wolfe is a self-made man," my brother said as we cruised 30A in his Dodge Charger. We were on our way to a party in Nowhere, wherever that was, but first we had to pick up Sophie.

"Oh yeah?" I said, not particularly interested in Junior Wolfe's origin story, but knowing I was about to hear it anyway.

"Yeah," Axl said, stopping to let ten people dressed all in white cross the road for a family photograph on the beach. "I mean, his father is obviously rich, but Junior only got a million dollars to start his company after college, and now he's one of the biggest developers on the Gulf Coast."

"You and I have significantly different definitions of self-made," I said.

Axl shrugged. "Well, his dad inherited half of Florida and just grows pine trees. Junior took a million dollars and turned it into millions and millions of dollars. He's ten times the businessman his father is."

This wasn't exactly true. Junior Wolfe's success as a developer was a direct result of the Panhandle's massive demand for new homes. Demand brought on by the large number of people who had no business owning homes now having recklessly large loans from recklessly greedy banks. Of course, I didn't know that then, but I knew from the tense conversation I overheard in the Wolfes' hallway that all wasn't well in Junior's kingdom.

"He's built huge developments in Grayton Beach, Seacrest, Destin, Niceville, Vermillion, all over," Axl said, taking such pride in Junior Wolfe's accomplishments you'd have thought he'd played a part. "It's amazing what he's done."

"Looks like he's having trouble finishing our neighborhood," I said, pouring sour milk over my brother's Cap'n Crunch.

"Yeah," Axl said as we reached the gate to Eden Shores, and he had his ritual football conversation with Clyde, the gatehouse guard. "The other day, I heard Mr. Wolfe telling Mrs. Wolfe the housing market is in a dip or something. He said it does this every decade, like a cycle or something, but it only hurts small-time developers and people who panic. They're so rich though, it doesn't matter."

When Junior Wolfe answered the door, he did not look like a

man who was so rich nothing mattered to him. He did not look anything like the twenty glamour shot versions of himself that dotted the empty lots on our street. His face was hollowed, with dark circles under tired eyes. His blue polo shirt hung loosely off his shoulders like he'd recently lost a lot of weight in an unhealthy way. Even his perfect swoop of blond hair was no more, and several follicles had jumped from the sinking ship.

"Good evening, Mr. Wolfe," Axl said, "we're here to pick up Sophie."

"Y'all come in," the real estate developer said, glancing nervously over our shoulders toward the private road.

We followed him into the Louvre, just as Sophie came downstairs in pajamas with an exfoliating mask smeared over her face. "I'm like, super sick," she announced, looking anything but. "Y'all go without me."

"Want me to stop by later?" Axl asked.

"Sure, whatever," Sophie said, before faking a cough and walking back upstairs, leaving Axl and me alone with her father, who exchanged a sympathetic shrug with my brother before escorting us back to the door.

As we walked, I cleared my throat to remind my brother I was still there, and he said, "Oh right, Mr. Wolfe, this is my sister, Izzy."

"Nice to meet you," I said, then curtsied and felt like an idiot.

"Nice to meet you too," Junior Wolfe replied.

As we reached the door, I said, "By the way, Mr. Wolfe, I'm writing a story on the 1983 state championship team for the *Bardo Breeze*, and I'd love to ask you some questions sometime about the season."

"Anytime," Junior Wolfe said, instinctively rubbing the championship ring he still wore.

"I'm particularly interested in Ricky Lee."

"Izzy," Axl snapped, but Junior Wolfe and I were now conducting an impromptu staring contest, and I couldn't look away.

"Of course," Junior Wolfe said after a long pause, his face softening slightly. "You can't write about that team and not write about Ricky. He was our best player by a mile."

"And you were one of the last people to see him alive," I said.

Axl elbowed me in the ribs, but Junior Wolfe and I had locked eyes again. Then his phone rang.

"Shit," he said, glancing at the screen. "I need to take this. I'm sorry, guys. Good seeing y'all though." Junior Wolfe opened the door and gave us a half-hearted thumbs-up before stomping back into his house and answering the call with, "Tommy, I was about to call you. No, I swear to God—"

<p style="text-align:center">~~~~~~~</p>

"Sorry your girlfriend is sick," I said as we left the Wolfes' house.

"She's not sick, she just hates hanging out in Nowhere," Axl said, "and you promised you'd drop all this murder shit."

"I know, but he looked so murdery, I couldn't help myself."

"I hate you," Axl said, but I could tell he wasn't too mad.

"You've got to admit," I said, "he's a weird dude."

"He's just super busy with work right now," Axl said, coming to his hero's defense. "He told me anyone can make money during a real estate boom, but only the best of the best can do it when the market goes down. And he's the best in Florida."

I had no reason not to believe my brother, apart from the fact Junior Wolfe looked like he was in the final stages of some terminal illness, but it turns out he was far from the best developer in Florida. He'd ridden the wave of easy money to great heights, but in his greed, he became reckless. When the banks started to sniff what was coming, the non-recourse loans dried up. The gamble-free money was gone. So Junior Wolfe committed the cardinal sin of real estate development. He guaranteed a loan with his own fortune. And now that the market had turned, what would be his largest development sat empty, and the bank was after Junior's money. His personal money. Every dime of it. The Hummer. The sporty European number with butterfly wings. The Bardo Beach palace. The piano, the artwork, the boat in the harbor, the twins' Xbox, every designer purse, shoe, and dress in Sophie's closet. Everything. Which explains why the man I met that night looked like the corpse of the man on the for sale signs on our street.

"The best," Axl repeated as we drove on toward the development that would end Junior Wolfe. Bardo kids called it Nowhere.

CHAPTER EIGHT

Nowhere was somewhere. Twenty miles northwest of Bardo in Vermillion, to be precise. It sat on the former site of Mystic Pines Golf and Yacht Club, which sounds swanky, but was, in reality, a homemade golf course and driving range squeezed into thirty-seven acres by a man named Perry Harkins. Perry, whose mobile home doubled as the course's clubhouse and whose pontoon boat rationalized the liberal use of "Yacht" in the club's name, mowed his links twice a month with his own John Deere, and local hacks paid him $5 for unlimited daily play. The course's condition, as you've likely deduced, was not a big draw. However, Perry let golfers bring their own beer and play shirtless in the summer, which kept the five-dollar bills rolling in.

In true Florida Man fashion, Perry Harkins died in 2005 when a black bear, drunk on a cooler of Natty Light accidentally left on the sixteenth green, stumbled into his trailer and ate most of him. Perry's three grown children, realizing new housing developments all but surrounded their father's course, sensed an opportunity and put the land on the market, asking twice its appraised value. There were whispers even then of the coming crash, but Junior Wolfe ignored them. He risked his personal fortune to secure the loan.

Junior Wolfe's smiling pre-crisis face greeted us on the billboard marking the entrance to Nowhere, a subdivision actually called Mulligan Shores. A model home sat empty just inside the ornate stone entryway, and a sign in the yard invited us to come inside and inquire about the home of our dreams. But the waist-high weeds in the yard indicated no one, apart from perhaps some upwardly mobile raccoons, had been inside in a long, long time.

"Yikes. Abandon all faith ye who enter here," I said, but Axl had no clue what I was talking about, so I asked, "This is really where Bardo kids hang out on weekends?"

"Until someone runs us off," Axl said as we drove deep into Mulligan Shores, where Junior Wolfe smiled out at us from the faded signs planted in hundreds of overgrown lots. Making a final turn that took us along Choctawhatchee Bay, I saw several cars in the cul-de-sac at the end of the road. Axl parked and strolled confidently into the crowd, and I followed closely behind. There were fifty or sixty people there, some sitting in cheap lounge chairs looking out on the water, others gathered around a keg on the back of a tailgate, all of them ignoring the speaker-rattling pleas of Lady Gaga to "Just Dance." I didn't recognize anyone and was about to ask Axl not to leave me alone when four girls pounced in front of him, hugging him too long and tight, safe in the knowledge Sophie Wolfe wasn't around.

The four girls resembled each other so closely, I felt one introduction would be sufficient. Still, Axl told me all of their names after they'd released him from their grasp. "Izzy, this is Margot, Anna Claire, Jillian, and the other Margot."

You all have very punchable faces, I thought. "Hi," I said, waving awkwardly at the four girls who were so drunk they could hardly stand without leaning on each other for balance.

"Izzy," one of them said while looking me over, "that's like a total stripper name." The other girls laughed, and I felt justified in hating them all without ever learning which one was which. Axl, who I'd hoped might come to my defense, just laughed and kept moving into the crowd, so I followed and wondered if I was about to spend the evening being introduced to people who'd proceed to insult me. But before we reached the group huddled around the keg, a hand fell softly on my shoulder, and I looked up to see Blaine, bushy eyebrows and blinding teeth, smiling down.

"Hey, you made it," he said.

"Blaine!" I said, with more enthusiasm than I'd intended. But he looked genuinely excited to see me too and asked if I wanted to meet some people.

"No," I said, "not at all."

He laughed. "Okay, how about a walk?"

"A walk sounds lovely."

We strolled along the bay, away from the party, and I kept my hand hanging unnaturally, hoping he'd hold it, but he never took the hint. I wondered if all the beer last weekend erased his memory of my overly aggressive flirting.

"How was week one at Bardo Academy?" he asked after a while.

"Fine," I said. "Most people either ignored me or wanted to talk about Axl, so not much different than Dandridge, honestly."

Blaine laughed and said, "Well, I promise not to ignore you or ask about Axl."

"Thanks," I said with a wink, then asked, "So, do cops never drive back here?"

"Not that I've ever seen," Blaine said. "Though if they did find us, there are a couple more abandoned neighborhoods in Vermillion we could move to."

"That is so crazy," I said, and pointing at all the empty lots to our left, added, "so they built all these roads but never got around to building houses on them?"

"I'm not sure what they were doing, but I've heard my dad say Sophie's dad bit off more than he could chew. I don't know if Junior doesn't have the money to build the houses, or if no one has the money to buy them, or what, but Dad thinks the Wolfes might lose everything."

"We stopped by their house on the way over here," I told Blaine, "and Mr. Wolfe looked like he hadn't slept in a month. Axl got all pissed because I asked him about Ricky Lee."

Blaine coughed out a laugh. "You asked Junior Wolfe about Ricky Lee?"

"Yeah. I'm writing about the murder for the school paper. Is that bad?"

"I didn't say it the other night because Sophie was sitting right there, but there are rumors Junior killed Ricky Lee so he could start the state championship game."

"Oh, shit. His face did turn white when I mentioned Ricky."

Blaine laughed. "It's just a rumor, I think. The financial stuff is true, though. I hear my parents talk a lot. Sophie's grandfather is richer than God, so he'd probably bail them out, but who knows, I don't think he and Junior get along. I'm surprised my father isn't giddier about it.

He thinks Sophie's dad flaunts his money, which is pretty rich, considering we live in a house the size of a Publix. I think it's his sports car, though. Dad is too fat to squeeze into one, and he resents Junior for it."

We walked through the empty neighborhood for over an hour, talking about Bardo and our life plans.

"My dad is super-obsessed with my future," Blaine told me at one point. "I almost didn't get to come tonight because I scored a 94 on our chemistry quiz yesterday, and anything that doesn't round up to one hundred is unacceptable."

"My mom hasn't looked at my report card since second grade," I said, "and if Axl ever made a 94, she'd kill the fatted calf."

"You're lucky," he said. "Dad is making me retake the ACT next month because he's convinced I've got a perfect score in me."

"What do you want to study in college?" I asked.

"I'd like to be an elementary school teacher," he said, "but I'm going to medical school."

"I don't think they require a medical degree to teach elementary school these days."

Blaine laughed. "Yeah, I guess I'm going to be a doctor. I mean, who can actually live on a teacher's salary anyway?"

"Teachers," I offered.

He flashed a condescending smirk, and I punched his arm. "Do you even want to be a doctor?"

"No. I pass out at the sight of blood. But what can I do? Dad won't pay for college unless it's business school, law school, or medical school. He'd cut me off and never pay for anything again. I don't want to sound like a spoiled brat, but I'm not going to take some vow of poverty just to prove a point. I'll get his money one day, then I can do what I want. But until then, it makes sense to play by his rules."

I found his line of thinking cowardly but also had to concede that I'd never had money and could not say with any certainty what I would or wouldn't do to keep it, so I smiled and said, "Well, tell your dad I'm more than happy to go to medical school too if he pays for it."

"I'll tell him," Blaine said with a laugh, then he sighed and added, "I can't wait to get out of this place." He picked up a rock and threw it into the bay. "Bardo by the Sea," he said, rolling his eyes. "You know, the developers thought they named the town after the Buddhist word for heaven, but "bardo" is actually their word for purgatory." He laughed. "God, it feels like it sometimes."

"Yeah," I agreed while thinking only a relatively benevolent deity would use 30A for purgatory.

Blaine's phone buzzed, and he checked a text message. "We should head back. People saw a black bear out here a couple of weeks ago."

Though I'd rather meet a black bear than more Margots, we went back to the party, which had doubled in size since our departure. I followed Blaine through the crowd, past the keg, and while I fished us a couple of Dr Peppers from a cooler, he spoke to someone who'd just pulled up in a van.

"Are you not drinking tonight?" I asked him moments later when he returned. It seemed he and I were the only ones who weren't.

Blaine groaned. "No, Dad is back in town, and he likes to play cop on weekends. He bought a Breathalyzer to randomly test me after I've been out because a DUI would ruin my chances for med school."

"That's ... normal," I said, following Blaine through the crowd while trying to process the fact his father owned a home Breathalyzer kit. We found my brother lying next to a Margot in the back of a truck bed, gazing at the stars together.

"Your boy show up?" My brother asked Blaine, sitting up with great effort.

"Slim never disappoints," Blaine said, discreetly placing something in Axl's palm.

Before I could inquire about this mysterious transaction, my brother fell back on the truck bed and said, "Thanks, and keep your hands off my sister."

Blaine blushed, mumbling something about not touching me unless I wanted him to, which made us both blush, then we walked over toward the bay and squeezed onto a rusty lounge chair together.

"It's really peaceful out here," I said, looking at the lights of 30A across the bay.

"It's about to be," Blaine said, pulling a small bag of pills from his pocket. He took out a light pink one and swallowed it with a swig of Dr Pepper before closing his eyes.

Perhaps I was more sheltered than I thought. Back in Dandridge, I'd been to keg parties, and occasionally someone would bring weed, but Blaine's little bag of pills freaked me out. My heart raced, and I broke out in a cold sweat. "You're taking drugs?" I asked, immediately regretting how much I sounded like the mom in a just-say-no commercial.

Blaine laughed. "Technically, yes, but it's not like I'm smoking crack. These are for pain, but they help anxiety too," he said, pointing toward the light pink pills. "They help me forget about my dad and school and all the shit I stress over all day every day for like eight glorious hours. They don't get me high or anything. I'm still me, just with none of the worries."

"Oh, okay," I said, thinking that sounded wonderful but still slightly terrifying.

"And these orange ones help me focus. I take them on weeknights when I'm studying and before I take the ACT. Nearly every kid in school is on them, but Dad won't let me get a prescription because he thinks it's a sign of weakness."

Blaine was right. He was the same person after taking the pill, just more relaxed. His eyes locked with mine more, and he laughed easier, and he even took hold of my hand after a while. But I still had to kiss him first, which finally gave him the confidence to kiss me back. Then he reclined the chair and pulled me on top of him.

Ten minutes. I had all of ten minutes to relish the fact I lived in a big, expensive house on the beach, I went to the finest high school in the Florida Panhandle, and I had a cute, rich boy kissing my neck in the best way imaginable. I had ten minutes to believe Pineview Villas was my distant past, and this was my new life. But it was all a fantasy. A construct of a desperate mind. Because no sooner had I accepted these things as my new reality, I heard my brother scream, "I am your golden-armed god!"

"Shit," Blaine said, as we both stood and looked back toward the party, where Axl stood on the roof of a truck, raising two beer cans toward the heavens. "I've told him not to mix that stuff with beer, but he—"

Blaine never finished his thought because my brother's eyes rolled back in his head, and he fell face-first onto the ground.

1983

Ricky Lee was nervous.

Pep rallies always brought him to the brink of puking, and his first one at Bardo Academy was no different. Ricky never understood the purpose of firing up the team so many hours before kickoff. Still, it got him out of class, so whatever.

"Good luck tonight," a classmate said, patting Ricky on the back as he passed him in the parking lot after school. It was the first friendly word he'd received all week, and Ricky wondered if it weren't a case of mistaken identity. Every guy on the team wore a jersey and blue jeans. Maybe this kid wished all the players good luck and didn't realize his mistake until it was too late. "Trailer trash parking only" was still faintly visible on the asphalt below Ricky's car, despite the janitor's best efforts to pressure wash it away.

Maybe the kid hadn't seen it.

Maybe he was hedging his bets.

The first game was at home versus Milton, a school Bardo Academy hadn't beaten in its six years of existence. In fact, they'd never even scored, and old men at the Bardo Diner still talked fondly of that one time they got close.

Milton won the toss, kicked the ball to Bardo, and Ricky led his offense onto the field, standing taller than his biggest lineman. The team huddled around him, and Ricky leaned in.

"Look at me," Ricky shouted, and the team obliged. "We're about to do things you've only dreamed about."

"Trips right, 951 post, on one."

"Trips right, 951 post, on one."

"Ready … break."

The huddle broke, and Ricky grabbed Mason Driscoll by the arm as he ran out wide. "Don't drop it," Ricky said with a wink, and Mason nodded.

The snap was low, and the protection wasn't great. Ricky side-stepped a Milton defender no one remembered to block, then he uncorked the prettiest spiral ever thrown in the short history of Bardo Academy. Mason Driscoll caught it in stride fifty yards downfield, and Ricky nearly beat him to the end zone, pumping his fist in celebration.

Ricky's teammates, who'd tolerated him at best through two-a-days, all came by the bench for a high five or pat on the helmet. Even Junior Wolfe, who didn't need an Old Testament prophet to tell him his reign as king was near its end, reluctantly walked over for a fist bump. But the Bardo Academy crowd hadn't seen anything yet. Ricky threw four more touchdowns and ran for another, and when he took a knee after the final snap and raised the football to the heavens, he might as well have raised a scepter.

The king was dead.

Long live the king.

Luckily for Junior Wolfe, Ricky was a benevolent and forgiving monarch. It was Ricky who insisted Junior come to the impromptu victory party on Bardo Beach. Junior balked at first but quickly relented.

If you can't be the king, be the king's wingman.

They rode together in the new Pontiac Firebird Dalton Wolfe had just given Ricky in exchange for his private commitment to attend Florida State, both of them slightly on edge since they'd woken up that morning hating each other's guts. But from that day forward, they were rarely seen apart.

The quarterback and his backup, a most unlikely friendship.

CHAPTER NINE

"Would you like a drink from the machine?"

Blaine and I were in the ER waiting room at Sacred Heart Hospital, waiting to hear about Axl.

"No thanks," I said, counting the goosebumps on my legs. It was a muggy Florida night, but the emergency room was a meat locker, and the flickering fluorescent lights above had already given me a splitting headache. My first headache since our move to Bardo. We switched to some seats nearer the bathroom in case I had to vomit.

Axl had landed funny on his arm, and as he came to, some guys helped him up and ushered him to his car while he shouted he was okay. But when someone pointed out his rapidly swelling wrist, he nearly passed out and conceded he ought to have it looked at. I drove him to the hospital, with Blaine following behind. A nurse took Axl back immediately, but that was an hour ago, and we hadn't heard anything since. I tried to and failed to stop imagining doctors in the back sawing off my brother's arm while he bit down on a stick.

"Maybe you should call your mom now," Blaine suggested, and I murmured my consent.

I hadn't called her yet because it was still before curfew, and I'd hoped the doctors could fix Axl's arm and sober him up while they were at it, and we could make it home before she knew anything. But it was a quarter after eleven now, and we'd never make it, so I stepped outside and called. We lived half an hour away, but she burst into the ER fifteen minutes later.

"Where is he?" Mom shouted to me across the waiting room.

"He's in the back somewhere," I said, crossing the room so I didn't have to shout too. "I don't know where they—"

"Where the hell is my son?" Mom shouted at the triage nurse, who pushed her chair back several feet from her desk and must have pressed an alarm, because several large men rushed into the lobby and surrounded by mother.

"My son, Axl Brown, he's hurt his arm. I just want to see him," Mom said in a more reasoned tone, and all but one of the large men left the waiting room. Mom provided the triage nurse with her identification before shouting at me again. "How could you let this happen? How could you be so stupid, Izzy? You know your brother is the only reason we're living here. The only reason you're going to that school. And you go off and let him risk everything we've worked for."

I wanted to tell her we hadn't worked for any of this. It had fallen on our heads like seagull shit. But I'd never seen my mother so angry, and sometimes she carried her father's old revolver in her purse, so I bit my tongue.

"Axl was just goofing off, Mrs. Brown," Blaine said, coming to my defense.

"You stay out of this, eyebrows," my mother snapped, and Blaine hid behind me. "Goofing off, wait, was Axl drinking, Izzy? Did you give him alcohol?"

I stifled a laugh at the thought I'd given Axl alcohol. I rarely took more than a sip at parties, because without even trying, I could easily rattle off the names of half a dozen close relatives who'd drank themselves to death, not to mention my father, who Mom claimed threw up in the delivery room moments after our births, because for him any occasion was the right occasion for a handle of Jack Daniels. But this never concerned Axl. I doubt it had ever crossed his mind. He'd drank since we were fourteen, and last year he'd gone to school still hungover on Mondays more often than not. He told me once it numbed the stress of playing quarterback. He was typically a quiet drunk. Not the sort who'd loudly proclaim his deification on a truck roof. The pills were new, though, and I didn't know what they'd done to him.

"No, Mom, he wasn't drinking," I lied. "He was just showing off to impress some girls."

Mom cursed under her breath and turned to yell at the triage nurse who'd yet to provide her with any information, just as Dalton Wolfe, panting for breath and holding his chest, charged into the waiting room.

I thought for a moment he was dying of a heart attack, but after several deep breaths with his hands on his knees, Dalton Wolfe straightened up and barked, "Where's Axl?" I pointed toward the back, and he grabbed my mother by the arm and stormed toward the examination rooms like he owned the place. Technically speaking, he didn't own the place, but he had built the ER. I hadn't noticed it yet, but his fat face was on the bronze plaque above our seats. He'd also built the cancer center and bought the hospital's ECMO machine. Legally this didn't exonerate Dalton Wolfe from the several HIPPA violations he committed by stalking through the ER, my mother in tow, looking in every room they passed until they found Axl. But no one from the CEO to the janitor would say anything to him about it. Eventually, they found my brother, his right arm, his throwing arm, wrapped in ice.

Now that Mom was there, Blaine suggested we leave before Dalton Wolfe came back out and killed us.

"He's not going to kill us," I said. "He's nice. Like a grandpa."

"He might have acted like a grandpa when he talked your brother into coming to Bardo, but he's not nice. He goes to our church—actually, he built our church—and even my dad is terrified of him."

This didn't jibe with the jolly man I'd bear-hugged in our trailer, but half an hour later, Dalton Wolfe stomped back into the waiting room and made a beeline toward me.

"Hi, Mr. Wolfe," I said as Blaine hid behind me again. Dalton Wolfe ignored my greeting, stuck a ring-covered finger in my face, and snarled, "Listen up, girl, you've been here one week, and you've already jeopardized your brother's future. You'd better hope to high hell that arm of his can still sling a ball the way it could, or y'all just might find yourselves back in Dandridge living in one of my trailers for the rest of your sad-ass lives."

"Mr. Wolfe, Izzy didn't—"

Blaine, bless his heart, tried to come to my defense, but Dalton Wolfe turned and left without another word. An hour later, a muscle-bound nurse pushed Axl out in a wheelchair, which was entirely unnecessary for a sprained wrist, but whatever. There was no charge, of course. Dalton Wolfe took care of everything, and after the discharge nurse explained this to Mom, she glared at me one more time and left with my brother.

Blaine and I walked outside, and as we stood by Axl's car in the parking lot, my body began to thaw in the warm Gulf breeze.

"You okay?" he asked, giving me a half hug. "Want me to follow you home?"

"I'm fine," I said, though I wasn't. "Are you okay, though? Should you drive? You took that pill."

Blaine laughed. "I'm fine. A little sleepy, but it is one in the morning. I told you, those pills just take away stress. You'd have to take several at once to get messed up. I'm not stupid, Izzy."

"What about Axl?" I asked. "What was he on that made him black out and fall off a truck?"

Blaine shook his head. "Same thing, only he takes it for pain. His doctor gave it to him when he got hurt in the spring. His ankle was still giving him trouble when his prescription ran out, but they're not hard to find. You just can't mix that stuff with alcohol. I've told him that a dozen times, but Axl can be an idiot."

"Don't I know it."

"Well," Blaine said, taking my hand and squeezing it, "when can I see you again?"

"Whenever," I said, "assuming I'm not grounded for Axl being a dumbass."

"How about tomorrow? We always have lunch after church. You can come with us, meet my parents."

I hesitated here because I was operating under the assumption if Blaine and I became a thing, we'd be the sort of thing he'd want to hide from his parents, not flaunt in front of them at Sunday lunch. But he read my hesitation as a lack of interest and said, "But if you don't want to, it's cool, we can take things slow and—

"No, I'd love to," I said, and he smiled in relief.

"It's a date," he said and kissed me goodbye on the forehead.

I sat in our driveway for half an hour, not eager to go inside. Axl's light was off upstairs. I figured he was in bed, passed out. But the kitchen light was on, and Mom would be perched on a barstool, waiting to eviscerate me for the sin of having a careless brother.

When I finally found the courage to go in, Mom was there, but she didn't scream. She just flashed a sad smile and motioned for me to sit next to her, so I did.

"Sorry I hollered at you at the hospital."

"It's okay," I lied.

"No, it ain't," Momma said. "I know you're a good kid, and your brother, well, he's the life of the party, ain't he? It's wrong of me to expect you to protect him. Hell, my brother wouldn't have listened to me when we were y'all's age. But if Axl screws up now, it could cost us everything. So I'm gonna need you to watch out for him, okay? For me. For you. For all our futures. Izzy, I know it ain't fair for me to even ask, but you've got to help me. You understand?"

I understood my mother was scared of her own son. Scared to punish him and risk angering him in the slightest. Scared, I guess, that Axl would hold a grudge and not buy her a big new house when he cashed his NFL lottery ticket in a few years. It was about the saddest thing I'd ever seen.

"I'll try," I said, hugging Mom before climbing the stairs to my bedroom. Even though I was exhausted, it was well after 3 a.m. before

I finally fell asleep, and a house-shaking rumble of thunder woke me three hours later. I stared at the ceiling fan and cursed. My head pounded so hard I knew I'd throw up later that morning. In the time it took me to sit up, I realized the worries and anxiety I thought I'd left behind in Pineview Villas had finally tracked me down. It only took two weeks.

I couldn't fathom how anyone could ever truly feel good about their life when it could all turn to shit so quickly.

CHAPTER TEN

Blaine picked me up Sunday morning for church, kissing my cheek on our porch when I greeted him at the door. Giggling, I twirled to show off my little green dress after he complimented it, and holding the umbrella, he walked me to his car, a Mercedes SUV I suspect he didn't pay for by mowing lawns over the summer. Seeing him again lifted my spirits from a morning spent in bed with a raging migraine, and a frantic half-hour spent fretting over arriving woefully under or overdressed for the service. But Blaine wore a skinny tie with khakis, and I thought we looked like we belonged in a magazine advertisement together. For a minute, all felt right in the world again.

"How's Axl?" he asked as we drove out the gates of Tartarus Shores, heading west toward Bardo.

"Fine," I said. "The swelling went down in his wrist. He'll be ready for the first game Friday."

"Oh, good, because our backup quarterback sucks."

I laughed and said, "I'm worried about him, though. The doctor gave him more pain medicine."

"Probably the same stuff he's taken since hurting his ankle this spring," Blaine said. "He'll be fine. We just have to keep him from mixing it with alcohol again. Or catch him next time he falls off a truck."

We parked on a narrow redbrick Bardo street and walked down the sidewalk, passing a dozen overpriced cottages whose pastel shingles, white picket fences, and oyster shell drives blurred together until they were only distinguishable by the small, decorative signs informing passersby where the owners resided the rest of the year. The Rutherfords, Vail, Colorado. The Hawthorne Family, Atlanta. Beckett and Kitty Kincaid, The Woodlands, Republic of Texas. *The Brown Family, Pineview Villas Trailer Park*, I thought to myself and stifled a laugh.

Saint Anastasia Church sat tucked between two of these homes, hidden under the everlasting branches of an ancient live oak tree.

"What a cool old church," I said.

"It's actually brand new," Blaine replied. "They just built it to look old. Everyone here went to All Saints until two years ago when the church split over gay people."

"Which side is this church on?" I asked.

"Against," Blaine said, slightly embarrassed.

"Oh, so not such a cool old church," I said, and Blaine shook his head in agreement.

Two men in seersucker suits welcomed us with smiles and bulletins before ushering us through giant red doors. Inside, the church was all vaulted ceilings, dark hardwoods, and stained glass, a stark contrast to my childhood church, Dandridge Church of God and Prophecy, which met on Highway 79 in a metal building that doubled as a gymnastics studio six days a week. There were no electric guitars or drums either, and I silently thanked God because my head couldn't handle a rock concert that morning.

Entering the church, Blaine bowed toward the golden cross hanging above the altar. I wasn't sure what to do, so I nodded in the cross's general direction and followed Blaine to our pew.

"My folks are down front," he whispered, waving toward a crowded pew left of the altar. Blaine's father nodded back in our direction. He was short and round, with bushy eyebrows and big ears, features he didn't pull off half as well as his son. His mother, Katherine Park, smiled and returned his wave.

The service began, and though the bulletin had detailed instructions, I spent the first fifteen minutes in a general state of confusion. There were calls and responses, then a hymn, but I apparently grabbed the wrong book because when I turned to page 433, there were no lyrics to be found. Blaine came to my rescue, holding his hymnal where we both could see it, but I wasn't about to sing in front of him, so I mouthed the words and listened to his cracking tenor.

I've learned through the years staying impossibly busy can keep my anxiety at bay, at least for a while. The problem is, there are paces I cannot run at very long, and when I inevitably crash, I'm left exhausted and anxious, which is worse than only being anxious. That morning, Saint Anastasia offered a short reprise from my troubles because I spent most of the service struggling not to make a fool of myself. But when the priest began his homily, a fifteen-minute snoozer on the parable of the rich fool, my thoughts drifted back to Axl, Mom, and Dalton Wolfe and how we were now only one misstep away from moving back into a trailer park surrounded by rattlesnakes.

But we were, if anything, a family of missteps, and by the end of the sermon, I'd all but decided to go up front and petition God to use any and all miracles necessary to keep us in Bardo. I'd seen my mother do this several times through the years when money was short, or when Axl had a big game. The last time she tried was before the state championship game. Axl threw three interceptions in a blowout loss that felt like a damning indictment of the power of prayer. Still, we were currently living in a million-dollar beach house, so maybe the Lord does work in mysterious ways.

However, Blaine's church did not afford parishioners an opportunity to bum-rush the altar and beg. We did go up front for bread and wine, but it was all very organized. There were no tears, no pleading or bargaining, and no women rising from their knees with mascara streaming down their cheeks. I'm not sure this silk suit and pearls crowd needed anything from God anyhow. I left with a vague feeling they viewed the service more as an opportunity to tell the Almighty that all was well and keep up the good work.

"Sunday greetings," Elton said, tapping me on the shoulder after the service.

"Hey, Elton," I said, and he stared at my fist before reluctantly bumping it. "You go to church here too?"

"Affirmative," he said, pointing to his mother, who was talking to the priest. "Mother has several theological disagreements with the priest but says this is the closest thing in Bardo to the Church of England. My mother is from England, and double-barreled names are—"

"Yes, you've told me. Have you cracked the case yet?"

"Negative, but I did spend several hours in the microfilm room of the Bardo Library yesterday searching for articles I had previously overlooked."

"I guess that's one way to spend your Saturday."

Elton ignored this and said, "I discovered that Ricky Lee received death threats before the Cowden game. However, the police determined it was only ex-teammates playing a prank."

"Or was it?" I asked. "I wonder if we could find one of his ex-teammates to talk to?"

"Leave that to me," Elton said with a dramatic finger snap, then turned away without another word.

After handshakes and hugs, Blaine and I stood outside under his umbrella, singing a painfully obvious Rihanna song, and waiting for his parents. He pointed out a former Louisiana governor just as Dalton Wolfe stepped through the red doors with Ella Kay on his arm. I'd forgotten Blaine told me the night before he'd built their church. Apparently, they'd sat right behind us, and I quickly thanked God for not letting me notice them because I'd have certainly hyperventilated if I had. Thankfully, Mr. Wolfe didn't see me as he passed, and before I could say something to Blaine, his father walked over and said, "We have reservations at Great Southern Cafe for lunch."

"See you there," Blaine said, and again we walked hand in hand to his car.

Driving toward Seaside, I admitted to Blaine I was anxious about having lunch with his parents.

"Not as nervous as me. I swear, sometimes my mother thinks she's the queen of 30A. I've seen her make waitresses cry for bringing out the wrong salad dressing."

"I think your mother is sweet," I said.

"And I think you don't know my mother," Blaine teased. "She likes you, though, so she'll be on her best behavior. But Dad has a lot going on at work, so he's been in a mood lately, plus he's always grumpy after church. A dollar says he makes at least one racist comment before appetizers."

The patio at Great Southern Cafe was closed due to Hurricane Gustav's outer bands, which were intermittently battering 30A throughout the day, so we met his parents inside, where they'd already been seated in the restaurant, which, like a lot of 30A, somehow felt casual and elegant all at once. They stood, and Blaine introduced me. Thomas Park, Blaine's father, who'd removed his coat and rolled up his sleeves to better blend in with the lunch crowd, formally shook my hand. Mrs. Park put a hand on my shoulder and said how nice for me to join them for lunch.

We sat, and while the others carefully considered their menus, I quickly decided on a Caesar salad because it was the cheapest thing available.

"Izzy," Mr. Park said, after announcing his intentions to order Grits à Ya Ya, "Blaine tells us you're new to Bardo."

"Yes, sir," I said. "We moved here from Dandridge."

"You've got cousins in Dandridge." Katherine Park said to her husband.

"Who?" Tom Park demanded.

"Carl and Tina."

"Oh, God," Mr. Park said, his eyes returning to his menu, "I don't claim them."

A waitress took our order, and the conversation turned to school.

"Izzy, how was your first week at Bardo Academy?" Katherine Park asked.

"Amazing," I said. "I loved every minute." This wasn't exactly true, but I saw no reason to burden her with my classmates' chilly reception.

"And the *Bardo Breeze*?"

"It's great," I said. "Elton and I are researching a story on the 1983 state championship team."

"That was your team, Thomas," Mrs. Park said to her husband, but he was too busy dumping several packets of sugar into his tea to hear.

"And we're trying to solve Ricky Lee's murder while we're at it," I added.

"Oh, Izzy," Katherine Park said, her look telling me I'd said something wrong. But her face quickly softened, and putting a hand on mine, she added, "I only ask you to be respectful with that. There are a lot of painful memories buried with Ricky's story, and not everyone in Bardo wants them dug up."

I nodded. "Of course."

Mrs. Park smiled kindly and asked, "Speaking of football, is your brother ready for the first game Friday?"

"Yes, ma'am," I said, "I think so."

"I can't believe the academy still lets these football players in after all the trouble we've had through the years," Mr. Park said, his attention now returning to the conversation.

"What's that supposed to mean?" Blaine snapped.

"Watch your tone, son," his mother admonished.

"It means we pay a small fortune to send you to that school, and if we wanted you to learn with riffraff—not that your brother is riffraff," Tom Park added, waving a hand toward me, "we'd have put you on a yellow bus and sent you on your way."

"Holy shit," Blaine muttered under his breath, and his mother shot him a look.

"Tell me, Izzy," Tom Park asked, "do you play a sport?"

"No, sir."

"Then how are you able to attend Bardo Academy?" he asked.

"Dad," Blaine huffed.

"I'm curious, son. Tuition is a barrier for the siblings of most Bardo students on athletic scholarships."

"Dalton Wolfe helped me get in," I said, my face starting to flush.

"Oh, Lord," Mr. Park said, frowning when his wife snatched the sugar away before he could add more to his tea. "Dalton Wolfe has more money than sense. We've got to get him off the board of trustees."

"Good luck with that, dear," Mrs. Park said, "he only built the school."

"Yes, well, charitable donations do not give him the right to turn Bardo Academy into his personal playground," Mr. Park said, after taking a sip of his tea and finding it lacking. "As president of the foundation, no one is better positioned than you to take the school back from him."

"Oh, are we telling each other how to do our jobs now?" Mrs. Park snapped, and her husband quickly looked away.

"Can we talk about anything else?" Blaine asked, but his suggestion fell on deaf ears.

"You see, Izzy, Dalton doesn't have kids in school anymore, so what does he care if the school is full of football thugs, so long as they go to Florida State," Mr. Park said. Then, noticing his son glaring across the table, he again waved a hand toward me and added, "Not that your brother is a thug, but some of the boys Dalton has brought in, well, they belong in prison, not a private school. Like that Black boy in your grade."

"And ... you owe me a dollar," Blaine said.

"Who, Elton?" I asked.

"No, not Elton," Mr. Park said, literally rolling his eyes at me. "That kid is too weird to be a thug. But his father was."

"I'm shocked you wear that state championship ring everywhere since you're so ashamed of your teammates," Blaine said.

"Enough," Katherine Park said, so firm that the table went awkwardly quiet. We all paused to sip our drinks, and while I silently prayed for an asteroid impact, Tom Park turned to me and, in a more conversational tone, asked, "Is Dalton Wolfe putting your family up somewhere too? Rent around here isn't attainable for everyone."

"Yes, sir," I said, with all the politeness I could muster. "He bought one of Junior's houses on Rosemary Beach, and he's renting it to us."

"Junior Wolfe," Mr. Park scoffed. "Speaking of people who belong in prison."

The rain picked up, beating hard against the windows, and Mr. Park rambled on for several minutes on a myriad of topics ranging from food stamps to affirmative action. A thousand and one smart-ass replies filled my brain, but I bit my tongue. Mom raised me better than to insult the person buying my lunch, even if he was an asshole. Mrs. Park stared out the window at the deluge, having tuned her husband out, something I suspect she often did. And Blaine kept trying to change the subject, but his father was on a roll, hardly pausing to take a breath. My chest grew tighter as Mr. Park circled back around to Bardo Academy and the perils of letting just anyone through its pearly gates. My face flushed with a mixture of anger and embarrassment, and my headache returned with a vengeance. I wanted to ask Blaine to take me home, but I couldn't find my voice, and the world around me grew dark. I was about to pass out. I could feel it coming. So, I employed my one homemade remedy to stave off an anxiety attack. I ran, literally, out the front door into the rain.

Blaine found me minutes later in the children's section of Sundog Books, soaked to the bone and crying while the staff eyed me with suspicion.

"God, Izzy, I'm so sorry," he said, holding me tight, my head now buried in his chest. "He's a monster, and I should have never let him near you. I'm so sorry."

I told Blaine it wasn't his fault. If anyone knew you couldn't choose your parents, it was me. Then I asked if he had any of those little pink pills left.

CHAPTER ELEVEN

Leaving Seaside, my headache reached meltdown levels, and the glare from oncoming headlights and the squeaking windshield wipers only threw fuel on the fire. When we stopped at a crosswalk to let a couple run across the street to Bud and Alley's, I opened my door and vomited, which scared Blaine but made me feel slightly better. Axl was on the couch when I got home, watching the Braves play the Nationals on our giant new television. I hoped he wouldn't notice as I ran upstairs to my room, but a minute later, he knocked on my door.

"You okay?" he asked, stepping inside before I could tell him to go away.

"Fine," I said, though the left side of my head throbbed like a demented carpenter was steadily hammering a three-inch nail into my eye. "Just a headache."

"You don't look fine," he said, flopping onto the bed next to me.

I shrugged, hoping he'd go away, but he didn't.

"Is it Blaine?" he asked. "I don't want to kick his ass, but I will."

I laughed despite myself and shook my head no.

Axl stood and walked over to my balcony window and stared out at the rain for a moment. "It took me a couple months to get used to this place," he said, turning around.

"I seem to recall you begging Mom to come back home for several weeks."

Axl smiled at the memory. "I mean, everyone was nice to me, but they didn't think I belonged. Not really. I still feel like it's all a mistake, you know?"

I nodded. I knew exactly what he meant.

"Do you remember my first varsity touchdown pass for Dandridge?"

"I know you're going to find this hard to believe," I said, "but I haven't gotten around to committing your football highlights to memory."

Axl shot me a bird and said, "First play, first game. The corner bit hard on an out and up, and I hit Patrick Cothran in stride. Prettiest spiral I'd ever thrown, and I was so juiced I almost beat Patrick to the end zone. I pumped my fists and shouted like a madman until a linebacker pointed back down the field at the yellow flag on the ground and said, 'It's coming back, baby.' They'd flagged our left tackle for holding. Ten-yard penalty, repeat first down."

He sat back on my bed and said, "The last six months have felt just like that play. More perfect than I've ever dared to dream. But I can't escape the sneaking suspicion it's all gonna be called back."

"Yeah, me too," I confessed, "especially since the reason we're all here is currently wrapped in a bandage."

"Don't you worry," Axl said, standing and pretending to throw a ball with his off-hand. "I can always play lefty if I have to."

"All I do is worry," I said as he made his way toward my door. "It's all I've ever done."

"And how's that working out for you?" Axl asked.

I glared at him across the room, and he smiled and said, "Look, Izzy, it's all gonna work out in the end. It always does."

You hear about twins sharing a special bond, reading each other's minds and feeling the other's pain, but the closest thing Axl and I had was an uncanny ability to have the opposite reaction to nearly any situation. We were anti-twins, almost. He believed, despite what I considered overwhelming evidence to the contrary, that everything in the universe conspired together for our benefit. For Axl, offensive holding or a lost scholarship to Bardo Academy were just bumps in his road to preordained greatness. Perhaps he suffered from a lack of imagination. Try as he might, maybe Axl could not envision a future where his ability to heave a pigskin would fail to bring him the world on a platter. But, for all I knew, the prospect of a lifetime in Pineview Villas was all too real to him also, and he'd found denial a better coping mechanism than soul-crushing worry. Either way, I envied my brother's outlook, even if in the end, life would shit on us both.

I spent the next hour lying in bed with a wet rag across my face, but it didn't help. I was suffocating and needed out of that house. The first band of thunderstorms had passed, so I walked to the beach to try and clear my head. The sand was wet and dotted from rain, and thousands of jellyfish had washed ashore, covering the sand like translucent landmines.

Walking east, past the old pier on Inlet Beach, I didn't see a soul. It was spooky, like some end of the world movie, and turning back, I wished I'd brought a jacket because the wind was cold, and the darkening skies felt more like November than the last day of August. I finally passed a man walking his dog, but he didn't return my wave.

Another band of rain was coming. I could see the squall on the horizon, but I wasn't ready to go home yet, so I sat on the beach at the end of our street and watched the heavy wind whip the tops off waves churning in the Gulf. I wondered how long I could survive in that surf before I went under. Half a minute, maybe? The thought made me shiver, and I looked away.

After a few minutes, I pulled the little pink pill Blaine gave me from my pocket and examined it. It looked harmless enough, and if it helped my headaches and anxiety, what was the problem?

"And you're sure this is safe?" I'd asked when he dropped me off.

"It's exactly what a doctor would give you for headaches and anxiety," Blaine said with a reassuring smile. "You're not doing anything wrong, Izzy. Let me know if it helps. I can get you more."

I paced the beach for five minutes, threw several shells into the ocean, and cursed. *What the hell*, I thought, and popped the little pill without a glass of water to wash it down.

I suppose it was about a third of the way down my esophagus when the panic set in. I had visions of all the strung-out kids from the anti-drug videos they showed us during health class at Dandridge. That would be me, at best. At worst, the DEA or FBI or whoever arrested you for taking someone else's prescription medication was about to storm the beach and take me to some scary women's prison. But then, nothing happened.

My head still hurt, and a general sense of impending doom still weighed heavy on my chest. I laughed out loud. Blaine's silly little pill couldn't help me. Nothing ever could. The rain was close now, so I walked back home, stepping over several Junior Wolfe signs the storm had blown into the street.

"How's your headache?" Axl asked as I stepped through the door.

"It's fine," I said, because that's what I always said when someone asked about my headaches. I never was fine. More often than not, it felt like my brain had swollen several times its regular size, and relief would only come when it burst from my skull and killed me. But explaining this took time, and if I said I was fine, people usually left me alone to stare at the ceiling.

But no sooner had I said this to Axl, I blinked at him with a mixture of confusion and realization. "Whoa," I said, "it really is fine."

"That's good," he said, looking at me like I was crazy.

It wasn't just that my headache was gone, though. Eventually, they always went away but usually left me feeling hollow and exhausted, like I'd won the war, but at a great cost. Now I felt like I'd just awoke from ten hours of dreamless sleep. I was alert, lucid, and happy. No, more than happy, I was euphoric. Like, straight A's on my report card euphoric. Like, catch the cute boy in calculus class staring at you euphoric. I felt … I felt exactly like I did on the beach that morning soon after we'd moved to Bardo when I believed everything was going to be alright. Sensing this, my traitorous mind flooded with images of Axl breaking his arm and ending his football career and the three of us moving back to a trailer in Pineview Villas, but now the images didn't upset me. I felt so good, so charged and refreshed, nothing could worry me.

"I can get you more."

Blaine's words echoed in my head, and I smiled.

CHAPTER TWELVE

After scouring the internet for a couple hours, Elton tracked down one of Ricky Lee's former teammates, so on Tuesday afternoon after school, we went to Cowden, a one-stoplight town in north Okaloosa County that time had forgotten. I drove us in Elton's Escalade because his mother wouldn't allow him to drive outside of Bardo, and pulling into town, we passed a Dollar General, a Dollar Tree, a Family Dollar, a gas station, an abandoned gas station, and the old high school, which closed a decade ago when Cowden students were incorporated into neighboring Baker High. The downtown, if you could even call it that, looked like the set of a post-apocalyptic film I wouldn't watch alone. Of the two dozen storefronts, only two appeared occupied: a law office and a taxidermy shop. Thankfully, we visited the former.

"I'll be right with you," a voice boomed through a closed door when we entered the law offices of Tanner P. Cobb, Esquire, where diplomas and state bar certificates hung haphazardly on the grimy walls. Elton and I exchanged a shrug and waited on creaky pine floors while dust particles danced in the sunlight streaming through the street-front windows. Five minutes later, a toilet flushed, and Tanner Cobb waddled out wearing cargo shorts, sandals, and nothing else.

"He's an attorney?" I whispered to Elton, who seemed to momentarily doubt his own research.

"Well, if it ain't Stretch Armstrong and Pippi Longstocking," Tanner said. "What can I do for y'all?"

You can put a shirt on, I thought. "We need your help," I said.

"Y'all selling ads in the football program?" the lawyer asked, mercifully donning an ill-fitting Hawaiian shirt before flopping into his high-backed leather chair. "I'll take the cheapest one you got."

"We are investigating the murder of Ricky Lee," Elton said the way only Elton could say it.

"You're doing what now?" Tanner Cobb asked with a laugh.

"We're investigating the murder of Ricky Lee," I repeated.

"For shits and giggles," the attorney asked, "or are y'all from the internet or something?"

"We are with the *Bardo Breeze*," Elton said, and Tanner Cobb cocked his head and squinted.

"It's Bardo Academy's student newspaper," I clarified.

"Oh, Bardo by the Sea," Tanner Cobb said in his poshest accent. "So y'all are a couple of rich kids?"

"I am wealthy," Elton replied, matter-of-factly, "Izzy is poor. She is from Dandridge."

Tanner Cobb looked at me for confirmation, and I shrugged and explained, "My brother is on a football scholarship at Bardo, just like Ricky Lee. I got in because Dalton Wolfe really wants my brother to go to Florida State."

Tanner Cobb nodded in recognition. "Oh, I know all about Dalton Wolfe's little Bardo pipeline. Your brother any good?"

"I don't know, I guess."

"As a freshman, Axl Brown set the Florida High School record for touchdown passes with fifty-four," Elton said as if quoting from a statistics book only he could see.

"Damn, sounds pretty good to me," Tanner Cobb said, scratching at a spot on his beard like a flea-ridden dog. "Now, what did y'all want to know about Ricky? As you can see, I'm a busy man."

Elton looked around at the empty room in confusion, and I asked, "Did you know him?"

"Hell yeah, I knew him. I was his backup quarterback." Tanner Cobb must have read the skepticism on my face because he quickly added, "I put on some pounds in law school. Anyway, Ricky was a year ahead of me at Cowden. Best damn athlete this state has ever seen. He should have never gone to Bardo."

"Is that why Cowden students sent Ricky death threats? Because he left to play for Bardo?"

"Death threats?" the attorney asked, looking at us like we were idiots.

Elton handed Tanner Cobb the newspaper article he'd printed off at the library, and the attorney read it and chuckled.

"What's so funny?" I asked.

"I'd forgotten about this," he said, handing the clipping back to Elton.

"Do you know who made the threat?" I asked.

"Well, yeah, it was my sister and a bunch of her cheerleader friends. The week of the Cowden-Bardo game, they sent Ricky a drawing of a tombstone with his name on it, just like the one they sent to every other quarterback we played that season. The only reason it made the papers is because some Bardo parents got bent out of shape over a damn joke. Hell, a Walton County Sheriff's deputy came to school that week and interrogated a bunch of hundred-pound girls like they really had intentions of killing somebody. We all loved Ricky. Sure, we wanted to beat him, but I think most of us were happy he made it out of Cowden, you know?"

"So, you don't believe Cowden students were responsible for Ricky's death?"

Tanner Cobb stood to let us know our meeting was over. Elton and I stood too, and he walked us toward the door. "No, kids, they weren't. I suppose it was drug dealers like the Bardo police said."

"But you don't believe that," I said as the lawyer opened the door for us, "do you?"

Tanner Cobb sighed, closed the door, and in a lower voice said, "Well, no, I don't. Why the hell would a drug dealer stab a kid twenty times and dispose of the body? They wouldn't. If something went wrong, they'd shoot him in the head behind the 7-Eleven and leave it at that. Ricky's murder, I don't know, felt personal."

"Personal how?" I asked, leaning in. "Can you tell us what you know?"

"I don't know anything," Tanner said, "but I've heard a lot through the years. Courthouse rumors, speculating deputies, and one-upping lawyers, most of it bullshit, but probably some truth buried in there too." I took out my pencil band pad to take notes, but the lawyer shook his head. "But it's nothing I plan to share with the two of you.

"Why not?" I protested.

Tanner Cobb opened the door again and said, "The rumors I've heard involve some powerful folks, and those aren't the sort of rumors I like to spread because they have a tendency to come back around on you. The last thing I need is you two running around Bardo telling folks Tanner Cobb is up here in Cowden talking shit." He slapped Elton on the back and pushed us both onto the sidewalk. "Now, y'all make sure to check out our Dollar General while you're here in town. It's one of the nice new ones."

He closed the door, but I stopped it with my foot. "Please," I begged, "just tell us where to start."

Tanner Cobb closed his eyes and sighed. "Same place you always start, Pippi, the money. Figure out who got rich after Ricky died, and maybe you can figure out why Ricky died."

I nodded. "Thanks for your help."

"You're welcome," the lawyer said, rubbing his temples liked he'd made a big mistake. "But for shit's sake, kids, be careful. Remember, in the end, you're looking for someone who obviously doesn't have a problem slitting a teenager's throat. So maybe you don't want to find them.

1983

Ricky Lee was king.

Even dictators who double as their country's local deity have never felt the love and adoration Ricky felt whenever he parked his black Pontiac Firebird and strolled the halls of Bardo Academy. The football team was a perfect 4-0 for the first time in school history. A playoff berth inevitable, and whispers of a state championship grew louder by the day. All because of Ricky.

Ricky hadn't forgotten his first week of school.

The silent treatment.

The hateful graffiti.

The concealed laughter whenever he walked by.

He knew his newfound popularity had nothing to do with him and everything to do with his ability to throw a football better than any teenager on the planet. But so what? He wasn't popular at Cowden until sophomore year, when the starting quarterback broke his leg in the first game of the season. Ricky took the field pimpled and gangly. One of the poorest kids at an impoverished school. But by the time the game ended, he was dating the head cheerleader. This is not an exaggeration. Traci Thompson literally climbed down from a pyramid of peppy girls and asked Ricky to the homecoming dance during a fourth-quarter time-out. He said yes, even though Traci's boyfriend was in the emergency room with his leg in a cast, and she hadn't had an opportunity to dump him yet.

Don't hate the player.

Hate the game.

Bardo Academy's head cheerleader, reverently referred to as Her Majesty by friend and foe alike, was slightly more subtle in her pursuit of Ricky. First, she had to end things with Junior Wolfe, and he was not a guy you dumped during a fourth-quarter time-out. Junior was still one of the wealthiest and best-looking guys in school, so, even if he was no longer the starting quarterback, his popularity remained an entity unto itself. She'd have to let Junior down easily, because if Ricky broke his arm, who knows, she just might want her old boyfriend back.

Junior took the news in stride, and Her Majesty commended herself on a well-executed plan, not once feeling guilty about taking such a strategic approach to romance. Life was a game, and Her Majesty played to win. She came by it naturally. Her grandfather helped General Eisenhower plan the D-Day landings.

Her Majesty knew which bridges to cross.

And which bridges to burn.

Strategy was in her blood.

Ricky didn't necessarily care for Her Majesty. They had little in common, nothing to talk about, and making out with her in the back of his Firebird was not as much fun as he imagined. But that was no bother. Ricky never cared for any of the girls he dated at Cowden either. He was just happy to be back atop the social food chain because life was easiest there. Ricky never had to worry about finding a date or if he'd be invited to the weekend's big party. Ricky Lee was the king, and everybody loved the king.

Well, not everybody.

CHAPTER THIRTEEN

"Hello, I'm trying to reach Jack Duncan?"

"You got him."

"The Jack Duncan who served as Bardo's Chief of Police from 1977 to 1983?"

"The one and only. But listen, lady, if you're with the Fraternal Order, I've already given to the scholarship fund this year, so I don't—"

"No, sir, my name is Izzy Brown, and I'm a student at Bardo Academy. I'd like to interview you for our school's newspaper."

"Interview me? What the hell for?"

These days when people think of my home state of Florida, they think of Florida Man. Florida Man isn't a single person, but the headline-grabbing personification of our collective weirdness. You've seen the stories …

Florida Man Falls off Moving Car While Taking Selfie on Roof

Florida Man Arrested after Assaulting Crossing Guard with Arby's Roast Beef Sandwich

Florida Man Removed from Local Park for Practicing Karate on Untrained Swans

And while you'll get no argument from me that Florida is a weird-ass place, there is a simple explanation why you don't see these stories about Connecticut Man or Nebraska Man. Florida's public records laws, called the Sunshine Laws, are the most comprehensive in the United States. Crime information is accessible in close to real-time. So, when a reporter needs a quirky story on deadline, they know where to look, and Florida Man rarely disappoints.

The Sunshine Laws also made it easy to track down the thirty-seven Jack Duncans living in the Florida Panhandle. I'd called over half of them before we found the one we were looking for living on the bay in Panama City Beach. Elton and I wanted to talk to Chief Duncan because Tanner Cobb's advice to follow the money had gotten us nowhere. Junior Wolfe and Mason Driscoll were the last people to see Ricky Lee alive, so they were our prime suspects. But they were both born with silver spoons in their mouths, and killing a poor classmate wouldn't have made them any richer. We'd read every local newspaper story on the murder until our eyes crossed, but they mostly said the same thing. We needed fresh information, and we hoped Chief Duncan could provide it.

"We're writing a story on the 1983 state championship team," I said, which wasn't technically a lie, "and we thought you might have an interesting perspective."

"Well, I suppose I was at every game that season," Jack Duncan said with the voice of a man who'd had a fifty-year love affair with unfiltered Marlboros.

"Wonderful. Would you mind if a classmate and I drop by tomorrow after school for a quick interview?"

There was a long pause, and I worried Chief Duncan had hung up, but then I heard him breathing on the other end of the line. "I suppose that would be alright," he said. "Let me give you my address. It's—"

"Thanks, Chief, we've already got it. See you tomorrow around four."

"You don't have to keep apologizing."

"I know. I'm sorry."

"Apologizing for apologizing is just as bad."

Blaine smiled. On Thursdays, we had lunch together, which was nice, because after nearly three weeks at Bardo Academy, I hadn't made any other friends. My relationship to Axl meant I'd never remain anonymous, but being a curiosity wasn't the same as being popular, and at times I felt like my brother's press agent.

"His wrist is fine."

"Florida State, I think."

"Boxers, and yes, that was a weird question."

I feared if a Bardo student actually asked me a question about myself, I'd die from shock, but it appeared I wouldn't have to worry about that.

Blaine and I were sitting across from each other eating food that was, disappointingly, no better than Dandridge High School's notoriously gross lunchroom cuisine. Like every other day that week, he spent most of our conversation apologizing for how his father acted at lunch on Sunday.

"Okay, I'll try and stop," Blaine said, downing a mouthful of fries. "But you'll be happy to know I overheard Dad telling Mom this morning he thinks he has a kidney stone."

I laughed. "Now, that does make me happy. Please do keep me updated on any excruciating pain your father may experience."

"Speaking of," Blaine said in a lower voice, "how'd that work on your headache?"

"Way better than Advil," I said. "It was amazing."

I hadn't had a migraine since the weekend, and I'd been so busy running around with Elton trying to solve a murder, I'd momentarily stopped worrying about Dalton Wolfe kicking us out of Bardo. Still, I thought about how Blaine's pill made me feel a lot, and I wished I had more of them, you know, just in case.

"Good," Blaine said. "I'm supposed to get with my guy tomorrow. I'll grab you some to keep at the house when your headaches come back."

"Thanks, Blaine, but I can't afford to—"

"My treat," he said, holding up a hand. "Seriously, they're not expensive, and if they help you feel better, I want you to have them."

I smiled, a wave of calm washing over me at the thought of having round-the-clock access to the way that pill made me feel.

"Hello, Izzy, Blaine."

"Hi, Mrs. Park."

"Hi, Mom."

Katherine Park smiled and turned to me. "Izzy, will you drop by my office at the beginning of extras today? I promise not to keep you long."

"Yes, ma'am," I said.

"Thank you. I'll see you then," she said, tousling her son's hair and leaving us to finish lunch.

"Any idea what that's about?" I asked Blaine after she left.

He shrugged and smiled. "She probably wants to tell you about Dad's kidney stone too."

"Have a seat, Izzy," Mrs. Park said when I entered her office. "I promise not to take up much of your time." I did as I was told, and Katherine Park removed her glasses, took a deep breath, and said, "Izzy, my husband can be an ass." I coughed out a laugh, and Mrs. Park flashed a conspiratorial smile. "He's under immense pressure at work, but that does not excuse his behavior at lunch on Sunday, and I need to apologize."

"It's okay," I said.

"No, it's not okay, and if you're gracious enough to share a table with us again, I promise you, Thomas will be on his best behavior."

"Thank you," I said, "I'd like that."

Mrs. Park seemed relieved to get this off her chest, and she walked me to the door with an arm around my shoulder. "I've bumped up Blaine's allowance this week," she said. "He's to take you somewhere nice for dinner to make up for it."

"That's not necessary," I said.

"Oh, but it is," Mrs. Park said. "Righting wrongs is what separates us from the animals."

"And opposable thumbs," I said, and Mrs. Park snorted something like a laugh.

"Thank you for stopping by, Izzy," she said, reaching for the door. "I'm sorry I kept you from the newspaper. Speaking of, how's your investigating going?"

"Not great," I said. "I've tried to talk to people at Bardo Bikes, Bardo Books, Bardo Boards, Creamery by the Sea, some shop that only sells T-shirts with Bardo written on the front, and that little boutique on 30A where the salespeople are all beautiful and apparently paid to be rude to you." Mrs. Park laughed like she knew the place. "But no one wants to talk to me. It's like they're afraid if they admit someone was murdered here, their property values will fall."

Mrs. Park shook her head and smiled. "Izzy, you're too young to be that cynical. It's like I said the other day, Ricky's murder was hell on this community. Don't be surprised if people are hesitant to talk about it."

"We did meet with a shirtless attorney in Cowden who played football with Ricky, but he wasn't much help." Mrs. Park squinted at this information but didn't say anything. "And we're interviewing Jack Duncan this afternoon. Elton thinks he'll have a ton of new information, but I'm not holding my breath."

"Jack Duncan," Mrs. Park said, straining to place the name. "Do you mean Chief Duncan?" I nodded, and Katherine Park laughed to herself. "Chief Duncan. I haven't thought about that man in ages. He was quite the celebrity around here during the investigation. On television every night talking about the murder. Ugly as sin." I laughed, and Mrs. Park said, "As I recall, he quit and moved away soon after the case closed. The rumor was he had a breakdown and couldn't handle police work anymore. So, he's moved back to the area?"

"PCB," I said. "Elton tracked him down online."

Mrs. Park considered this for a moment. "I guess people just can't stay away from these beautiful beaches."

"I guess not," I said before going on my way.

CHAPTER FOURTEEN

After school, Elton and I made the short drive over to Panama City Beach to meet Jack Duncan, former police chief of Bardo by the Sea. I hadn't been to PCB in years—our rare beach outings were usually to Destin because Mom liked to go outlet shopping on the way home—but the skyline shocked me. A seemingly endless line of towering condominiums stretched the length of Front Beach Road, and when the prime real estate had run out, they'd thrown up giant buildings across the street. A few projects were in various stages of construction, but the lack of cranes and workers in hardhats made me wonder if they'd be finished anytime soon. It turns out the bottom had already fallen out of the market. After a decade of meteoric growth, it would be eight years before another condominium would rise on Panama City Beach.

We drove past several Alvin's Islands, more restaurants with the word "Dick" in the name than I thought necessary, a store that appeared to specialize exclusively in condoms, the ruins of Miracle Strip Amusement Park, and Ripley's Believe It or Not! museum, because what family beach trip is complete without forking over thirty bucks to stare at some shrunken heads.

"Are you sure this is the place?" I asked Elton as we reached the bay and turned down the palm-tree-lined driveway of a white stucco mansion Tony Montana would be proud to call home.

"Affirmative," Elton said.

"Doesn't it seem like a lot of house for a retired cop?" I asked.

"It is seventeen thousand square feet," Elton recited from the public record he'd found.

"Right, and that's a huge house," I said, but Elton only shrugged as we parked next to a fountain on the crushed gravel driveway in front of the castle. Elton rang the bell, but no one answered, so I knocked, and he rang the bell again. I borrowed Elton's phone—Axl hadn't given me his hand-me-down iPhone yet—but a recording told me Chief Duncan's number "… has been disconnected or is no longer in service."

"Maybe he's around back," I offered, and we walked around the house, where a perfectly manicured St. Augustine lawn ran down to a three-hundred-foot pier, but no boat was moored to the dock. We waited around for half an hour before finally admitting we'd been stood up. With nothing left to do, we drove back to Bardo.

"Holy hell, Jack Duncan's house cost two million dollars," I said, looking at the public record on Elton's phone.

"Affirmative," Elton said.

We were back at my house, sitting around the breakfast table, speculating if Jack Duncan had forgotten about our interview or if he'd skipped town on his boat. The latter admittedly seemed farfetched, but so did a retired cop living in a bayside fortress.

"And you didn't think this was information I'd want to know?"

"It is irrelevant," Elton replied.

"Tanner Cobb told us to follow the money, and it looks like a lot of the money ended up with the cop who investigated Ricky Lee's murder."

Elton thought about this for a moment. "Every house in Bardo costs more than his house. Your house costs more than his house. It is not that much money."

I shook my head and blinked in disbelief. "Dude, you know Bardo isn't real, right? Like, no one in the real world lives this way."

Elton stared back blank-faced. I suppose if you were born and raised in Bardo, places like Pineview Villas felt as fictional as Middle Earth.

"Okay," I said, rubbing my temples to fend off a headache, "we need to find out all we can about Jack Duncan. Did he come from money? Did he win the lottery? Did he invent the internet after leaving Bardo?"

Elton took his phone back and began researching Jack Duncan, and I went to the medicine cabinet for some Advil just as Mom walked in from work.

"Hey, baby girl," she said, kissing my head before tossing her travel mug into the sink. "Another headache?"

"Another day."

"I didn't know you still had them. I thought maybe—"

"Living in a nice house would help? Nope, it turns out my brain is screwed up regardless of what zip code I'm in."

Mom frowned. "You know we've got good insurance now. If you want to see a doctor, I can make you an appointment."

Short of laying my head on a railroad track, there wasn't much I wouldn't have tried to get rid of my migraines before Blaine gave me that pill. But with the promise of more to come, I was content to take ibuprofen and suffer in silence for now.

Still, I think about this conversation often. It's funny how there are several forks in the road of life, yet some people seem destined to arrive at the same place no matter their path. Depression and anxiety are complicated. Treatment is nuanced, and counseling takes time, and honestly, our health care system isn't set up to deal with the roots of the disorder, but boy, can we ever treat the symptoms. Like pain. Doctors can treat pain with the illegible stroke of a pen on a prescription pad. And in 2008, in Florida, doctors wrote more opioid prescriptions than any other time and place in human history. Had I let my mother make me an appointment, it's a near certainty they'd have sent me to the pharmacy with a prescription for enough pain pills to kill an elephant. Back then, they'd give you opioids for a hangnail before even considering nail clippers.

"Seriously, I'm fine," I said, and Mom noticed Elton sitting at the breakfast table.

"Are you not going to introduce me to your boyfriend?" she asked, approaching the table. "Hi there, I'm Izzy's mom, Brandi Brown."

"Elton Jones-Davies," Elton said without looking up. "I am not allowed to date."

Mom turned to me, band I shrugged. "Well, nice to meet you, Elton Jones-Davies," she said with a laugh before walking back to the counter and sifting through the mail she'd brought in. "Junk, junk, bill, junk, and one for Izzy Brown," she said, handing me a small card.

I squinted at the envelope. There was no return address, just my name typed on the outside. Mom went upstairs for a shower, and I sat across the table from Elton and opened the note.

I read it six times before taking a breath.

Dear Izzy,

You're a curious girl. Nothing wrong with that. Curiosity should be encouraged. However, there is a line, and your inquisitiveness has crossed into the realm of meddlesome. You've been offered a tremendous opportunity here in Bardo. It would be a shame to lose it by continuing to stick your freckled little nose where it doesn't belong. So, Izzy, please accept this gentle reminder to focus on your studies, enjoy your high school experience, and don't go digging in the sand for skeletons that are best left buried. Otherwise, another quarterback might find himself floating in the Gulf, along with his sister.

Be well,

A Concerned Neighbor

"Elton, I've got good news and bad news."

"I prefer good news first."

"I think we're looking in the right direction."

He looked up. "And the bad news?"

I passed him the note.

CHAPTER FIFTEEN

"Who do we play tonight?"

"You join the team?"

"You. Bardo. Whoever."

"We play Vermillion, and they suck."

It was the Friday morning of Axl's first game as starting quarterback for Bardo Academy. He stood next to our sink finishing a bowl of cereal while I sat at the breakfast table, contemplating my half-eaten Pop-Tart. I'd been up half the night debating how to tell him about the note I received the day before. I knew he'd be pissed I hadn't stopped investigating Ricky Lee's murder. Plus, on the selfish side, I worried he might not play well if he knew someone had threatened to murder us and dump our bodies in the Gulf. And if he didn't play well, Dalton Wolfe might not see the point of keeping him on scholarship. He needed to know, though, if not for any other reason than to watch his back. Besides, Axl never worried about anything. This probably wouldn't bother him either.

I opened my mouth to tell him, just as Axl placed his bowl in the dishwasher and said, "It's stupid."

"What? Wearing a football jersey with dress pants?"

Axl popped his jersey and said, "Whatever. I make this look good." He sat next to me, took a bite of my Pop-Tart, and said, "No, tonight is stupid. I mean, Vermillion sucks. We're going to crush them. But this is my first game, and I missed most of spring practice with my ankle. Coach Martin told me yesterday we'll keep the gameplay simple. Start with some easy throws. Bubble screens and shit. But still, I don't know. I'm just … nervous."

I laughed out loud before I could stop myself.

"Thanks for the talk, sis," Axl snapped, standing to leave, but I grabbed him by the arm, and he sat back down.

"I'm sorry," I said, playfully shoving him, "I wasn't laughing at you. But you're never nervous. About anything."

Axl let out a deep breath. "I know, it's just …"

"What?"

"Football used to be just football, you know? It was a game. It was fun, and I was great at it. But now there's all this pressure. And I'm not talking about on the field. That still doesn't bother me. But if I don't play well, Mr. Wolfe might not see the point in paying for us to live here anymore. It's like I'm playing for you and Mom now too."

I loved him then. Loved him the way I did when we were kids, and he'd check the closet for monsters. Loved him the way I did in seventh grade when Bobby Singleton popped my bra strap and Axl gave him a black eye. And I knew he loved me too, because Axl, the boy who never worried about anything, was worried about letting down Mom and me. I wrapped my arms around his broad shoulders and squeezed. "Hey," I said, "you're going to play great. You always do."

I didn't tell him about the note.

The game kicked off at 7 p.m. at Dalton C. Wolfe Stadium. I sat next to Blaine and Sophie in the student section, and we cheered the team onto the field while the marching band played the fight song. Bardo got the ball first, and after the kickoff, Axl led the offense onto the field. He took the first snap and stood tall in the pocket, surveying the field with a calmness you cannot teach. He looked so big out there, like an adult playing with children, and when a Vermillion defender finally fought through the line, Axl eluded him with a nonchalantness bordering on arrogance. Then my brother cocked his right arm. The right arm he'd hurt falling face-first off a truck last weekend. The right arm Dalton Wolfe coveted perhaps more than his own. Axl's pass screamed straight through his crossing receiver's hands, ricocheted off his left shoulder pad, and bounced into the waiting arms of an unsuspecting Vermillion defender. I've no doubt there were groans of dismay from the Bardo fans as their opponent raced into the end zone and celebrated the pick-six with his delirious teammates, but I couldn't hear them. I couldn't hear them because the Vermillion fans, who like the rest of the area public schools, were sick and tired of Bardo Academy plucking their star players away, celebrated the touchdown like they'd won a world war.

I dropped my head in my hands as Axl jogged despondently off the field.

"Was that bad?" Sophie asked.

"It wasn't good," Blaine said, consoling me with his arm.

Bardo played the rest of the half conservatively, running the ball and slowly pounding Vermillion into submission. The home team led 24-7 when the bands took the field for their halftime shows, and I excused myself to the restroom.

"Friday salutations."

"Hey, Elton," I said, bumping into him near the concession stand. "I didn't know you were here tonight. I didn't see you in the student section."

"I find the volume of our classmates a hindrance to my viewing pleasure," he said. "So I sit in the press box and help Archie with the video board." He gestured to Archie, a small, bespectacled boy standing beside him.

"Nice to meet you, Archie," I said, extending my hand.

"I prefer not to shake hands, but it is likewise nice to meet you," Archie said, and I realized that somehow, Elton was the cool one in this relationship.

"Well, you guys are doing a great job," I said. "The replays were perfect."

Archie thanked me with an awkward bow before walking away.

"It is not a difficult job," Elton said, "though last year, someone pressed a wrong button, and everyone in the stadium was subjected to security camera footage of Mrs. Jones and Mr. Phillips doing a sexual intercourse in the chemistry laboratory."

"Yikes," I said, trying and failing not to picture what that would have looked like. "And let me guess, Bardo splurged for the high definition security cameras?"

"With audio," Elton said, shivering at the memory. I laughed, and he added, "On the murder front, I uncovered information concerning Jack Duncan this afternoon."

"Quieter, you donkey," I said, shushing him. "Did you forget about the note?"

Whereas most sane people would consider a death threat ample reason to call off an amateur murder investigation, I decided we should press on, only be quieter about it. Besides, Ricky Lee's death threat was a harmless cheerleader prank. Mine probably was too. Right?

"Apologies," he said before continuing in the loudest whisper imaginable. "After obtaining satellite imagery of Jack Duncan's boat, I—"

"Wait, what?"

"Google Maps," he clarified. "I have determined he owns a seventy-five-foot Sunseeker yacht, valued at roughly 1.8 million dollars."

"Good Lord," I said. "And did you find his parents? Did he come from money?"

"Ralph Duncan was a policeman in Panama City. Brenda Duncan taught elementary school. Mr. Duncan died in the late nineties, and Mrs. Duncan currently resides in a nursing home. I discovered no evidence to indicate they were wealthy."

"Weird," I said, rubbing my chin. "And do we know what Jack did after leaving Bardo?"

"He worked in sales for C. E. Petroleum in Odessa, Texas, for twenty years. I found a photograph of his retirement party in a company newsletter archived on their website. They gave him a cake shaped like an armadillo."

I squinted at Elton before asking, "And how much do C. E. Petroleum salesmen make?"

"I do not know what they made in 1983, but a job listing I found today boasted of a starting salary of thirty-eight thousand dollars plus benefits."

"So not enough to live in the Taj Mahal and drive a boat the size of the *Titanic*?"

"Measuring eight hundred and eighty-two feet from stern to bow, the *Titanic* was significantly larger than Jack Duncan's yacht. In fact—"

"It was an exaggeration, Mr. Wikipedia," I said, giving him a hug he flinched away from.

"Sorry," I said.

"I do not mind hugs," he said, "they just always catch me off guard."

"Noted," I said with a smile, then added, "and good job on the research."

Elton dramatically saluted me for no reason and turned to walk back to the press box before I stopped him.

"Hey, and you didn't tell anyone you worked on this, right?"

"No one asked," Elton said.

"Well, if they do ask, lie." Elton looked scandalized by this suggestion, so I added, "We've got to make it look like we've given up looking for the killer. The note was a prank, but even so, the investigation will go smoother if no one knows we're still investigating."

"You believe the note was a prank?" he asked.

"Yeah," I said without conviction. "No one would hurt us."

If only that were true.

CHAPTER SIXTEEN

Blaine's house was every bit as redonkulous as Sophie Wolfe's, though it somehow felt more lived in. More of a home. The Wolfes' living room had a museum-like quality that put me on edge. There was too much glass and crystal and marble to ever feel at ease around, and though the Wolfes were, to borrow a phrase, richer than shit, I feared they'd enforce a "you break it, you buy it" policy. On the contrary, the Parks' living room was full of books, family photos, and big, comfortable furniture, all angled toward a giant television currently tuned to the local news in hopes of seeing highlights of Bardo's 48-7 victory over Vermillion.

"Here we go," Axl said when the station came back from commercial break, and the sports segment began. But the clips were all from the first half and only showed Axl's interception followed by two rushing touchdowns for Bardo.

"That sucked," Axl said when the highlights ended.

"Dude, you played great in the second half," Blaine said.

"Yeah, but how are News Channel 7 viewers supposed to know that? Someone give me a phone. I'm calling to complain."

"Hello, News Channel 7," I said, holding my phone to my ear, for I was now the proud owner of a hand-me-down iPhone, "I'd like to see another replay of Axl Brown's interception. Yes, the one returned for a touchdown."

Axl threw a pillow at me and laughed. He was in a good mood thanks to the three touchdowns he'd thrown in the second half of the blowout win. I also suspected he'd taken something after the game. He wasn't drinking, though, because Blaine's parents were home. Well, his mother was. His father was mercifully out of town on business. So at least I didn't have to worry about him falling off a vehicle and prematurely ending his football career.

"I'm bored," Sophie said, yawning loudly. She stood and began perusing a bookshelf in the corner.

"You must be bored if you're considering reading," Blaine said, and Sophie shot him a bird.

She came back to the couch with an old Bardo yearbook and curled up next to my brother. They flipped through the pages, marveling together at the staggering display of early-eighties fashion. "Your mom rocked this *Flashdance* sweatshirt," Sophie said to Blaine.

"I didn't know your mom went to Bardo," I said.

Blaine nodded. "Yearbook editor. Prom queen. You name it. Dad went here too."

"Please, tell me your dad still has this Michael Jackson jacket," Sophie said, holding a page for us to see.

"I doubt he wants any reminders of how skinny he used to be lying around the house. I think he even tossed out his old letterman's jacket."

Axl took the yearbook from Sophie and began counting. "Eleven, twelve, thirteen. Thirteen zippers. Why would anyone ever need thirteen zippers?"

"It's weird to think your father played football," I said to Blaine.

"He was on the team," Blaine said. "To say he played is a stretch."

A small part of me wanted to interview Blaine's father about Ricky Lee and the 1983 team, but a much larger part of me would rather swim in a riptide than ever speak to him again.

Blaine grabbed the controller to change the channel, but I asked him to wait. Dalton C. Wolfe Stadium was back on the screen, but now a reporter was interviewing a man who looked like a young George Clooney. The graphic at the bottom identified him as State Rep. J. Mason Driscoll.

"He's too old for you," Blaine said, and I shushed him.

"Bardo Academy is home, and it's always nice to come back home," Representative Driscoll told viewers before flashing a mouthful of pearly whites.

The interviewer asked Driscoll something I didn't catch because Sophie was telling Axl that Michael Jackson needed those zipper pockets to keep his switchblade knives, which were vital in dance fights. The Representative smiled again and said, "No, that's the furthest thing from my mind. As always, I'm focused on the citizens of Florida's Fifth District. They sent me to Tallahassee to stand up to Hollywood's liberal elites and to fight for traditional family values, and that's what I intend to do."

Back in the studio, the bleached blonde anchor in a red dress said, "Despite denials, sources tell News Channel 7 the Representative will soon establish an exploratory committee. If elected, Driscoll will become the first United States Senator from Walton County."

"He's running," Blaine said, now flipping the channel to ESPN. "I was in the car with Dad last week when he called to ask for money."

Whoa. I'd always hedged toward Junior Wolfe killing Ricky Lee, but now I almost wanted it to be Mason Driscoll. Scandals involving Florida representatives are a dime a dozen. One was arrested last week for attempting to breed an alligator with his pet tiger. But if I brought down a candidate for the US Senate, Ivy League, here I come. Unless, of course, the *Washington Post* wanted to make me the LeBron James of investigative journalism and hire me straight out of high school.

"Was he friends with your dad in high school?" I asked Blaine.

"Not that I know of," Blaine said. "Driscoll was popular. Dad, not so much."

"No wonder," Axl said, still flipping through the Bardo yearbook. "Your dad apparently wore his Michael Jackson jacket every day."

Blaine laughed and said to me, "Dad is rich, though, and politicians need money, so they're friendly now, I guess you'd say."

"Are we seriously sitting here on Friday night talking about senators?" Sophie asked, sighing dramatically. "Why didn't we go to the party at that ugly girl's house?"

"Because her parents came back in town, and it was canceled," Blaine reminded her.

"Bitch," Sophie said before announcing her intentions to go home. She turned to Axl and added, "Come on if you want to make out. Otherwise, I'm going to bed."

Axl tossed the yearbook into my lap and said, "Hasta mañana, losers," before following Sophie down the beach to her house.

I opened the yearbook when Blaine went to the kitchen to pop some popcorn. No one had signed it, which made me sad until I realized it was his father's, then I felt guilty about how happy it made me.

Blaine returned, and pointing at a bespectacled kid with a relief map of acne on his forehead, said, "That's Dad."

Nice face, I thought. "You look like your mom," I said. Then in my poshest accent, I added, "Thomas B. Park III. It's a shame you're not Thomas the Fourth."

Blaine laughed. "Oh, I'm totally Thomas the Fourth. The B stands for Blaine."

"My fancy-ass boyfriend," I said, immediately regretting it since we'd yet to have the boyfriend-girlfriend discussion. But when he leaned in to kiss me, I knew I'd unilaterally defined our relationship. "Not now," I teased, pushing his face away. "I'm looking at this."

Blaine huffed and began quickly turning the pages for me. "There's Junior Wolfe, there's Mason Driscoll, there's Selena Mink."

"Who?" I asked, squinting at the photo of a scowling girl.

"Principal Baugh," Blaine said. "She and Mom were cheerleaders together." I scrunched my face in disgust while struggling to imagine Principal Baugh waving pom-poms, and Blaine continued, "There's Ricky Lee, and there's Mom."

"Katherine Ewing," I said, looking at her photograph. "She was beautiful."

"I guess," Blaine said.

I kept flipping through the yearbook, and Blaine ran upstairs because he said he had something for me. When I came to a photograph of Mason Driscoll, Junior Wolfe, and Ricky Lee celebrating a victory in some forgotten game, I snapped a picture of it on my phone and texted it to Elton because I now had those capabilities.

Me – We need to talk to Mason Driscoll.

Elton – Affirmative. I will make an appointment.

Me – Can you do that?

Elton – I am a taxpayer, am I not?

"Put these in your purse," Blaine said, returning to the couch and handing me a pill bottle.

I took the bottle and shook it, surprised at how heavy it was.

"Thank you," I said, "but you seriously didn't have to—"

"You're welcome," he said, putting an arm around me. "There is no need for you to suffer when you don't have to." Then he tried to kiss me again, and this time, I let him.

I let him until I was late for curfew.

1983

Ricky Lee was oblivious.

At Cowden, Ricky was worshiped, but he didn't have friends. Everyone was friendly, sure. Beyond friendly, even. Ricky was the quarterback, and quarterbacks are gods, but can man befriend a god? Classmates idolized Ricky, but they didn't know him. Even Traci Thompson, Ricky's girlfriend of two years, would later concede the boy was a mystery.

"I guess he liked football," she'd say.

What else?

"I don't know. We didn't talk much."

But in Junior Wolfe, Ricky found a kindred spirit. Yes, they'd both carried the mantle of starting quarterback, but they rarely talked football. Instead, new wave music was a popular topic of conversation. The boys discovered their mutual appreciation of The Cars, Blondie, and Duran Duran, along with a shared loathing of any song by Journey. Junior even gave Ricky his Sony Walkman because what was forty bucks to the son of Dalton Wolfe? They didn't share a taste in cinema, though both enjoyed debating and asserting their superior taste. One Saturday, after a blowout win for Bardo the night before, they spent most of the day at the Panama City Mall watching a double-feature of *Risky Business* and *Return of the Jedi.* Junior preferred the Tom Cruise flick, while Ricky favored Harrison Ford, though even he struggled to justify the inclusion of Ewoks.

That Ricky now dated Her Majesty never seemed to hinder the budding friendship. Junior felt relieved to be free from her grasp and even offered his new best friend advice on keeping her content.

Write notes and send flowers.

Take her to restaurants where everyone will see you together.

Treat her like the queen.

From the outside, all appeared well at Bardo Academy. But if high school is an ecosystem existing within a delicate balance, Ricky Lee was the invasive species. When Ricky took Junior's starting position, his girlfriend, and became his best friend, he set in motion a chain reaction of social unraveling, unlike anything the school had ever seen. At least three cheerleaders dumped their boyfriends in hopes of finding themselves on Junior Wolfe's arm. Those jilted boyfriends stole the girlfriends of other unsuspecting classmates, and on and on down the social food chain.

However, perhaps no one resented Ricky's arrival more than Mason Driscoll, for it was Mason, Bardo's most eligible bachelor, who'd lost his best friend.

Mason and Junior used to listen to Depeche Mode and rip on Journey.

Mason and Junior went to see *The Outsiders* and *WarGames* on opening night.

Mason and Junior used to bitch about Her Majesty being a bitch.

But no more. Now, when Mason hung out with Junior and Ricky, he felt like a third wheel. If he was invited at all.

At the 1876 Centennial Exposition in Philadelphia, kudzu was marketed to American farmers to stop soil erosion. The invasive vine, which grows a foot a day, now covers over seven million acres of the American south. The stuff surrounded the ramshackle house Ricky grew up in on the outskirts of Cowden. He sometimes wondered if the relentless vines had consumed his childhood home now that he and his father were no longer around to cut them back. But what did Ricky care, really? He had a new life, and it was perfect. Or so he thought.

Ricky Lee was oblivious to the damage he'd caused.

Invasive species always are.

CHAPTER SEVENTEEN

You can't turn on the news these days without hearing about opioids, but I didn't know what they were before I took one. This is due in part to my own naivete. A lot of kids at school knew what they were—Axl and Blaine certainly did. Still, the opioid epidemic wasn't a topic of national conversation yet, and by the time I learned what they do, it was too late.

Growing up, when Mom didn't want to talk on the phone, she'd take it off the hook so callers would hear a busy signal. This is how opioids work. They tell your brain to take its receiver off the hook, and when pain calls from your leg or back, no one answers. Opioids also release a reward chemical called dopamine, flooding our brains with warm feelings of pleasure and satisfaction and a not-so-subtle reminder to take more of them, and soon.

The pill Blaine gave me, OxyContin, was the drug of choice in the wild west that was the 2008 Florida pharmaceutical scene. Abusers would crush and snort them, getting a whole day high all at once. But I didn't take them to get high yet. Back then, when I took a pill, I just felt … relieved. Relieved there was an answer to my migraines and anxiety. I wasn't buzzed or spaced out. No one could look at me and tell I'd taken anything. I was myself, just the best version of myself. I felt like a computer, reformatted after years of contracting viruses and malware. I felt new. Fresh out of the box. I still had the same problems. It's not that I wasn't aware of them. But how could any problem be that bad if I felt this good?

A week passed with little to report on our Ricky Lee investigation. I hadn't given up, but with Chief Duncan missing in action and Axl's warnings not to upset Junior Wolfe, that only left Representative Driscoll, and I doubted he'd ever make time to talk to a couple of meddling kids who couldn't even vote. We could only read the same old newspaper articles so many times, there were no public records since the case never went to trial, and I couldn't exactly barge into the Bardo police department and demand to see their evidence collection. Actually, I could, and I did, and get this, the original Bardo police station, along with any evidence from Ricky Lee's case, went up in flames early New Year's Day, 1984. Fireworks, they said. Yeah, right.

Friday night, Bardo traveled to God-forsaken Washington County for their second game, but my ultimate goal in life was never to return to God-forsaken Washington County, so I didn't make that trip. Without my help, the team returned victorious, Axl having broken some single-game record for passing yards and finding his big dumb face all over the newspaper. I spent an hour with Mom on Saturday morning driving around Bardo, buying every copy of the *Walton Observer* we could find. Why she thought we needed more than one copy, I'll never know, but I guess we had the money now, so why not splurge.

Things with Blaine were good. Okay, better than good. We hung out every day after school, and as promised by his mother, he took me to dinner at Café Thirty-A on Saturday night to make up for that awful lunch with his father.

"Don't you love the fall?" he asked me over appetizers—jumbo lump crab cakes that cost more than I'd ever spend on an entree, much less a starter.

"It was ninety-three degrees today," I replied. "Not exactly pumpkin spice weather."

"True," Blaine said with a laugh, "but it's a lot easier to get a table here now that the tourists have thinned out, and it didn't take me twenty minutes to drive the mile to your house."

"I have noticed fewer cyclists on the roads for Axl to almost kill on our drive to school."

Blaine rolled his eyes. "Don't get me started on the bikes. I will never understand why these people want to ride on 30A when there is a perfectly suitable path right next to it. It's like they wake up every morning wondering how they can make the most congested road in Florida just a little worse."

"Preach on," said a man at the table next to us, whose dinner companions did not agree with his and Blaine's views on sharing the road, thus starting an argument that would last through dinner and probably continues to this day.

"You should consider the lobster," Blaine said, pointing at my menu.

"Forty-five bucks?" I asked. "Is it some rare albino lobster? I'm not sure I'd feel comfortable eating an endangered species."

Blaine laughed. "I promise you my father won't miss forty-five dollars."

"How is ol' Thomas these days?"

"I haven't seen him all week," Blaine said.

"Some weeks are better than others," I said with a wink.

"He's been in Atlanta meeting with boring old men in suits. Something's going on with the bank, but Mom won't say what." Blaine tried to play this off, but I could detect a hint of worry in his voice. Then I saw him discreetly take a pill over dessert and the concern melted away.

I'd had two headaches since Blaine gave me my own bottle of pills, matching my weekly headache average for as long as I could remember. But now I simply opened my nightstand drawer, popped a pink miracle into my mouth, and, voilà, instant normalcy. Just knowing that bottle was in my drawer had kept my anxiety at bay for the most part. I even considered taking one every morning before school because they energized me in a way that's hard to describe, but I figured that would set a bad precedent, so I resisted.

For a while.

"We have an audience with Representative Driscoll today," Elton said on Wednesday afternoon while we worked on our 1983 state championship story during last period extras. Well, while Elton worked on the story and I played on my new phone and ignored Denham Frost's dirty looks.

"Wait, really? How'd you pull that off?"

"I called him and asked."

"Nice work, Big E.," I said, offering a high five he just stared at.

"His office is in Rosemary Beach," Elton continued, "but we have to visit my house first."

"What for?"

"Mother insists on meeting the person I have spent so much time with recently," he said, and my heart raced.

"Wednesday greetings, Mr. Jones-Davies," said Clyde, the gatehouse guard to Eden Shores, with a toothy grin.

"Wednesday greetings, Clyde," Elton replied.

"And is that our quarterback's little sister with you?"

"Big sister, by six minutes," I said, and Clyde laughed as he opened the gate.

"Good Lord, Elton, I didn't know you lived in here," I said as we drove into the neighborhood.

"It is public record," Elton said.

"Well, yeah, but …" I said, searching for a smart-ass reply but losing my train of thought when Elton parked at the giant blue house between Sophie's and Blaine's. "Wait," I said, "this is your house?"

"Affirmative," Elton said matter-of-factly.

"So, your dad is … Mustang Jones?"

"Affirmative," Elton repeated and climbed from his Escalade without another word.

By now, I considered myself an old pro at walking into gigantic oceanside mansions, but Elton's was larger than both Sophie's and Blaine's. Best I could tell, it was the biggest house on Bardo Beach, and inside, the decor was minimalist and modern, like the interior of an alien spaceship from a planet that had outlawed any color not on the gray scale.

Walking through the living room, a giant furry dog of an indeterminate breed came bounding up. Elton ignored it and kept going into the kitchen, but I stopped and scratched the four-legged Brillo pad, making a new best friend in the process.

"You must be Izzy," a woman said, walking into the living room. "I'm Elton's mother, Holly."

Elton's mother was tall and unfairly attractive. I'm talking Halle Berry on a good hair day attractive. And she spoke with a British accent—the fancy kind, not the chimney sweep kind. We shook hands, and Holly Jones-Davies offered me something to drink before asking me to have a seat on her spaceship couch, facing out the giant picture window toward the Gulf. "Elton tells me the two of you are working on a story about Bardo's first state championship team," she said, sitting next to me.

"Yes, ma'am," I said, hoping Elton hadn't mentioned our part-time murder investigation.

"Hopefully, my husband will find the time for an interview this fall."

"He was on the 1983 team?" I asked.

"He was, though he seldom speaks of it. Terrance's Bardo Academy experience ..." She paused to find the right words. "It left much to be desired."

"Oh," I said, a thousand questions flooding my mind, all inappropriate to ask this woman I'd just met.

"How has your Bardo experience been so far?" she asked.

"Oh, great," I said. "Elton has been a big help, and I'm friends with your neighbors, Blaine and Sophie.

"Ah, yes, the neighbors," she said and started to add more, but seemed to reconsider, perhaps believing her thoughts inappropriate to share with the girl she'd just met.

Elton came back from the kitchen wearing a milk mustache. "Have you finished vetting Izzy?" he asked.

"I suppose I have," his mother said with a laugh, standing to hug her son and wiping the milk from his upper lip while he squirmed away. "He's a good lad," Holly Jones-Davies said. "You understand why I'm a touch overprotective."

"Yes, ma'am," I said, winking at Elton.

"So, you're off to interview the next junior senator from the great state of Florida?"

"We are," I said. "I'm shocked he's taking the time to meet with us."

"Yes, well, Elton's persistency tends to wear people down." I smiled, and Elton's mother said, "Mason Driscoll has been after Terrance to campaign for him for years. When he starts hounding Elton, remind him Terrance says Democrats buy grills too."

I laughed. "Don't worry. I'll always look out for Elton."

"That's all I needed to hear," Holly said before walking us to the door and hugging her son goodbye until he fought free of her grasp.

CHAPTER EIGHTEEN

"Elton," I asked, navigating his Escalade through 30A traffic toward Mason Driscoll's office in Rosemary Beach, "how long have we known each other?"

"Twenty-four days," Elton said without hesitation.

"Right," I said, laughing off the robotic quality of his reply, "and not once in those twenty-four days did you think it worth mentioning your father is, like, super-famous?"

"It never came up," he said, and I glared at him. "Besides, you never referenced your father."

I huffed. "Fine, my father's name is Rodney, and he left my mother when I was three. Last we heard, he married a one-legged stripper, lives in Nebraska, and works as a stay-at-home chemist."

"Your father is a chemist?" Elton asked.

"A meth dealer," I clarified, and Elton's mouth fell open. "Now, tell me about your dad."

"What would you like to know? I have read his autobiography twenty-three times."

I glanced over to see if Elton was joking, which of course, he was not. "How did he meet your mother?" I asked.

"She worked for an advertising agency, and he met her in England while promoting his new Nike cross-trainers. My father asked her to dinner, and they married three months later in a small cathedral in London."

"How romantic," I said, but Elton remained unmoved. "Okay, tell me about this grill he invented."

"He didn't invent it," Elton said. "My father lacks the mechanical inclination to change a lightbulb, much less invent an electric grill. I once saw him spend seven minutes trying to open our garage door with the television remote."

"Then why is his name plastered all over it?"

"After retiring from the NFL, my father gained a lot of weight, and Mattesserie, the company that invented the grill, approached him with a sponsorship offer. All my father had to do was lose fifty pounds, attribute his healthy new lifestyle to the grill, and pitch it relentlessly on television for the rest of his natural life."

"And when he dies?"

"They have licensed his likeness in hologram form for eternity."

I laughed, even though Elton was serious. "And they pay him for that?"

"Three million dollars a month since 1994," Elton said, and I coughed so hard we nearly hit a palm tree, then I spent the better part of the next minute multiplying large numbers in my head.

"So that's what he's doing now? Traveling the world selling grills?"

"No, he's in Connecticut right now. He's an NFL analyst for ESPN in the fall. The rest of the year, he promotes the grill at all the big cooking expos around the world."

"He sounds super busy," I said. "When was the last time you saw him?"

"March 31st," Elton said automatically.

"I'm sorry," I said.

"For what?"

"That you haven't seen your dad since March."

"He said if I went out for the football team, he would come to my games, but I prefer not to sweat."

"Florida is a great place to live if you prefer not to sweat."

"Mother often talks of moving back to London, but my father claims to like it here," Elton said, not catching my joke. "However, Mother believes he only likes having the largest house in Bardo and paying for me to attend Bardo Academy."

I felt terrible for Elton. His parents' marriage seemed rocky, even if he didn't realize it. And I couldn't escape the sneaking suspicion Mustang Jones didn't know how to relate to the brilliant, eccentric, sweat-phobic boy that was his son. On the bright side, Elton hadn't picked up on any of this. Otherwise, he'd probably be on the football team, trying in vain to impress his absentee father.

"Okay," I said after a while, "what did your mother mean when she said your dad's Bardo Academy experience left much to be desired?"

Elton thought for a moment as if trying to recall that passage from the book. "My father was the first Black student at Bardo Academy, and in 1983 the school was not properly evolved on issues of race. Coach Wallace did not want my father on the team, and a majority of parents did not want him attending the school, but Dalton Wolfe did."

"And Dalton Wolfe writes the checks," I said, thinking back to my horrible lunch with Blaine's parents.

"Bardo did not run the ball often in 1983. Coach Wallace built his offense around Ricky Lee, and he used my father primarily for blocking. But when Ricky Lee died, the game plan changed drastically. Coach Wallace did not have faith in the backup quarterback, so the load fell to my father. In the title game, he rushed for over three-hundred yards and seven touchdowns. Overnight, he went from an unknown high school senior to a cannot miss five-star recruit. He signed with Florida State, won the Heisman Trophy, and played six seasons with the Houston Oilers before breaking his leg in a playoff game. Do you want to see the video? It is gruesome."

"Uh, no," I said, and Elton shrugged.

We passed the faux-Mediterranean whitewash of Alys Beach, and turned into Rosemary Beach's quaint downtown, where a security guard was admonishing a gang of kids for performing skateboard tricks on the wall of the picturesque post office. "Representative Driscoll's office is in there," Elton said, pointing next door to the Sugar Shak. I nervously parked the giant Cadillac between a couple of two-door Mercedes. And as we walked into Representative Driscoll's office, I asked Elton, "Do you think your dad would talk to us about Ricky Lee?"

"I will ask Mom to text him and see," Elton said, insinuating he didn't even have his father's phone number.

"Cool," I said, as Tanner Cobb's words echoed in my ears. "Start with the money. Figure out who got rich after Ricky died, and maybe you can figure out why Ricky died."

Mustang Jones went from a forgotten running back to a top

recruit in seven short days, and twenty-five years later, he had more money than I could calculate in my head. And besides, it's not like he'd be the first former NFL running back accused of a brutal murder. My heart raced as we entered the building to talk to Mason Driscoll. The case was heating up again, and I even had a new suspect.

Too bad it was Elton's father.

CHAPTER NINETEEN

I blame my own political naiveté for expecting Rep. Driscoll's office to be in some flag-draped federal building where he sat all day in his American flag tie listening to constituents and solving their problems. In reality, Florida's state representatives make less than thirty grand a year, only work sixty days each winter, and spend the rest of the year campaigning like hell to get re-elected. Like most state legislators, Driscoll had a much more lucrative day job. He was a real estate attorney for D. C. Wolfe Properties.

"Mr. Jones-Davies," Mason Driscoll said, meeting us at his office door and vigorously shaking Elton's hand with both of his, "how long has it been? Have you been well? Still collecting those little Lego men? And how's your old man? What country is he hocking those fat-burning grills in today? Uzbekistan? Turkmenistan? And your mom, is she good? Could there be a nicer lady?"

Elton took a step back, unsure which question to answer first or how many Driscoll had even asked.

"And you must be Izzy," Rep. Driscoll said, turning to me with a smile and a handshake.

"Hello," I managed, coughing out the greeting with great effort. Mason Driscoll was probably the best-looking man I'd ever seen in person, and I had trouble looking directly at him and forming coherent sentences.

We followed Driscoll into his office, where framed photographs of him and everyone from George W. Bush to Bobby Bowden covered the walls. "Izzy, I saw your brother play in the season opener," Driscoll said after we'd taken our seats across from his giant desk. "That young man has an NFL arm. I know Dalton can't wait to see him play for the Seminoles. He might even win a Heisman Trophy like Elton's daddy."

I turned to Elton and smiled, but he continued to process all the questions Mason Driscoll asked when we entered the room.

"So, what can I help y'all with today?" Driscoll asked, clapping his hands together and bringing them to his chin. "Elton, you mentioned you're writing a story on the '83 team."

"Affirmative," Elton said, speaking for the first time, but when he left it there, I had to pick up the slack.

"We're writing a story about the school's first state championship for a special homecoming game edition of the *Breeze*," I said, "and since you were an integral part of the '83 team, we hoped you'd share some memories."

Mason Driscoll smiled and touched his state championship ring. "I don't know how integral I was to the team's success, but I did catch a few passes that season."

"From Ricky Lee," I said, and Rep. Driscoll nodded.

"What was he like?" I asked.

"Ricky? He was the best pure passer I've ever seen. I know tales of high school glories tend to expand like waistlines, but I kid you not, I saw Ricky ring a trash can from forty yards away six times in a row one day after practice. He didn't miss the seventh either. He just got bored and walked away."

"Were the two of you friends?"

"Yes, well, no, not at first," Driscoll said, smiling at a memory. "Junior Wolfe was my best friend, but he and Ricky hit it off, and I was jealous."

Jealous enough to murder him, I thought. "Tell us about the '83 season," I said.

Driscoll went all Uncle Rico on us for several minutes, detailing his athletic achievements in such detail I found him much less attractive than I had moments earlier.

"You said you were not friends with Ricky Lee at first," I said when the politician took a moment to catch his breath, "but you were with him the night he died. Had the two of you patched things up?"

"Oh sure," Driscoll said after a moment's thought. "Ricky and I, we came from significantly different backgrounds. I grew up here on 30A. He was a Cowden farm boy. But Ricky, he wasn't your stereotypical jock. Looking back, I'm not even sure if he liked football. Sure, he was amazing at it, but I think he viewed the game as a way to get out of the sticks. Ricky was into music, he'd started playing guitar, and he read obsessively. Ricky was, he was …"

I took notes while Mason Driscoll spoke, but when he hesitated, I glanced up to see him crying big fat crocodile tears.

"I'm sorry, guys," he said, pulling his American flag handkerchief from his pocket and wiping his eyes. "Losing a classmate is hard. You'd think it gets easier with time, but the older I get, the more I'm reminded of the life Ricky never got to live."

I'm not proud of this, but my first reaction to Mason Driscoll's tearful performance was to ask what politician worth their weight in votes can't cry on demand.

"What can you tell us about the night Ricky died?" I asked after he'd dried his eyes. But perhaps I came on too strong because Mason Driscoll pressed a button on his desk phone, and two seconds later, a secretary popped in to let him know his next appointment had arrived.

Rep. Driscoll stood and ushered us toward the door. "Not much," he said, answering my final question. "We'd spent most of that Saturday celebrating our semifinal win. Celebrating too hard, probably, but kids will be kids, I suppose. Ricky, Junior, and I were on the beach until late, and when Junior and I went home, Ricky went to buy drugs. The scary thing is none of us knew he had a problem. So, y'all watch out for your friends, you hear me?"

Mason Driscoll locked eyes with me when he said this, and for a split second, I wondered if this man could sense I had an illicit bottle of pills in my room just by looking at me. But the panic passed, and Driscoll bid us goodbye, standing in his doorway as Elton and I made our way out of his office toward the parking lot. "Oh, and Elton," he said, and we both turned around, "you tell Mustang I'm still waiting on that endorsement."

"Democrats buy fat-burning grills too," Elton said after a long pause, and Rep. Driscoll just laughed, flashing more teeth than a shark.

CHAPTER TWENTY

On Friday, Bardo vanquished the rival South Walton Seahawks in spectacular fashion, with Axl accounting for six of the seven touchdowns. After the game, what felt like the entire student body went to Nowhere and partied late into the night. I'd taken a pill for a migraine that morning, my fourth of the week, and was hesitant when Blaine offered me a cup of red punch that smelled like strawberries dipped in rubbing alcohol. But it was over twelve hours since I took the pill, so I drank the punch and thankfully had no desire to climb onto the roof of a parked car. Two more cups later, Blaine and I snuck off into the woods for some privacy, bears be damned. Considering the punch somehow smelled like it contained more than 100 percent alcohol, it was no surprise I woke Saturday morning with an embarrassing bruise on my neck and a raging headache. I took another pill and slept past noon.

After breakfast or lunch or whatever you call the Pop-Tart you eat at 1 p.m., I went outside for some vitamin D. Walking toward the beach, I took note of how much our street had decayed in the short time we'd lived there. Sprinkler heads dotted the dusty, overgrown lots, but no one had bothered to turn them on since we moved in, and consequently, the imported palm trees lining both sides of the road were either dead or well on their way. The water in the fountain at the end of the street was green and stagnant, and summer storms had blown over most of Junior Wolfe's for sale signs. I stopped and stared at one of the few signs still standing. Both the face and phone number had faded past recognition, and fire ants raced up and down the stick. Before the crash, Junior Wolfe must have felt like he was planting magic beans every time he stuck one of these signs into the ground. But now the drought had come, and his stalks had withered and died.

When I reached the sand, I sat and closed my eyes and soaked in one of those brilliant Emerald Coast days you get in late September tucked between the summer vacationers and October snowbirds. The temperature was Goldilocks perfect, and no cloud would dare harass such a perfectly blue sky. A pod of brown pelicans flew by in formation, flapping their wings hard, then skimming just above the blue-green Gulf for several yards, the tips of their feathers all but touching water. I watched them until they were out of sight, then stood and dipped my feet in the surf, realizing I hadn't actually gone swimming since the move. Before living here, I assumed I'd jump in every day, but we're not all characters in a Jimmy Buffett song, and life gets busy regardless of scenery.

Somewhere, Elton was digging through Mason Driscoll's campaign documents, looking for something but not exactly knowing what. The Representative's relationship to the Wolfe family was evident and in the open for anyone to see. But maybe we'd find something fishy, like ties to Jack Duncan, the former Bardo police chief.

My focus was now on Elton's father because he obviously benefited the most from Ricky Lee's death. Finding information on Mustang Jones was not difficult. I'd watched a documentary about him on YouTube the night after we interviewed Mason Driscoll. But the video glossed over his short time at Bardo Academy, only mentioning he led the team to a state championship. I needed to talk to someone who knew him in school. I had a date with Blaine that night. If I saw his mother, I could ask her.

I hadn't forgotten about the note from a concerned neighbor who threatened to throw my corpse into the Gulf. Still, I hadn't received a second note, so maybe going radio silent on our investigation had thrown them off our scent. Elton and I made a list of everyone who knew we were researching the murder, and it was long. Long enough it felt safe to assume we'd never know all the people who knew. There was my mom, Axl, Sophie, her parents. Blaine, his folks, Tanner Cobb in Cowden, Denham Frost, several other newspaper kids who'd overheard us discussing the case, and dozens of random Bardo citizens I'd accosted on the beach, at football games, and in the crowded aisles of Bardo Market. But only Elton and I knew we were still at it, and so far, no new note. I'd even developed a convenient and comforting theory that Axl sent the note himself. He'd been the most vocal opponent of our investigation, so it was possible. Then again, the note didn't have any misspellings, so probably not.

"Beautiful day," a voice behind me said, and I turned around to see the oldest woman on Earth, squinting into the midday sun.

"Yes, ma'am," I agreed, her leathery skin making me wish I'd put on sunscreen before venturing outside.

"Years ago, it was always like this," she said, waving a hand at the empty beach where oil-covered tourists would usually lie baking in the sun.

"How long have you lived here?" I asked.

"In Florida? All my life. In that house," she said, turning and pointing between two mansions at a small beachside shack I'd never noticed until now, "since I retired in 1981."

"Oh, wow," I said. "I'm sure this place has changed a lot since then."

"For the worse," the old woman snapped. "Back in the day, just us misfits and screwballs lived down here. Weirdos drift toward the edges, you know. But we're dying off and being replaced by CEOs and their tennis-skirt wearing trophy wives. I used to live next door to a mullet fisherman, now I'm neighbors with some Fox News blowhard who thinks his property line extends all the way to Havana." She shook her head and extended a middle finger toward her neighbor's mansion. "This place is evil."

I laughed, but she didn't smile. "What makes you say that?" I asked.

"Do you read the Bible?"

"Not religiously."

The old woman snorted. "Well, it says the love of money is the root of all evil, and look around, money lovers as far as the eye can see. All these greedy men and their ridiculous castles. Two years ago, one of those sleazy developers offered me three million dollars for my place." She looked back at her ramshackle house and laughed. "Well, three million dollars for the land under it. Now you tell me what in the world would I do with three million dollars?"

I wasn't sure if this was a rhetorical question or not, so I shrugged, and the old woman said, "Exactly. I kindly told them to take their money and go see the devil in hell. I plan to die in that house, then my kids and their lawyers can sort it all out in court. That's what they get for never visiting."

I smiled and asked, "So, you lived here when the Bardo Academy student was murdered?"

"I found him," she said.

"Wait, what?"

"I found him. A few hundred yards from here," she said, pointing down the beach. "My late husband and I stumbled on him during our morning walk." She shook her head at the memory. "Awful, awful day."

"A friend and I are investigating his murder for our school newspaper," I told her. "We don't believe drug dealers killed Ricky."

"Of course they didn't," the old woman said before slowly bending over to pocket a shell she was eyeing.

"Do you know who killed him?" I asked.

She laughed bitterly. "No, and I don't want to. It takes a lot of money to cover up something that big. Your problem is, there are plenty of people around here rich enough to make it all go away."

"Don't I know it," I said.

"If I were you, I'd let it go," she said. "Whoever killed that boy would do the same thing to you and not think twice."

This was the second time someone had warned me the person I was looking for wouldn't think twice about killing me too. I thought about the note and shivered.

The old woman shook her head at me and added, "But I can tell by looking at you you're not the quitting type."

"No, ma'am," I said.

She finally smiled and looked off at the horizon. "I think about the poor boy's momma all the time. Don't you know she rues the day her family moved here?"

I thought about our own move to Bardo and wondered if we'd one day come to regret it too. Probably, knowing our luck.

"You be careful now," the old woman said, turning back toward her house.

"Wait," I said, something the old woman mentioned setting off alarm bells in my head. "Does Ricky Lee's mother still live around here? I'd love to talk to her."

"She moved away and hopefully never looked back," the old woman said. "But she wouldn't be hard to find. Folks never are unless they want to be."

1983

Ricky Lee was happy.

From the outside, this would seem obvious. Ricky was the star quarterback of the undefeated Bardo Academy football team, and he was breaking state and national records with every pass. The school's first playoff berth was in the bag, and whispers of a state championship grew louder daily, all because of Ricky. Last week, after he publicly committed to Florida State, the *Walton Observer* sent a reporter to school to interview Ricky for a front-page cover story. His parents framed a copy and hung it over their television, though Ricky never saw them read it.

Socially, all was well. Friday nights after games and Saturday afternoons, Ricky did whatever he wanted, but his Saturday nights belonged to Her Majesty. Thanks to small "loans" from Dalton Wolfe, every date night, Ricky took her to dinner at Délicieux 30A, the swanky and oh-so-pricey French bistro in Bardo's town square. Then they'd usually rent a movie and go back to her house. They'd had sex eight times, a number Ricky didn't have to try hard to recall, because for some odd reason, Her Majesty insisted on referencing the growing digit in every note she wrote him, and she wrote him several a day.

Yes, from the outside, Ricky Lee's happiness seemed apparent.

He was the star quarterback.

He drove a car straight out of freaking *Knight Rider*.

He was sleeping with the hottest girl in school.

But none of this made Ricky happy.

Football came easily to Ricky, but he didn't love it. Not the way he loved music and movies and books. But those things hadn't gotten him out of Cowden, and Ricky was a pragmatist. Once he got to Florida State, he could study whatever he liked. Dalton Wolfe and the coaches had promised him as much. And after he'd made his fortune in the NFL, he could do whatever he wanted with his life. Ricky viewed football as a sort of conscription he'd have to serve before getting on with the real business of living life. Football was the path to happiness, not the source.

Neither was Her Majesty. If Ricky were honest, he hated everything about her. Her Majesty's parents were divorced—her father now lived in West Texas, her mother in Bardo—and they competitively spoiled their only daughter to the point Ricky found her company intolerable. The sex was okay, Ricky figured. No better or worse than any of the girls from Cowden Ricky had slept with. But at least when he and Her Majesty were having sex, she momentarily stopped droning on about the Guess jeans she'd bought with the check her daddy sent. Deep down, Ricky knew it wasn't healthy to feel a sense of impending doom while driving to pick up your girlfriend for a date, but whatever—he'd move to Tallahassee in June and never think about her again.

No, Ricky's happiness could be entirely attributed to his friendship with Junior Wolfe. Though they'd grown up worlds apart, Junior and Ricky had more in common than they would have ever dreamed. Ricky began spending several nights a week with the Wolfes since it saved him the half-hour commute from his parents' new house in Vermillion. The only problem was he typically went to school more exhausted than usual after a late night of beating Junior at Atari.

After games on Friday nights, Ricky and Junior often skipped the parties and cruised 30A in Ricky's car. On Saturdays, they took to the sea, cruising the shoreline and 30A's rare costal dune lakes in one of Dalton's boats. One day they discovered a secluded wooded inlet on Powell Lake, close to where a famous Australian golfer would one day build a golf course. From then on, that's where they'd drink their Saturdays away, listening to music and cracking each other up.

"Wait, don't you have a date tonight?" Junior asked on what Ricky would remember as the best day of his life. A day when they'd stayed in their secret drinking spot well past sunset.

"Shit. I'm dead," Ricky said. He was already an hour late to pick up Her Majesty.

Junior laughed at him the entire ride back to the dock, but Ricky didn't care.

For the first time in his life, Ricky Lee was happy.

CHAPTER TWENTY-ONE

Perhaps there is a delicate way to tell a friend you suspect his father to be a cold-blooded murderer, but I could not think of one, so for the better part of a week, I avoided talking to Elton about the case. He was still researching Mason Driscoll, and I'd also sent him down the rabbit hole of finding Ricky Lee's mother, but when he'd give me updates, I'd just nod and quickly start a *Millennium Falcon* vs. USS *Enterprise* debate, which he couldn't resist. "While technologically advanced, the hyperdrive on the *Millennium Falcon* is significantly less reliable than ..."

Things would have been easier had Elton not worshiped the ground his father walked on, something I could not relate to in the slightest. I only had two memories of my father, one disputed, both shitty.

The first, denied vehemently by my mother, involved the day he left. It was 1995, early October, and Hurricane Opal had just ravaged the Gulf Coast. He left three days later, on a Saturday, claiming he'd found work clearing debris from the hundreds of homes destroyed in

Escambia County. This much my mother concedes. What she contests is my insistence I saw him go. That even to this day, I still vividly recall sitting on the couch with Axl, watching *Rugrats*, and seeing him stumble through the den, all his belongings and all my mother's valuable belongings in a duffle bag slung across his back. She disputes he stopped on his way out and stood in front of us, and we both shouted at him for blocking the television. She refuses to accept he kissed my brother softly atop the head before waving his tobacco-stained fingers in my direction. But he did, and he was gone.

"Izzy, that just did not happen," Mom said anytime I'd share this memory.

"You weren't there," I'd reply.

My rebuttal always stung more than I intended, but it was true. She wasn't there. She was at work, waiting tables at the Dandridge Waffle King. Axl and I were alone in our trailer for eight hours before she finally came home. We'd just turned three.

"Well, first of all, Rodney took the damn television," Mom would always answer, "and second, he would've kissed you both."

"Well, he didn't."

"Well, that doctor said you can't remember things that far back, so it must have been a bad dream or something."

Because we stopped seeing the local pediatrician during elementary school on account of her insistence that Mom pay her bills, "that doctor" could have alluded to any number of general practitioners working at the Dandridge doc-in-a-box through the years. Mom began taking me to see them for my migraines when I was eight or nine, and after ruling out allergies and tumors and aneurysms, one of those ever-changing white coats referred us to the local psychiatrist, but she didn't accept Medicaid, and Mom couldn't afford brand name cereal, much less seventy bucks a week for me to lie on a couch and talk about my feelings. So, recalling their six weeks of psychiatric training from medical school, several of these locums tried counseling me themselves, once a month, in fifteen-minute increments. This did not help my headaches. But when, at his request, I shared my earliest memory with one of the doctors, he confirmed my mother's belief it was likely false, citing infantile amnesia, a term I suspect he'd just googled.

"You weren't there," I told the good doctor, and Mom told me to shut my mouth.

Eventually, they diagnosed me with anxiety and depression and prescribed an antidepressant, but Mom couldn't afford the copays, so she started giving me a Goody's headache powder every morning with my bowl of Fruity Rings. This did not help my headaches either, but I stopped complaining because what was the use?

My second, irrefutable memory of my father concerned the birthday card he sent Axl and me for our eighth birthday. We were born on August 1st, but the card showed up around Halloween, with no return address, probably because Dad owed years of alimony, and if Mom knew where he lived, she'd have driven there and beaten the money out of him. The postmark said the letter came through Nebraska, though, and for a while, Axl and I bounced around a theory that Hurricane Opal scared our father so bad he moved to the smack middle of the country for safety. The card, covered in daisies and featuring a sappy poem written in a curly script neither of us could read, looked like something you'd grab for your grandmother last minute. When Mom opened it, two crumpled five-dollar bills fell on our dirty floor.

Axl snatched both bills, and after Mom wrestled one away from him and gave it to me, she sat us on the couch and said, "Those are a birthday present from your daddy. He wrote here that he loves you and not to spend it all in one place." The next time Mom took us to K-Mart, we did just that.

My mother was pretty. Perhaps, in all the wrong ways, since she seemed to only attract men like my father or worse. My quality of life ebbed and flowed with these men. Some were useless but harmless, like Todd, the El Camino driving pothead who'd come over stoned, eat every Dorito in our kitchen, then sleep in our tub for the next sixteen hours. Others were useless and scary, like Donnie, who gave my mother black eyes for four months until she chased him out of Pineview Villas with a butcher knife one cold January night.

None of my mother's boyfriends ever touched me. One might have, but he was small, and at thirteen, Axl beat his ass outside our trailer, then pelted his Camaro with rocks while he sped away, never to return. Whenever a new man would show up at our trailer, I could usually give them a once-over and tell how much trouble he'd be before he even opened his mouth. There was usually something in the eyes that said, "Better stay clear of this one and hope he moves on soon." It's a skill I wish I hadn't needed, but it served me well through the years.

Axl and I hoped Mom would date a higher caliber of man after our move to the beach. Surely strung-out rednecks were harder to come by in Bardo by the Sea than Dandridge by the Landfill. But when I walked back to our house from the beach after talking to the old woman who discovered Ricky Lee's body, there was a beat-up white van sitting in our driveway. Thinking back through Mom's Rolodex of shitty boyfriends, the worst ones always drove vans. I cursed and silently prayed that our air conditioner had blown and this vehicle belonged to the HVAC man, but the entirety of my life experience led me to quickly deduce that wouldn't be the case.

"There you are," Mom said as I walked through the door. She was on the couch next to a man wearing a wife beater with white jorts. Dammit to hell.

"Izzy, this is my friend, Lenny Roach."

I snorted out a laugh before I could stop myself. Typically, we'd hear about Mom's boyfriends before we met them. When they had normal enough sounding names, Axl and I would hold out a false hope they'd be normal enough people. But Lenny Roach's name made no pretense he'd be good for my mother in any way.

"Call me Slim," Lenny Roach said with a wink, then propped his likely stolen Air Jordans on our coffee table.

"Sure thing, Lenny," I replied, and he laughed. The laughter was good. A stern glare here would mean bad news for Mom down the road, but Lenny wasn't a hothead, it seemed. At least not sober, which I assumed he was at 2 p.m. on Saturday afternoon, but you never knew with these guys.

I turned to Mom and said, "I'll be upstairs if you need me."

She smiled and nodded, and Lenny snapped his fingers and pointed at me in a super douchey way. Perhaps my Spidey sense was off, but this one seemed okay. Goofy, but okay. Sure, when it came, the breakup would be ugly. Lenny might even swipe our toaster walking out the door. But in the end, I thought he'd be one of the least memorable participants in Mom's cavalcade of deadbeats.

CHAPTER TWENTY-TWO

"I found Ricky Lee's mother."

"You drowned what?"

"Found. Located. Discovered."

"Who?"

"Ricky Lee's mother."

It was Friday, pep rally day, and against school spirit protocol, Elton and I sat on the back row of bleachers in Bardo Academy's Dalton C. Wolfe gymnasium while our classmates stood and implored the football team to win their fourth game of the season by loudly repeating some of the lamest cheers in the history of cheerleading.

"Really? Where?" I asked.

"Cowden," Elton said. "It appears she returned soon after Ricky's murder."

Elton said this during a lull in the cheers, and the girl in front of us spun around and looked down, but she quickly turned back when I flipped her double birds. Looking back, perhaps I shared some of the blame for not making many friends at Bardo Academy.

"Can we call her?" I asked. "Did you find her phone number?"

Elton shook his head. "It is either unlisted, or she does not own a phone."

I thought for a moment. "You up for another trip to Cowden?"

"Negative. I have Tae Kwon Do this afternoon."

"You take Tae Kwon Do?"

Elton blinked at me. "I just told you I did."

"Right," I said. "Okay, what about Sunday?"

Elton hesitated, letting the sophomore class finish a cheer about blood making the grass grow, even though Bardo had artificial turf. "I prefer to watch my father's NFL show on Sunday morning," he said once we could hear each other again.

"We can leave after lunch," I suggested.

"He does another show in the afternoon."

"Okay, fine, what about after school on Monday?"

Elton checked his mental calendar and nodded vigorously. "Affirmative."

On Saturday, after a big Bardo victory over Rutherford, in which Axl tossed four touchdowns and ran for two more, Blaine picked me up for date night. After a lifetime of embarrassment over our Pineview Villas accommodations, I instinctively blocked my boyfriend at the door, but like always, he squeezed past me to say hello to Mom. They were both Miami Dolphins fans, and their pastel-clad heroes had defeated Tom Brady's Patriots the week before, so they had a lot to discuss. Plus, I suspected he had a crush on Mom. Boys always did. She was young compared to the rest of our friends' parents—she looked like me, only taller and prettier and, well, chestier—and she was always overly friendly to Blaine, perhaps to make up for yelling at him and making fun of his eyebrows the night they met in the Sacred Heart emergency room.

"And what big plans do the two of you have for this evening?" Mom asked while Blaine and I sat at the kitchen bar, watching her prepare dinner.

"Dinner at The Red Bar," Blaine said.

"Yum, I might join you," Mom said. "I've always wanted to hear their jazz band."

"Come with us," Blaine said, and Mom laughed and brushed his arm a little too flirtatiously for my taste.

Blaine blushed and added, "Later we'll probably hang out with Axl and Sophie at her house. Watch a movie or something."

I'd hoped we'd watch a movie at Blaine's so I could talk to his mother about Mustang Jones, but his father was back in town and in a lousy mood.

"Well, that sounds like a fun evening," Mom said, snapping two handfuls of spaghetti noodles and dropping them in a boiling pot.

"What sounds fun?" Lenny asked, walking into the kitchen from the hall bathroom. Mom began to explain, not noticing Lenny's peculiar smirk.

"Lenny Roach," Lenny said, walking over to shake Blaine's hand.

"Blaine," Blaine said.

"You got a last name, Blaine?" Lenny asked.

"Park," Blaine added reluctantly.

"Well, it's a pleasure to meet you, Blaine Park," Lenny said with an odd chuckle.

"Yeah, you too," Blaine said, standing and putting his hand on my back, suddenly eager to leave.

"Y'all have fun tonight," Mom called after us, but we were already out the door before I could reply.

Axl and Sophie were outside on the middle deck finishing a meal Rosalia had begrudgingly prepared when we arrived at the Wolfes' mansion.

"Mom has commandeered the downstairs television," Sophie said, pointing through the window at a woman on the couch holding a basketball-sized glass of wine. "On Saturdays, she watches *Snapped* and drinks until she passes out, but we can watch the movie in the twins' playroom."

"What is *Snapped*?" I asked.

"Some true crime show about women who snap and kill their husbands," Sophie said. "Mom probably thinks it's an instructional video."

"Oh," I said, because what else can you say to that?

"What'd you rent?" Blaine asked as the four of us ascended the stairs.

"*Superbad!*" Axl said.

"Again?" Blaine asked.

"Again," Sophie said with a dramatic sigh.

"What? It's hilarious," Axl said. "McLovin!"

The twins' playroom was 1,600 square feet of couches, arcade games, ping-pong and pool tables, and possibly the largest television ever produced by the good people at Samsung. Two identical nine-year-old boys sat three feet from the screen, rapidly hitting buttons on their controllers.

"Shoot her!" one of the twins shouted.

"Die, bitch!" the other replied.

On-screen, a nurse collapsed in a hail of bullets, and as the twins celebrated their victory over an unarmed healthcare worker, I shook my head in disbelief.

"Get out," Sophie told her brothers, "we're watching a movie in here."

The twins ignored this and continued their spree of digital violence until Sophie unplugged their PlayStation mid-game.

"Get out, or I'm showing Mom that screenshot of your browser history," Sophie said. The twins stomped out, but not before calling their sister every curse word they knew, which was apparently all of them plus a few I'd never even heard.

While Sophie tried to start the movie, Blaine grabbed Axl by the shoulder, and the two of them walked out onto the top deck to talk. "Secrets don't make friends," Sophie called after them, but they ignored her and shut the door. Blaine had acted weird all through dinner, asking me more than once about Lenny. "Not long," I said when he inquired how long he'd dated my mother. "A couple of weeks at most. I doubt he'll be around long. They never are." This appeared to relieve him momentarily, but he asked the same string of questions again during dessert.

I watched my brother and boyfriend have an animated conversation through the glass before realizing I had an opportunity to ask Sophie something without either of them around.

"I had no idea Elton's dad was Mustang Jones," I said.

"Crazy, huh?" Sophie replied, her efforts to start the movie yielding nothing but a solid blue screen so far. "Elton can barely tie his shoes. You'd never know that weirdo was the offspring of some famous athlete."

I'd forgotten I didn't particularly like Sophie, but she didn't take long to remind me.

Do you take bitch lessons, or does it come naturally? I thought. "Have you ever met Mustang?" I asked.

Sophie rolled her eyes and nodded. "He coached the soccer team Elton and I played on in elementary school. God, he was scary. Always yelling at us for not hustling or some shit. He hasn't spent much time in Bardo since he accepted his son would never be a football star, which is fine with us. Dad heard Mustang was a gang banger in Pensacola before Grandpa moved his family to Bardo. Said he killed a homeless man as part of his initiation."

"Holy shit," I said.

Sophie nodded gravely as Axl and Blaine came back inside, both looking like they'd received a dire prognosis. Sophie finally got the DVD player working, then the four of us sat in the dark and watched the movie. But it's hard to laugh when you're pretty sure your friend's dad is a killer.

CHAPTER TWENTY-THREE

After one of the more awkward date nights of my life, Blaine drove me home, and we half-heartedly made out on the porch until a flock of giant 30A mosquitos chased him home. My head was pounding now from stressing out about Elton's dad, so I took another pill, my second of the day. Once I felt normal again, I pored over all the newspaper clippings we had from the fall of '83, looking for mentions of Mustang Jones but not finding many. From what Elton's mother said, most people at Bardo didn't want him there to begin with, so I doubted he was partying with classmates the night Ricky Lee died, but how could I know for sure? The answer drove down my street.

It was sometime after 2 a.m., and I was on my balcony, watching the moon drift across the sky when a familiar sports car rumbled past our house and parked next to the fountain in the circle. The door opened skyward, and a man stepped out and walked through the dunes to the sea, but this time I caught a better glimpse of him. Perhaps my second pill of the day gave me the courage I typically wouldn't have found, but I left the house barefoot to catch up.

I found Junior Wolfe a few hundred yards down the shore, sitting on the beach with his chinos rolled up to mid-calf. He was drawing in the sand with a stick of driftwood when I approached, but he didn't look up until I said, "Hi, Mr. Wolfe." There was no trace of recognition on his face, so I added, "I'm Izzy Brown, Axl's sister."

"You're out awfully late, Izzy Brown, Axl's sister," he said with a smile before turning back to the ocean.

Junior Wolfe wore an FSU cap, so I couldn't tell how much more of his hair had fallen out since I'd last seen him. But even in the moonlight, I could see he'd lost several pounds he could ill afford to lose. His baggy golf shirt ballooned out in every direction at his waist, where he'd cinched his belt to the last notch. I wondered if he might keel over soon and if the life insurance money would be enough to keep his family out of the poorhouse. Uninvited, I sat next to him.

"Have a seat, stay awhile," he said with a laugh.

"I've seen you come down here before," I said.

"I'm sure you have," he said. "I come here to think." He looked at me, smiled again, and added, "And there's a lot to think about these days, don't you think?"

Junior was a different person than the man I'd met a month earlier. He laughed and smiled so easily I thought he was either drunk or had just received some good news from the bank. He was in such a good mood, I pressed my luck. "Did you know this is close to where they found Ricky Lee's body?"

"This is exactly where they found Ricky's body," Junior Wolfe replied, and I gasped involuntarily. "You and Terrance's boy are investigating his murder, correct?"

"How'd you know?"

"Bardo has grown, but it's still a small town at heart. And there are no secrets in a small town." He tossed his stick into the water and asked, "How's your investigation going? Any leads?"

"I'd rather not—"

"Tell me I'm your prime suspect?" he said and laughed. "You're not going to hurt my feelings. I was one of the last people to see Ricky alive. I had the most to gain from his death. I know the rumors, Izzy. I've heard them for twenty-five years."

"Mason Driscoll was there too."

"Yes, he was. But what would Mason gain from killing Ricky Lee?" Junior asked with a shrug. "A quarterback with half the arm strength and none of the accuracy. Mason played wide-receiver. He wouldn't want me throwing him passes in the state championship game."

"I guess not," I said.

"Who else you got?" Junior Wolfe asked, now excitedly turning to face me. "I know a smart girl like you has moved beyond the usual suspects."

"Mustang Jones," I said, and Junior raised an eyebrow.

"Okay, explain."

"Well, in the end, he benefited the most, right? He went from a nobody to a can't miss recruit overnight because Ricky wasn't there to play quarterback. I know his family didn't have the money to pay off the cops, but your father did, and since Mustang signed with FSU, it makes sense he'd cover up the murder. Sophie told me tonight you said Mustang killed a homeless man in Pensacola for his gang initiation, so—"

Junior Wolfe began laughing so hard I shut up. "Sorry," he said, waving a hand in apology. "I didn't mean to laugh at your theory.

Honestly, it's not that bad, and my father is entirely capable of doing what you suggested. Does Elton know his father is your prime suspect?"

"No," I said, "not yet. I'm trying to investigate him on my own, but I haven't found much. Do you know where Mustang was the night Ricky died? Did he party with you on the beach?"

"He did not," Junior Wolfe said. "Terrance's parents belonged to a rather intense branch of the Seventh-Day Adventist Church. Are you familiar with them?"

I shrugged. "Is that the church on Saturday one?"

"It is, and this particular congregation met all damn day. They'd start around nine in the morning, go well past lunch, then come back at eight and sing until their throats were raw. There are only about sixty souls who could tell you Terrance Jones was dozing off in a back pew the night Ricky Lee died."

"What about the homeless man from Pensacola?"

"Never happened," Junior said, shaking his head. "The Minks started that rumor so their precious Selina wouldn't have to attend school with a Black child. Terrance Jones wouldn't hurt a fly. I've told Sophie that several times, but listening comprehension has never been my daughter's strong suit."

The relief must have been evident on my face because Junior Wolfe smiled and patted me on the back. He climbed to his feet, brushed the sand off his pants, and helped me up. "I guess that puts your investigation back at square one."

"I guess so," I said.

"Would a confession help?"

I smiled weakly.

"Okay," Junior Wolfe said, holding his hands up in surrender. "I killed Ricky Lee."

I instinctively took a step back, prepared to run if I had to. I suspected a killer wouldn't confess and just let you walk away.

"But not the way you're thinking," Junior added, with a sad smile.

"What does that even mean?" I asked. "Do you know who killed Ricky or not?"

"I've put together a theory over the years," Junior Wolfe said and walked past me to leave. "It wouldn't hold up in court, but I feel pretty good about it. The shame is, I've been too much of a coward to do anything about it. It would have cost me too much."

"Please," I begged. "I need your help."

Junior Wolfe stopped and looked back. "Izzy, why are you doing this?"

I thought for a moment. Sure, I began the investigation with selfish means. I wanted to be a famous investigative journalist—the next Nellie Bly. I wanted a college scholarship, and I knew solving a twenty-five-year-old cold case would trump the greatest college essay of all time. But that night in the emergency room, when Dalton Wolfe screamed at me and threatened to send us back to his trailer park, I began to understand how places like Bardo chewed up and spit out poor kids like Ricky Lee. Poor kids like Axl and me. And now, more than anything, I wanted justice. I was almost obsessed with it.

Junior Wolfe laughed bitterly after I told him this. "Justice for Ricky," he said. "You understand solving the murder won't bring Ricky back from the dead."

"So, I should just let the killer get away with it?"

"Why not?" Junior asked. "You see, that's what I find comforting about the concept of heaven and hell. Whoever did this to Ricky will get away with it for what, sixty or seventy years at most? But then they'll burn for eternity."

"I'm not sure I share your confidence in the universe getting this right in the end."

"I'm not that confident either, to be honest," Junior said with a sigh. "But here's what I do know. Whoever killed Ricky was powerful enough to get away with it. If you somehow caught them, you'd go down too. They'll ruin your life, Izzy. So, if I were you, I'd keep my head down, get out of this place, and never, ever look back."

He turned to leave again, and I called after him. "But what if I can't do that? Will you help me? It's the right thing to do."

Junior Wolfe looked back and smiled. "It's too late for me to do the right thing," he said. "I'm going to hell either way."

CHAPTER TWENTY-FOUR

Monday, September 29, 2008, might always go down as the strangest day of my life. It started off well enough, jumping Elton in the hallway and giving him the first of two dozen begrudgingly accepted hugs. I was so relieved to learn his father wasn't responsible for Ricky Lee's death I couldn't help myself, even if I couldn't tell Elton the reason behind my elation. From there, things took a turn for the worse. Blaine hardly spoke to me during first period AP English, then he left campus with his mother around ten, and I didn't see either of them the rest of the school day. We were supposed to get together to "study" that evening, but I had a sneaking suspicion he'd text soon to cancel.

After school, Elton and I drove to Cowden in his Escalade. Ricky Lee's mother lived alone on five acres of overgrown pine thicket just north of town. According to the obituary Elton found online, Ricky's father died five years ago after a one-sided confrontation with a freight train. The Lees' dirt driveway meandered through the kudzu-covered trees, past a small overgrown family cemetery. Slowing down, I spotted

Ricky's name on faded white cross, and shivered. The driveway stopped at a dilapidated house in a small clearing, where an old black sports car sat rusting near the tree line, and a white pickup truck was parked in front of the house, but the flat tires indicated it hadn't left the property in some time.

"You sure this is the place?" I asked, not anxious to leave the safety of the car.

"Affirmative."

I glanced over at Elton, who apparently hadn't watched enough horror films to know we were on the set of one.

"Alright, you ready?" I asked, but Elton wasn't sure how to reply to a question so banal, so we climbed from the car and stepped onto the creaking porch. I knocked softly at first, then harder, then nearly jumped out of my skin when a voice from behind asked, "Y'all from the church?"

We turned to see an old woman carrying several empty mason jars and staring at us through thick glasses. Thanks to an internet background check Elton paid twenty bucks for, we knew Ruby Lee had her only son Ricky when she was twenty-five and that now she was sixty-eight. But this woman looked twenty years older than that, hunched over and beaten down by life.

"No, ma'am," I said, "we're students from Bardo Academy."

"Well, don't just stand there," she said, "help me with these jars."

Elton and I took the jars off her hands and followed her into the house, where a gas furnace ran full-blast, despite the pleasant late-September day outside.

"You said you were students?" Ruby Lee asked, not inviting us to sit.

"From Bardo Academy," I said, nodding. "We're writing a story about the 1983 State Championship team for the student newspaper." I waited for Ruby Lee to acknowledge that her son played on this team, but when she didn't, I added, "And since your son, Ricky, was the starting quarterback, we hoped you could share some memories with us."

"I never saw Ricky play football," Ruby Lee said bitterly.

"Wait, never?"

"Nope. I didn't go to a single game. Didn't want him playing, to be honest. I just knew he'd get hurt. All that football nonsense was his daddy's idea. Benny was always saying, 'Ruby, that boy is gonna make us rich.' Now they're both dead, and I ain't rich." Ruby Lee stood and said, "Football," like it was a swear word, then she hobbled down the hallway. Elton and I exchanged a shrug and followed her.

We found Ruby Lee in a bedroom down the hall, digging through a cluttered closet. "About a year after Ricky died, somebody from that school of yours dropped this off at our house," she said, removing a large cardboard box from the closet and dropping it on the bed. "I think there's a yearbook in here and whatever else they found in his locker." She walked past us back into the hallway and said, "Maybe you'll find something to help write your little story."

We opened the box and started going through it. There was a yearbook on top—the same yearbook I'd flipped through at Blaine's house—but there were no signatures or well-wishes in Ricky Lee's since he'd died before ever receiving it. Ricky's school notebooks were inside, full of doodles and song lyrics and the occasional homework. I made Elton remove the old gym clothes that hadn't been touched and therefore hadn't been washed in a quarter century, then we shuffled through several football programs, old editions of the *Bardo Breeze*, issues of *Sports Illustrated*, *Rolling Stone*, and *NME*, and even the tombstone drawing Cowden cheerleaders sent Ricky before their game. There were also dozens of notes folded into perfect rectangles with little "pull to open" tabs on the side.

I picked a note and opened it, realized it was from Ricky's girlfriend, then gasped and clutched my chest when she mentioned having sex for the seventh time the previous weekend and how she preferred the blanket on the beach to the backseat of Ricky's Firebird.

"What is it?" Elton asked, looking up from a yellowing issue of the *Walton Observer* that he'd apparently decided to read cover to cover.

"Nothing," I said, blushing at the note, which was signed with love and a little drawing of a cat.

I read at least twenty of these notes, which, while revealing an embarrassingly exact accounting of Ricky's sex life, did not shed any light on his murder.

"Find anything interesting?" I asked Elton.

"Yes," he said, showing me the old newspaper, "The United States invaded the island nation of Grenada."

"Okay, not what I—wait, really? Why?"

"I will let you know when I finish the article," he said, returning to the paper.

I smiled and shook my head. All that was left in the box was a Sony Walkman, several cassette tapes of bands I'd never heard of, and a large hardback edition of *A Tale of Two Cities*. I was about to walk back into the kitchen and try my luck with Ruby Lee when instinctively I picked up Ricky's copy of the Dickens tome. I'd written a paper on it at Dandridge and wanted to read the famous opening lines, but when

I opened the book, they were not there. Ricky had carved out a secret compartment in the pages, and inside he'd hidden several more notes. I took one out, opened it carefully, and read.

"Who is Dan Marino?" I asked Elton, who was now scanning the classifieds from a twenty-five-year-old newspaper.

"Dan Marino is an NFL Hall of Fame quarterback who played for the Miami Dolphins from 1983 until his retirement in 1999," Elton said without turning from his paper. "He still holds several passing records and made a cameo appearance in *Ace Ventura: Pet Detective.*"

"And who is Don Strock?" I asked.

Elton looked up, and for a moment, I thought I'd stumped him. But the answer came to him with the snap of his fingers, and he replied, "Don Strock was Dan Marino's backup."

The quarterback and his backup.

"Oh my God," I said, dropping the note and covering my mouth in shock. "Elton, Ricky Lee had a secret."

"What?"

"He was in love … with Junior Wolfe."

1983

Junior Wolfe was on fire.

A dozen psychics with a thousand tarot cards could have never predicted the senior year he was currently enjoying. And to think, it all began so badly. First, Ricky Lee took his starting job on the football team, then his girlfriend, then his crown as king of Bardo Academy. But instead of rivals, Junior and Ricky became friends. Best friends.

Sure, they argued like an old married couple, but they were rarely apart. They hung out after school, after football games, and whenever Ricky could escape Her Majesty for a few hours on the weekend. Rumors began when they started skipping out on post-football game parties and disappearing together on Saturday afternoons, but not those sorts of rumors. It was widely accepted in the Bardo Academy locker room that Junior and Ricky had befriended two dancers at Show-n-Tail, a Panama City Beach topless bar, and whenever they could get away to watch their girls dance, they did.

Junior started the rumor.

Ricky verified it.

No one was the wiser.

Only Junior and Ricky knew they spent most of their free time in the woods off Powell Lake, listening to music, arguing about movies, and drinking themselves into mellow stupors.

The night it happened, they were both six beers deep, lying on their backs, staring at the canopy of pine trees and listening to the water slosh against the shore.

"God, I can't wait to get out of here and never come back," Ricky said to the sky.

"I'm enjoying your company too," Junior snapped back.

"Not what I meant," Ricky said, and Junior huffed with fake indignation. "It's just, ever since I was a kid, I knew there was so much of the world I'd never get to see. But now … now I'm going to college, and if things work out, I'm going to be filthy rich. Then … then I'll be happy."

"And you're not happy now?" Junior asked.

Neither one of them knew for sure how it had happened, but that was the exact moment they realized they were holding hands. Junior sat up, his heart beating so hard it scared him. He took a deep breath to calm himself, but it didn't work, so he took another and looked at Ricky, who was twice as scared. Junior had fought against the current for as long as he could remember, not realizing it was taking him where he needed to go all along.

He closed his eyes.

Leaned down.

And drifted away.

Two glorious hours later, it was dark. Junior stood from the blanket, wiped his chapped lips with his sleeve, and grinned. "Wait, don't you have a date tonight?"

"Shit. I'm dead," Ricky said, and they both laughed. "Maybe she'll dump me and get back together with you."

"You wish," Junior said, grabbing Ricky's hand. "But hey, if you're free tomorrow, we can take the boat out again."

"I'm definitely free," Ricky said.

Junior Wolfe was on fire, and he couldn't wait to be alone in the woods with Ricky again.

The only problem was, they'd never been alone in the first place.

CHAPTER TWENTY-FIVE

I'm not proud of it, but I pocketed all of Ricky Lee's secret notes from Junior Wolfe and brought them back to my house. It appeared Ricky's mother hadn't opened her son's box of belongings in decades, if ever, so I doubted she'd notice the absence of seventeen notes she likely never even knew existed. Plus, I needed them as evidence to solve Ricky's murder, so the end was justified, even if Elton the Boy Scout loudly protested my means the entire drive back to Bardo.

"In the state of Florida, a person convicted of second-degree petty theft faces up to sixty days in jail and a $500 fine."

"Borrowing is not a crime," I said. "As long as we give the notes back when we're done, we're good." Elton considered this for a moment, but didn't buy it and continued to repeat the maximum punishment for second-degree petty theft until I reminded him that he was an accessory to my crime.

Thankfully, Mom and Lenny were gone when we got back to my house, and Axl was probably off somewhere with Sophie, testing out her birth control. I made us peanut butter and jelly sandwiches for dinner, my culinary specialty, then we took the notes upstairs to my bedroom and laid them out across the floor.

"We cannot be certain these are from Junior Wolfe," Elton said, grabbing a note at random and examining the signature. "He didn't sign his name."

"Ricky was the starting quarterback, and Junior was his backup," I said. "Who else would send Ricky notes addressed to Dan Marino and sign them from Don Strock?"

"Occam's Razor says the simplest solution is almost always the best."

"You think Don Strock sent these notes?" I asked.

Elton thought for a moment. "Yes."

"I think your logic is flawed, Spock," I said, then marched him downstairs to the kitchen, and in a drawer, found the laminated folder welcoming us to our Wolfe-built home. Behind instruction manuals for the dishwasher and microwave was a facsimile of a hand-written letter from Junior Wolfe, boasting of our amenity-rich home's superior construction quality and thanking us for our wise purchase.

"The handwriting is similar," Elton conceded upstairs after comparing the letter to one of the notes, "but we cannot rule out forgery."

"I think we can," I said, opening notes at random and comparing the handwriting. But then I opened one written in harsh, angled cursive and said, "Whoa, but this one is different." I read the note and gasped. It was full of physical threats and homophobic slurs, ending with a promise to leave Ricky paralyzed on the fifty-yard line. There were several faded signatures at the bottom and a date at the top.

"October 17, 1983," I said, reading the date aloud.

"A Monday," Elton said, because he could do that with dates, and it never failed to amaze me.

"Do we know who Bardo played that week?" I asked, already suspecting the answer.

"On Friday, October 21, 1983, Bardo Academy defeated Cowden High School by a score of 49-7," Elton replied. "Ricky Lee accounted for all seven touchdowns and was penalized three times for excessive celebration."

"Tanner Cobb, you piece of shit," I said, and Elton stared at me in confusion. I handed him the note. "This is the threat Cowden players sent Ricky Lee, not the silly tombstone drawing we found in his box. And not only that, they knew he was gay."

Elton read the note with wide eyes, then said matter-of-factly, "Some of these terms are no longer politically correct."

"No kidding," I said, taking the note back from him. "We're going to have to make another trip to Cowden."

"*Law & Order: Criminal Intent* comes on at eight, I cannot—

"Not tonight, you donkey. But soon. That shirtless lawyer has some explaining to do."

Relieved he wouldn't miss his television show, Elton and I spent the next half hour reading through the notes. Junior Wolfe had dated each page, and read chronologically, they told the story of a sweet but tragic high school romance between two boys who loved new wave music, disagreed on every movie they watched, and really, really hated the band Journey. The backs of several pages had hand-drawn maps to the same location on Powell Lake, where apparently Junior and Ricky would spend their Saturdays, away from prying eyes. I checked the map on my phone, only to see their old rendezvous was now the sixth green of a golf course.

"This is interesting," I said, showing Elton the note I was reading. "Junior gave Ricky girlfriend advice."

"You said Ricky was gay. I am beyond confused."

"He was gay, I think, but listen to this." I read the following passage from the note to Elton.

Her Majesty is pissed because you took her to the Vermillion Burger King for dinner. Look, she's exhausting, I get it. But it's not like you're going to marry her. Four or five hours a week is all it takes, and she'll provide all the cover we need. And don't feel guilty about using her. She already knows you're using her, only she thinks it's for sex. But even that doesn't matter, because she's using you too, for power. She only wants to date the alpha male of Bardo Academy, and that, my boy, is you. But if no one sees you together, are you really dating? That's why she's mad. Take her to dinner in Bardo, get a window table at Délicieux 30A or some other fancy place. If you can't afford it, let me know, and I'll get Dad to bump up your allowance. All Her Majesty needs to be happy is to be seen with the starting quarterback, so throw her a bone. Okay?

"Who the hell is Her Majesty?" I asked.

Elton shrugged. "Perhaps Queen Elizabeth the Second, by the Grace of God of the United Kingdom, Head of the Commonwealth, Defender of the Faith."

"Probably," I deadpanned. "I wonder if she was friends with the '83 Dolphins too."

Elton stared at me before turning back to the note he was reading.

"So," I said, thinking aloud, "Junior Wolfe gave Ricky Lee advice on how to keep his fake girlfriend happy as a cover for their own secret relationship." I rubbed my temples and tried to plan my next move. "Let's go back to your house," I told Elton. "I need to walk next door and have a little chat with Junior Wolfe."

What happened next was a blur. A door slammed downstairs, and the feet stomping through the house rattled my bedroom walls. I was in my room, with a boy, with the door closed, but if this was Mom, I doubted she'd be upset when she realized it was Elton. But as the stomps grew louder, I guessed it was Axl bounding up the stairs, and instinctively I swiped all the notes under my bed.

The door flew open without a knock, and Axl looked from me to Elton, then back to me. His face was pale, his breathing heavy, and when he opened his mouth to speak, the words wouldn't come out.

"What is it?" I asked, jumping to my feet. I feared something had happened to Mom, and tears welled in my eyes. Lenny didn't look like the abusive type, but I'd been wrong about her boyfriends before.

"It's Sophie's dad," Axl finally managed, giant tears rolling down his face. "He killed himself."

CHAPTER TWENTY-SIX

"Please slow down."

Axl and I were in his Dodge Charger, driving to the Wolfes' mansion in Eden Shores at speeds typically reserved for police chases.

My brother didn't register my concern over his driving, so when he blew through three consecutive crosswalks and ran two cyclists off the road, I yelled again, "Axl, slow down. You're scaring me."

He lifted his foot enough that I felt comfortable releasing the death grip I'd had on my door handle, and as the blood slowly returned to my white knuckles, I asked him, "Do you know what happened?"

"He shot himself," Axl said, shaking his head in disbelief. "Early this morning, they think. Someone found him in Nowhere, back by the water where we hang out."

"How's Sophie?"

"Not good. They told her during cheerleader practice this afternoon, and one of the teachers drove her home. I left practice and went over there as soon as I heard. One minute she's all quiet and sad. The next, she's hysterical and screaming. I don't ... I don't even know what to say to her. God, Izzy, I must have called you twenty times. Where were you?"

"I turned my phone off," I told him. "Blaine was all weird at school today, and I didn't want to talk to him."

I knew how trivial this sounded in light of the day's events, but Axl didn't snap at me like I'd anticipated. "Something happened with his dad's bank this morning," he said, pulling up to the guardhouse at Eden Shores, where a mournful Clyde let us through the gate without a mention of football.

"What happened with the bank?" I asked.

"I'm not sure," Axl said. "I think it might have had something to do with Mr. Wolfe's suicide, though."

Several cars were parked outside the Wolfes' house when we arrived, including Dalton's giant SUV, but I didn't see our benefactor among the adults gathered around Sophie's mother when Axl and I passed through the living room. We found Sophie upstairs, in her bubblegum-pink bedroom, which still contained more childhood dolls than I would have guessed.

"Thank you for coming over," Sophie said, sitting up from her bed and hugging me like we were old friends.

"Sophie, I'm so sorry," I said, and she smiled at me with bloodshot eyes.

"How are the twins?" Axl asked.

Sophie coughed out a laugh. "Fine, I guess. They're upstairs playing PlayStation like nothing happened." She began crying again, and Axl helped her back to her bed.

"Have you eaten anything since lunch?" Axl asked, and Sophie shook her head. "You need to eat something," he said. "There's a ton of food in the kitchen. Let me run downstairs and fix you a plate."

"I just don't get it," Sophie said after Axl left her room. "Like, I know Dad was super stressed with work. He was always on the phone arguing with the bank, and he was never in a good mood. I thought he was sick because he'd lost so much weight. But the last couple of days, he was himself again. He was funny and laughing. Last night he took me to Blue Mountain Creamery, and we got ice cream cones and talked for like an hour. I thought he was back. I thought he loved us again, but now …"

A senior boy killed himself during my freshman year at Dandridge. One of the several counselors they brought in to talk to us said when depressed people made up their minds to commit suicide, they often appeared happier, calmer, and more relaxed. I recalled the conversation I'd had with Junior Wolfe two nights ago on the beach and how even then, he was a different man from the one I'd met soon after moving to Bardo. It all made terrible sense.

Sophie started weeping again, so I sat next to her on the bed and put an awkward arm around her shoulder. "Of course he loved you, Sophie."

She tried to argue but couldn't get the words out through her sobs, and I was still holding her on the bed when Axl returned with her food. We watched Sophie push her dinner around the plate with a fork for several minutes before excusing herself to the bathroom. When she left the room, Axl confessed to me, "I don't even know what to say to her."

"You're here," I said, hugging my brother, "that's what matters."

He hugged me back, and I got a text from Blaine.

Blaine — Sorry about today. Shit hit the fan. Can we talk?

Me — I'm at Sophie's. Want me to walk over?

Blaine — Not a good time. Meet me on the beach instead?

Me — Give me a few minutes.

"Blaine wants to see me for a few minutes," I told Axl. "Will you be okay here?" He nodded, and I left the house through the kitchen, walking across the deck toward the stairs, when a gruff voice said, "Two months in Bardo by the Sea, and you're already too stuck up to say hello to the man paying your tuition?"

I turned to see Dalton Wolfe, sitting in an Adirondack chair with a drink in his hand and an empty bottle at his feet.

"Hi, Mr. Wolfe, I didn't see you. I'm so sorry about Junior."

"I don't know why," Dalton Wolfe said bitterly. "He was a terrible businessman, a lousy husband, and a miserable son."

I didn't know exactly what to say to this, so I didn't say anything, and Dalton Wolfe stood with great effort.

"All those fools in Junior's house crying like this is some damn surprise. That boy of mine has written checks he couldn't cash since high school, knowing all along Daddy would be there to bail him out. Hell, maybe I'm partially to blame here. If I'd have let him face the consequences just once, he might have grown up to be a man. But no, I didn't raise no man. I raised a coward. And now he's taken the coward's way out and left me with one last mess to clean up."

Being the daughter of a woman who dated her fair share of drunks, I know there's a stage of inebriation just shy of blacking out where people begin to offer unfiltered opinions and brutal honesty without much prompting. Over the years, I'd gotten no less than three of Mom's boyfriends to admit to being married, a confession that found them promptly thrown from our trailer and onto their no-good cheating asses. Judging by the way he stumbled around the deck, it appeared Dalton Wolfe had reached this stage. Though the man terrified me, I'd never have a better chance to ask him what I needed to know. I rolled the dice.

"Mr. Wolfe," I asked, "did you know about Junior and Ricky Lee?"

Apparently, I had miscalculated the amount of brown liquid Dalton Wolfe had consumed. His eyes bulged, and he charged across the deck like a grizzly bear, wrapping a giant paw around my neck. "What the fuck did you say to me?"

I tried to speak but couldn't, both from fear and a constricted airway.

"You listen to me," he snarled, "if I ever hear the name Ricky Lee come out of your mouth again, so help me God, I will ring your skinny little neck and feed you to the sharks. You understand me?"

I managed a nod, and something like fear flashed across Mr. Wolfe's face. He let go of my neck and stared at his hand like it belonged to someone else before slowly backing away from me. I think he'd just realized he was choking a teenage girl and was perhaps about to apologize, but I ran down the stairs to the beach in tears before I could find out.

CHAPTER TWENTY-SEVEN

Thankfully, Blaine wasn't on the beach when I got there, which gave me several minutes to calm down and let the breeze whip the tears from my eyes. Having an anonymous note vow to kill me and dump my body in the Gulf was one thing. Having a three-hundred-pound man deliver the threat personally while squeezing my neck in his giant fist was something else entirely. I cursed out loud and laughed to keep from crying again.

Pacing the sand for several minutes, I realized I hadn't miscalculated Dalton Wolfe's level of inebriation. In his right mind, a man like that wouldn't risk physically threatening a girl while several family members sat just inside. Sure, I'd overestimated the civility of our discourse, but I got the brutal honesty I was expecting, or, at the very least, an honest reaction. I'd hit close to home, and Dalton Wolfe responded with all the poise of a rabid dog. Of course he knew about Junior and Ricky. Why else would he react so viscerally? And this begged the question. Did Dalton Wolfe kill Ricky Lee when he found out about his relationship with Junior? He'd built Bardo's gay-unfriendly church,

I'd just witnessed a terrifying display of his penchant for violence, and he had the means to cover up his misdeeds. Unfortunately, he also paid my tuition and was responsible for my family living in a giant beachside house. Maybe this was what Junior meant when he told me if I went after the person responsible for Ricky's death, they'd take me down with them. Dammit to hell.

I checked the time. Ten minutes had passed, and still no Blaine. I texted him.

Me — Did you forget about me? I'm on the beach in front of your house.

Blaine — Sorry. Give me another minute or two. I'm trying to listen to my parents argue through the wall.

Me — Whatever they're arguing about, I'm on your mom's side.

Blaine — It's about the bank. I'll be down soon. Sorry!

Founded in 1937 by Blaine's great-grandfather, Thomas B. Park Sr., WalCo Bank was not a large financial institution in a global sense. With just under one billion dollars in assets at its height, it doesn't even qualify for the Wikipedia page of largest US bank failures. But the bank did have several dozen branches across Northwest Florida, and it had made the Park family wealthy beyond most people's capacity for dreams. The bank would have continued to make the Park family wealthy for many decades to come, too, had Blaine's father not fallen into the trap that was the Florida real estate scene of the early twenty-first century. Between 2001 to 2005, WalCo's development and construction loans increased sevenfold, to over $400 million, which is akin to a company blowing its entire advertising budget to paint their logo on the *Titanic*. What happened next was as inevitable as the tide.

"They closed our bank today," Blaine said, meeting me on the beach in front of his parents' mansion.

"What? Who?"

"The government," he said. "They took it over and sold it to some giant bank in Atlanta."

"They can do that?" I asked. I had no idea this was something that could happen to banks, though, in the coming years, it would happen to hundreds of them—one three hundred times larger than WalCo.

"Here, read this." Blaine handed me his phone, so I could read the article. I blinked at him in shock when I realized it was from the freaking *Wall Street Journal*.

—DeFuniak Springs

Paralyzed by millions of dollars in risky loans, WalCo Bank was seized and closed Monday morning by banking regulators.

SunTrust Bank of Atlanta, Georgia, will assume WalCo Bank's insured deposits, and its forty-seven offices will reopen Tuesday as SunTrust branches.

WalCo Bank becomes the nation's fourteenth bank failure of 2008 and the second in Florida.

The DeFuniak Springs bank suffered from the post-boom hangover facing several lending institutions throughout the country and Florida. Critics cite WalCo Bank's officers and directors' failure to properly vet borrowers and their approval of aggressive expansions during a time when more vigilance was required.

Wait, did your parents just lose all their money, I thought. "What happens now?" I asked. "Does your dad have to work for that bank in Atlanta?"

"I don't know," Blaine said, letting out a heavy sigh. "My parents are always so careful not to talk about money in front of me, but I heard Mom say something about the stock market crashing, and Dad telling her that was the least of our worries."

I didn't know it, but around lunchtime, the United States House of Representatives failed to pass a $700 billion financial bailout plan, sending the stock market into the largest single-day collapse in history. Yeah, it was an eventful Monday.

"Dad has been holed up in his office with his lawyers all afternoon. Apparently, the government froze some of our personal money. I'm worried, Izzy. I think he might be in trouble. All the people commenting on that article seem to think he's s going to prison."

I'm not proud to admit the thought of Blaine's father rotting in a prison cell warmed my heart, but here we are.

"Come on, you can't get worked up over a bunch of anonymous idiots on the internet."

"I wouldn't normally," Blaine said, "but right before I came down, I heard Mom yelling at Dad that he should have never stuck his neck out for Junior Wolfe. Dad said something I couldn't catch, then Mom said when the Feds came with handcuffs, Grandpa wasn't around anymore to get him out of it."

"Oh, God," I said, covering my mouth. "Do you think that's why Junior ..."

"Why Junior what?" he asked.

"Wait, do you not know?" I asked, and Blaine shook his head. "Junior Wolfe shot himself today. They found him in Nowhere this afternoon."

"Holy shit," Blaine said, pulling his hair with both hands. "Shit, shit, shit." I tried to hug him, but he pulled away and continued to pace small circles in the sand while cursing to himself. "Oh my God, I need to go check on Dad," Blaine said and turned toward his house. "Sorry," he added, looking back at me, "but if it's that bad, Dad might—"

"No, go," I said, not letting him finish his thought. "Just text me later, okay?"

"Okay," Blaine said and ran back up the dunes toward his house.

I sat on the beach for a while, not particularly relishing the thought of going back to Sophie's and possibly bumping into her crazy-ass grandfather again. Eventually, though, I found my nerve and ventured back, and as predicted, Dalton Wolfe had passed out in the Adirondack chair on the deck. Tiptoeing past the hibernating bear, I wondered if he'd even remember our incident from earlier. I hoped not.

I found Axl and Sophie still in her room. She hadn't eaten, but she was now laughing and telling stories about her father and how he used to take her exploring in the woods off Powell Lake when she was a little girl. Half an hour later, Blaine texted.

Blaine — Mom and Dad are okay. It's so weird. They're just sitting in the kitchen eating cold chicken and drinking beer like nothing happened. Maybe things are going to be okay. I'll see you tomorrow at school. I love you.

I'd never told a boy I loved you, and one had certainly never said it to me. I wondered if Blaine genuinely meant it or if he was just wrapped up in the emotions of the day. Either way, I smiled and texted back.

Me — I love you too.

CHAPTER TWENTY-EIGHT

School was understandably weird on Tuesday. Axl skipped to be with Sophie, so Mom dropped me off at Bardo Academy on her way to work. Blaine was there in person, if not in spirit, but his mother was still notably absent. Junior Wolfe's funeral was scheduled for 2 p.m. on Thursday at All Saint's Church in Bardo. Students who wished to attend were excused from class to do so, but I hadn't made up my mind if I wanted to go.

"I finally read through all of Ricky's notes to Junior late last night," I told Elton during last-period extras. He was hard at work on our actual assignment but paused to listen to me. "Junior suspected another student knew about them."

I pulled the note from my pocket and read it in a low voice.

"The only person who might suspect anything is Mark Duper. I know you'd rather not hear this, but last summer, he and I, well, we had the same thing going on. It didn't mean anything to me, I swear, but he knows we hang out all the time, so he'd be the one guy at school who wouldn't buy the strip club shit. He'll never say anything. He couldn't without outing himself. But just know that he probably knows."

I pocketed the note and asked Elton, "Was Mark Duper on the Bardo football team? I haven't seen his name in any of the articles we've found, but maybe if I can get my hands on a yearbook, I can find him."

"Mark 'Super' Duper," Elton replied automatically, "was born in 1959 in Moreauville, Louisiana. He attended Northwestern State University and played wide receiver for the Miami Dolphins from 1982 to 1992. A three-time Pro-Bowler and two-time All-Pro selection, the Dolphins inducted Duper into their Ring of Honor in 2003."

I blinked at Elton several times and looked behind me for a Mark Duper informational poster I'd somehow missed. When I offered no reply to Elton's biographical monologue, he returned to his work, and I rubbed my temples in thought. If Bardo's two quarterbacks referred to themselves at Dan Marino and Don Strock, then Mark Duper would have to be—holy hell.

"Elton."

"Yes?" He asked, not looking up from his work.

"Elton!"

"Please stop yelling," Elton cried, covering his ears.

"Sorry," I whispered and waited until Denham Frost and the rest of the *Bardo Breeze* staff stopped staring before continuing. "Mark Duper is Mason Driscoll."

Elton thought for a second and said, "That would make sense. Mark Duper was the leading receiver for the 1983 Miami Dolphins, and Mason Driscoll was Bardo Academy's leading—"

"You're burying the lede, Elton. Driscoll knew about Ricky and Junior because Driscoll had been with Junior too."

"Oh," Elton said, with much less enthusiasm than I'd expected. He turned back to his work but immediately spun back around with wide eyes. "Ohhh," he said again.

"Exactly. We've got to talk to the Representative again."

"I will secure an appointment," Elton said, pulling out his phone.

"No time for that," I said. "We'll see him Thursday at Junior Wolfe's funeral."

Nearly everyone in Walton County attended Junior Wolfe's funeral, however, All Saints Church would only accommodate two hundred of them, so Elton and I stood outside in the merciful shade of a live oak tree listening to the hymns and prayers drift through the open doors and up to heaven. Elton looked handsome in his dark suit, and he responded with customary confusion when I told him so.

A small graveside service for friends and family was to follow at the Wolfe family cemetery on some farmland north of Freeport. We watched several men in black suits carry Junior Wolfe's coffin to the waiting hearse, and the family followed close behind. Junior's widow, Leslie, her eyes red and puffy, held hands with her twin sons. Sophie came next, and Axl was with her, his strong arm around her shoulders. Finally, Dalton Wolfe and Ella Kay emerged from the church, their heads bowed solemnly.

"Hey guys," Blaine said, awkwardly shaking Elton's hand and hugging me when he left the church after the service. "Do you want to study tonight?" he asked. "It's been a weird week. I feel like I haven't seen you in forever."

"I'll have to check my schedule," I said with a wry smile. I knew what Blaine meant by studying and couldn't resist teasing him. When he smiled back, I added, "Just call me when you're on your way over."

Blaine left to ride with his parents to the graveside, just as Elton spotted Mason Driscoll. He and his wife were loading their three children into their Infiniti SUV, and we rushed over to catch him before they left.

"Representative, can we speak with you for a moment?" I asked.

Mason Driscoll smiled when he saw us and whispered something to his wife before ushering us a few yards away. "Elton, Izzy, how are you guys holding up?" he asked us, with fake political compassion oozing from every pore. "This has been one hell of a week. I know your school has amazing counselors if you need to talk to someone."

"We're fine," I said, "but how are you?"

Something in my tone must have made him uncomfortable because he glanced back at his SUV and said, "Look, kids, we've got to be at the graveside. If you still have some questions for the school paper, just email my assistant, and she can—"

"We know you were in love with Junior Wolfe," I said, cutting him off.

Mason Driscoll's jaw clenched so tightly we could hear his teeth grinding. He took a couple steps toward me, raised a shaky finger, and whispered, "You don't know what the hell you're talking about."

"I think I do," I said, pulling one of Ricky's notes from my purse for him to see. "Ricky Lee's mother gave us a box of notes from Junior." I turned and asked Elton, "Wouldn't you say about half mention the representative here?"

Elton shook his head, but I waved him off before he told Driscoll only one note mentioned him, and not even by name.

"Okay, look, we need to talk," Driscoll said, quickly looking around to make sure no one had heard any of our conversation, "but not today. Call me tomorrow. We can set up a time to discuss this in private."

"We'd prefer to discuss this matter in public," I said. "People who know your secrets seem to turn up dead."

Driscoll inhaled sharply like he wanted to scream at me but then seemed to remember where he was and thought better of it. "You've got it all wrong," he said in a low voice. "I'll tell you everything, I promise. It'll all make sense."

I knew what a politician's promise was worth, so I nodded and said, "We'll see," before walking away with Elton in tow.

1983

Mason Driscoll loved Bardo by the Sea.

The proximity to money and power gave him a glimpse of the life he wanted. All he needed was an opening, and now that he had it, an opportunistic kid like Mason wouldn't let it pass him by.

Dressed in his sharpest suit, Mason struggled to keep his wingtips from tapping out a beat on the marble lobby floor. He glanced at his watch, paced the room, and checked his reflection in the window.

"Mr. Driscoll," the gorgeous personal assistant said, stepping into the lobby, "Mr. Wolfe will see you now."

"Thank you," Mason said with a wink, and the woman, ten years his senior, blushed. Mason had just discovered this power. It would serve him well.

However, his charm wouldn't help with Dalton Wolfe, who was even larger than Mason remembered, even though he saw the man every week at football practice. But trapped in his office with the door closed, Mr. Wolfe's size felt oppressive. Mason loosened his tie ever so slightly and considered for the first time that perhaps he'd made a mistake.

"Well, Mason, to what do I owe the pleasure of your visit?" Dalton Wolfe asked, dropping into his leather chair like a ten-ton bomb. It was a Tuesday morning, and Mason had skipped school to be here.

"Mr. Wolfe, I—" Mason started, but his voice faltered.

"You what, Mason? I ain't got all day."

"Mr. Wolfe," Mason said, finding his courage, "I have some information that could save you from considerable embarrassment."

"Is that so?" Dalton Wolfe asked, cocking his head ever so slightly.

"Yes, sir," Mason said, "it's about Junior."

"All right, let's hear it."

Mason took a deep breath.

It wasn't too late to walk away.

It wasn't too late to run.

"Junior," Mason said, gulping for air, "Junior and Ricky Lee are running around together."

Dalton Wolfe squinted, and Mason knew he'd have to spell it out.

"They're in love," Mason said, his chest flashing so hot he feared he'd burst into flames.

Dalton Wolfe swallowed hard but didn't say anything. He just grabbed a pencil off his desk and tried to squeeze it into sawdust.

"Anyway," Mason said, "I just thought, you know, that you'd want to—"

"Who else knows?" Dalton Wolfe demanded.

"Just me," Mason said.

This time Dalton exhaled and nodded. "Mason, I appreciate you coming to me with this," he said, standing and moving toward the door. He opened it, and Mason stood to leave, but then he stopped.

This was his chance.

This was what he came for.

It was now or never.

"Mr. Wolfe, I need to ask you for something … in return."

"Return for what?" Dalton Wolfe barked.

"My … silence," Mason said, trying not to wilt under the big man's glare.

Dalton Wolfe took two steps toward Mason, blocking out the sun and any hope of escape. "Did you come here to blackmail me, boy?"

"No, sir," Mason managed, backing up until he bumped into Dalton's desk. "But I did you a favor, and I feel entitled to ask for one in return."

"You feel entitled," Dalton Wolfe said with a bitter laugh. "Okay, let's hear it then."

Mason Driscoll laid it all out for him. His parents weren't poor, but undergraduate tuition at any of the several Ivy League schools he'd been accepted to would stretch them, not to mention law school. Mason needed help, and when he was out, he'd need campaign money. He wanted to be a United States senator, and who knows, maybe president one day.

Dalton Wolfe belly laughed and said, "Son, you seriously want me to pay for your college and promise to fund some future political campaign when I don't even know the first thing you believe in?"

"Ask me about anything," Mason said, standing straighter. Dalton Wolfe picked abortion, and Mason Driscoll proceeded to argue for a woman's right to choose so effectively, Dalton Wolfe had to fight the urge to write a check to Planned Parenthood then and there. But then Mason stopped and countered with an equally convincing pro-life defense, and when he finished, Dalton Wolfe couldn't help but smile.

"Mr. Wolfe," Mason said, "I'll believe whatever you want me to believe."

Dalton Wolfe had an eye for talent, and staring at the boy standing across from him, he tried to imagine him a few years down the road when he'd filled out his father's suit, and his peach fuzz had turned to stubble. Sure, it was a long shot, but considering the embarrassment this kid saved him from, helping with his tuition was a small price to pay. And if the bet did pay off, he'd have this up-and-coming young politician in his pocket from day one. My God, the possibilities were endless.

"Senator Driscoll," Dalton Wolfe said, extending his giant hand, "I think we can work something out."

CHAPTER TWENTY-NINE

"Well, well, well, if it ain't Manute Bol and Anne of Green Gables," Tanner Cobb said as Elton and I entered his law office on Friday afternoon, the day after Junior Wolfe's funeral. The attorney wore a lifeguard tank top under an unbuttoned floral print shirt, and after he hid the Victoria's Secret catalog he was "reading," he said, "Y'all do know I value my time at a hundred bucks an hour, so if you expect me to keep participating in these little conclaves, you might have to start ponying up."

"I am extraordinarily wealthy," Elton said as a matter of fact.

"That's right, I keep forgetting," Cobb said, lightly smacking his own forehead in jest. "Now, what can I help y'all with today. Still trying to solve Ricky Lee's murder, or have you moved on to the Kennedy assassination?"

I cleared my throat. "Did the Bardo police know about the death threat you sent Ricky Lee?"

Tanner Cobb's demeanor changed. "I told you that was our cheerleaders playing a prank."

I shook my head, pulled the real death threat from my pocket, and held it for the lawyer to see. He lunged for it across his old wooden desk, but I yanked it back and wagged a finger at him. "I didn't write that," he snapped.

"You signed it, you dumbass."

"It was a joke," he said, changing directions.

"I didn't ask if it was a joke. Did the police know?"

Tanner Cobb inhaled sharply and said, "They never asked me about it. I guess they never found it."

"Because if they had, you'd have been a prime suspect in Ricky's murder," I said.

The lawyer ran a hand through his bushy hair and motioned for us to sit across from him. "Look," he said in a more confessional tone, "that note reflects rather poorly on my teammates and me, but I didn't kill Ricky Lee. I couldn't have. The weekend he disappeared, I was with my family in Birmingham, celebrating my Maw-Maw Helen's eightieth birthday."

I frowned at the lawyer and asked, "And your family can vouch for this?"

"Well, Maw-Maw Helen died twenty years ago," he said, "but I suppose the rest of my family would corroborate. I don't suspect they'll need to, though. What do you think will come of all this? Y'all really think the police are gonna reopen a twenty-five-year-old cold case just because the two of you found a note? Speaking of, where the hell did you find that thing anyway?"

"We are asking the questions here," Elton barked, slamming his fist on the desk so hard that Tanner Cobb and I both jumped. "Sorry," Elton said, turning to me, "I have watched an excess of *Law & Order* since we began this investigation."

"Ricky Lee's mother let us go through a box of his high school belongings," I told Tanner Cobb, "and we found your note, among other things."

"So," the lawyer said, raising his hands in a shrug, "now what? Y'all here to perform a citizen's arrest?"

I shook my head. "We know you didn't kill Ricky Lee."

"Do you now?" Tanner Cobb replied arrogantly, but I saw his shoulders relax ever so slightly.

"But we also know you'd rather this note not go public. I suspect a front-page story in the *Walton Observer* about the Cowden attorney who sent Ricky Lee a death threat full of homophobic slurs just weeks before his murder wouldn't be good business."

"So that's it," Tanner Cobb said with a bitter laugh, "y'all drove all the way here to extort me. Well, listen up, I'm not about to let a couple of snot-nosed trust-fund babies hold me hostage over a damn note I wrote when I was sixteen."

"Izzy isn't a trust-fund baby," Elton said, and Tanner Cobb shook his head in confusion.

"We don't want your money," I said, and the lawyer turned back to me. "We want information. For instance, all those horrific names you called Ricky in the note, was that just locker room talk, or had you heard something?"

Tanner Cobb looked up at his water-stained ceiling, exhaled loudly, and turned back to us. "A little of both. We all called each other names like that back then. Doesn't make it right, but we did. Hell, our coaches even called us some of those things. But there was talk about Ricky too. After he left for Bardo, his ex-girlfriend, Traci Thompson, told a bunch of us guys Ricky couldn't always … perform, if you get my drift."

I rolled my eyes and said, "We get it," though I'm not entirely sure Elton did.

"And if a guy couldn't perform for Traci Thompson, well, I don't know what to tell you."

"So that's all you've got?" I asked. "A bitter ex-girlfriend talking trash."

"That's not all. A fella in my class at Cowden named Tony Craven had a rich cousin that went to Bardo. He told Tony that Ricky was dating some hot cheerleader there too but spent all his time running around with Junior Wolfe. I mean, that doesn't prove anything, but it's enough to start a rumor."

"Did you think Ricky was gay?"

Tanner Cobb rubbed his chin in thought. "Nah, not really. We were just pissed off he left Cowden. We wanted to win a third state championship, and with Ricky gone, it wasn't happening."

"You said everyone was happy for Ricky that he got out of here."

"Yeah, well, I lied," Tanner Cobb said with a grin.

"Okay," I said, taking out a pen and pad, "tell us the rumor you've heard about Ricky's murder."

"Nope."

"Let's go, Elton," I said, standing up, "we'll drive right past the *Observer* offices on the way home."

"Fine, sit down," Tanner Cobb said in defeat. He put his palms on his desk and leaned in. "But you got to promise me you won't run around Bardo telling people you heard this shit from me."

"We promise."

"Okay," the lawyer said, looking behind us to make sure no one was coming in, "but again, this is probably just courthouse bullshit.

Still, I've heard it so many times I suspect there might be some truth in there too. Hell, I even heard a Walton County judge give his rendition after downing sixteen beers at a tailgate party in Tallahassee. The story goes, one day, Dalton walked in on Ricky and Junior doing some gay stuff. Old man Wolfe went off the rails and killed Ricky with his hunting knife, then paid the Bardo cops to make it all go away."

Holy shit. I set my pencil down and stared across the desk at Tanner Cobb, who merely shrugged. "Okay," I said, thinking aloud, "why wouldn't Junior turn in his father?"

"Because his daddy was rich as hell," Tanner Cobb said like it went without saying. "I heard Dalton all but disowned Junior but promised to give him a million dollars to make his own way. I guess Junior took the deal. Anyway, that's what I've heard."

Axl told me Junior got a million dollars to start his business after college. Is this what Junior Wolfe meant when he told me it was too late for him, he was going to hell either way? Had he remained silent all these years because his father paid him off?

I turned to Elton. "Let's get back to Bardo. We've got a lot of work to do."

"Listen now, y'all can't go printing that shit I just told you. I wouldn't put it past Dalton Wolfe to sue a student newspaper reporter to the moon and back for libel."

"Don't worry," I said, as Elton and I reached the door, "we'll never reveal our source." I held up the note Tanner and his teammates sent Ricky and added, "But we're keeping you on retainer in case we require any future legal advice. And you'll work pro bono."

"That's Latin for free," Elton added.

"Yeah, Stretch, I know," Tanner Cobb said, and we left him there, slumped in his chair.

CHAPTER THIRTY

After leaving Tanner Cobb's office in Cowden, Elton and I raced back to watch Bardo Academy host Marianna in the fifth game of the season. I sat with Blaine in the student section, watching Axl fling the ball all over the field in a game that was out of reach midway through the second quarter. I felt terrible for my brother. He thought of Junior Wolfe as the father we never had, and on our drive to school that morning, I'd noticed him wiping away a tear. But at least Axl had found a way to channel his emotions into something positive, and he was having one of the best games of his career.

"How are things at home?" I asked Blaine after a quarter of hardly speaking.

"Huh?"

This had gone on all week. He was never present, even the night before when we "studied" in my bedroom, and I had to repeat every question I asked at least once.

"I asked, how are things at home with your parents?"

"Fine," he said. "I guess."

"Did you ever hear them talking about Sophie's dad? Do you think his suicide had something to do with the bank going under?"

"I don't know," Blaine said, with more than a hint of agitation in his voice, so I left it at that, and we watched the rest of the half in silence.

When the teams went to their locker rooms at halftime, I excused myself and met Elton, who, per usual, was in the press box, helping Archie with the video board. We walked toward the concession stand, stood alongside the chain-link fence behind the north end zone, and waited for our meeting to commence. A minute later, Representative Mason Driscoll joined us.

"Good evening, Representative," I said, looking straight ahead as the Marianna High School marching band took the field to perform a medley of Beatles hits.

"Tell me what you know," he said, skipping the pleasantries.

"We know you and Junior Wolfe had a secret relationship."

"And you think you know this because of some old note you found?" he asked, trying to take back control of the situation.

"Yes," I said. "We have thirty notes to Ricky Lee, signed by Junior Wolfe, mentioning you by name." This wasn't exactly true, but Mason Driscoll didn't need to know that. "Thirty notes I suspect the police never found, or you'd have been the prime suspect in Ricky's murder." Driscoll snorted his opinion of my theory, so I added, "I don't know if it's enough evidence to re-open the case, but I suspect my uncle at the *Walton Observer* would win a Pulitzer for his story on the homosexual high school romance of Florida's most homophobic politician." This wasn't exactly true either. My only uncle was a bouncer at Club La Vela in Panama City, but again, what Mason Driscoll didn't know wouldn't hurt him.

"You wouldn't dare," Driscoll snarled.

"I would," I said, turning to face him. "I don't believe in outing people, Representative, even people as despicable as you. But I will if I have to."

Mason Driscoll closed his eyes and took a deep breath to compose himself. "Look, if you're after money, I don't have as much as you'd think."

"We don't want your money," I snapped, offended at the accusation.

"I am already wealthy," Elton said, exasperated. "Why does everyone assume I need their money?"

Driscoll noticed Elton for the first time, shook his head in confusion, then asked me, "What do you want then?"

"The truth."

A man approached to shake the representative's hand and inquire about his plans to run for the US Senate, and after he left, Driscoll looked up and down the fence line and said in a low voice, "Fine. Junior and I messed around some junior year of high school. We both drank a lot back then and smoked a lot of dope, which explains it. But I'm not gay."

"Of course you're not," I said, "lots of straight boys kiss each other." Driscoll looked pissed off enough to hit me in public, so I backed away a couple steps and said, "But for the sake of argument, let's assume you're straight. I still don't understand why someone with your past would spew all that homophobic shit every time someone points a camera at you."

"Because that's what my donors want me to say," Driscoll said in an angry whisper. "Look, I don't care what people do in their bedrooms, but the people who write me large checks do, and if they want me to promote traditional family values and keep the taxes low on timberland, that's what I'll do."

"My God, so you're just pretending?"

"We're all pretending," Driscoll said, not hiding his condescension. "But I am a happily married man, and none of that stuff in high school meant anything to me."

"'Come Together'," I said, naming the marching band's current tune. "Is that from *Sgt. Peppers*?"

"*Abbey Road*," Elton replied.

"Look, are we done here?" Driscoll asked, starting to walk away.

"Did you know about Junior and Ricky?" I asked.

"Sure," Driscoll said, quickly growing exasperated by my interrogation, "I knew what they were up to when they'd run off together. I was probably the only person at school who did. And yeah, I was pissed off at Junior, but only because we were friends. We used to go to movies together, listen to music, and ride around on Saturday nights, getting into trouble. Ricky took my place, and I resented him."

"Enough to kill him?" I asked.

Driscoll rolled his eyes. "Drug dealers killed Ricky Lee."

"And you buy that?"

"We all took drugs," Driscoll said, "that's what Bardo Academy is known for."

Perhaps the pills made me paranoid, but again Driscoll seemed to give me a knowing look when he said this. I tried to shake it off, then told him, "I saw Junior Wolfe on the beach a couple nights before he died. He told me he believed some powerful Bardo people covered up what really happened to Ricky."

Driscoll shrugged. "It's possible. You've got to remember, the

Bardo police department wasn't the NYPD. It was Jack Duncan, two deputies, and three golf carts. They didn't even have patrol cars. Chief Duncan interviewed me once about the night Ricky disappeared. It took less than five minutes, and he never spoke to me again. Those notes of yours must have been in Ricky's locker, but he never found them, which tells me he wasn't looking very hard. But before you ask, no, my parents were not involved. My father was an orthodontist, and my mother took valium and told the house cleaner when she missed a spot. We could barely afford to live in Bardo, much less pay off the cops to make a murder go away."

While I made a mental note to have Elton verify this, the three of us paused to watch a Marianna majorette twirl two flaming batons to "Maxwell's Silver Hammer."

"So," I asked Driscoll once the batons were safely extinguished, "you never confronted Junior about him and Ricky?"

"Nope," Mason Driscoll said, thinking he was off the hook.

"Fine," I said, calling his bluff and turning to walk away, "I'm going to call my uncle now."

Driscoll grabbed my shoulder, and Elton knocked his hand off me before either Driscoll or I realized what had happened. We both looked at Elton in shock, and Driscoll raised his hands in apology to the gentle giant before turning to me and saying, "I never confronted Junior, but ..."

"But what?"

Driscoll closed his eyes. "But I told his father."

"You told Dalton Wolfe about Junior and Ricky?" I said, much louder than I'd meant to, and Driscoll shushed me.

"Look, you've been in Bardo long enough to know how much

people here care about their image, and no one more than Dalton Wolfe. I knew if I could save him from a scandal, keep some tarnish off his name, he'd be in my pocket for a long time. Besides, I was pissed off at Junior, and I wanted to hurt him."

"My God," I said, thinking about what Tanner Cobb told us that afternoon and Dalton Wolfe's violent reaction at Sophie's house the night Junior died. We knew Mason Driscoll worked for D. C. Wolfe Enterprises and Dalton was his largest political contributor, and he'd just told us his disgusting rhetoric came straight from his donors. Holy hell. Dalton Wolfe killed Ricky Lee and covered it up.

"I know what you're thinking," Driscoll said, snapping me back to the present.

"No, you don't," I shot back.

"You think Dalton killed Ricky and covered it up. Well, he didn't."

"Forgive me if I don't take a sleazy politician's word for it."

"You leave Mr. Wolfe alone," Driscoll said, finding one last reserve of courage to confront a hundred-pound girl. "I know for a damn fact he didn't kill Ricky Lee, and if you piss him off, you and your family will find yourselves back living in the sticks before you can say white trash."

"I'll worry about that, Representative. You just stay out of our way. They say the worst thing that can happen to a politician is to get caught in bed with a dead girl or a live boy. Well, I've got notes tying you to a dead boy. So keep your head down, and maybe you'll still have a job when we finish ours."

CHAPTER THIRTY-ONE

After spending every weekend night together since the beginning of school, Blaine and I didn't have a date on Saturday night. He just never asked, and I wasn't going to beg, so by sundown, I'd resigned myself to a lonely evening in my room, plotting a way to confront Dalton Wolfe while Mom and Lenny watched Tina Fey impersonate Sarah Palin on *SNL* downstairs. Lenny had become a permanent fixture around our place, and to be honest, I didn't hate him. There was a certain up-to-no-goodness about him that all my mother's boyfriends possessed, but he was nice enough. He brought Mom gas station flowers, paid for their dates, and, best I could tell, didn't have another family across town. In the sad pantheon of my mother's romantic liaisons, Lenny Roach was a regular Romeo.

On Sunday, Blaine called and apologized for going AWOL the day before without offering any explanation, but then he and his mother were both missing in action at school on Monday and Tuesday. I texted to check on him both afternoons, and he said he was fine, just had a lot going on at home, whatever that meant. Wednesday morning,

Blaine was back, waiting by my locker when I arrived, and he hugged me in the hallway for what I considered an awkwardly long time.

"Are you okay?" I asked him. It crossed my mind he might have some terminal illness.

"Yeah, fine," he said, seeming anything but. "Can we hang out tonight?"

"Of course," I said.

"Great, I'll pick you up for dinner," he said before walking out of school. I didn't see him again until he rang our doorbell that evening.

We had a super awkward dinner at Angelina's in Seagrove. I ate two pizza slices, Blaine hardly touched his one, and every conversation I tried to start crashed on takeoff. So we spent most of the meal staring at the checked tablecloth and listening to a man at the bar boast loudly about the cheap Blue Mountain Beach land he'd just bought off some bankrupt developer.

"Let's go to my house," Blaine said after dinner, then reading my apprehension, added, "Dad's not home."

Clyde, the gatehouse guard, let us into Eden Shores, and when Blaine parked outside his parents' mansion, I grabbed his hand.

"Are you dumping me?" I asked. It was the last thing I wanted, but it was my best guess as to what the hell was up with him, and anything would beat this horrible purgatory we'd been in for the last week.

"No," he said, stung by the accusation. "God, no, Izzy, that's the last thing I want to do. It's just …"

"Just what?"

He started to tell me but reconsidered. "Come inside, you'll see."

Of the three Eden Shores mansions I'd been inside, Blaine's had felt most lived in, but no more. Gone was the living room full of books and family photographs. The comfortable sofas and chairs were no more. Even the massive television had disappeared. All of it replaced by cardboard boxes piled high in the corner, giving the giant room all the feng shui of a black hole.

"We're moving," Blaine said.

"What? Where?"

"Montenegro."

"Montenegro? Is that in Florida?" I asked. It didn't sound like it, but my geographic knowledge south of Orlando was spotty at best.

"Europe," Blaine said, shaking his head. "I had to google it too. It's a tiny country on the water close to Italy. Dad took off Saturday without even saying goodbye. He landed a job there with some big European bank. Apparently, it's a tremendous opportunity for our family, but ..."

He burst into tears, and I wrapped my arms around him. "But I don't want to leave," he managed through sobs.

"I know," I said. "I know."

After crying for several minutes, making out with me for half an hour, then crying some more, Blaine was himself again. The weight he'd carried for the past week had lifted, and all that remained was the crushing realization that our time together was quickly coming to an end.

"Remember the first time we made out in here?" Blaine asked, pointing toward where his couch used to sit.

"Vaguely," I teased, looking at the spot on the floor and half-expecting to see a small plaque commemorating the event.

"That Taylor Swift song was on," he said.

"'Love Story'," I said. "I always think of us when I hear that song."

He kissed me again, and I asked, "When do you and your mom leave?"

"We're here until the end of the month," he said. "I guess we can still go to the homecoming dance if you want to."

I smiled. "More than anything."

We sat on the floor for an hour, discussing the prospects of a transatlantic long-distance relationship, both of us vowing to make it work, neither of us believing we could.

"We could run away together," I suggested, half-joking, but half not.

"Run away? And just be poor?" he asked.

"We could get jobs, or rob banks."

"I do look good in a ski mask," he said, but something in his laugh told me if push ever came to shove, he'd never choose me over his parents' money.

Later, when Blaine went to the kitchen to grab us a couple of Cokes, I peeked into one of the moving boxes. Inside were dozens of books once displayed in the living room, including several Bardo Academy yearbooks. I pulled the 1982–83 edition off the top and assumed it was Blaine's mother's copy and not his unpopular father's since several signatures were inside the front cover. Many girls told Kat Ewing they loved her like a sister, others told her never to change, and others still pledged they would be best friends 4-ever. A boy named Jeremy was the first to sign Katherine's crack. And over half of the inside back cover contained a rambling sonnet from none other than Junior Wolfe. After quoting half the lyrics of "Faithfully" by Journey, Junior Wolfe penned some of the mushiest lines in the history of teenage romance, including this doozy of a closer.

"You have me, Kat, heart and soul, and I promise to love you so long as blood flows red through my veins. Yours forever with love, J-Wolfe."

My face scrunched in disgust, and I vowed to burn my yearbook on the spot if a boy ever wrote something that gross inside.

"What are you looking at?" Blaine asked, coming back into the living room with our drinks.

"Your mom's old yearbook," I said, closing it and putting it back in the box. "I didn't know she dated Junior Wolfe."

"Yeah," Blaine said, "sophomore or junior year, I think. Sophie always says we could have been brother and sister, but I've told her that's not how it works."

I laughed, and Blaine said, "I guess they'll ship my yearbook to Montenegro," then he lost it again and burst into tears. I spent the next half hour holding him on the floor, promising him it would all work out, and he finally pulled himself together enough to drive me home. It wasn't until I crawled into bed that the emotions of the evening finally hit me. It's not that Blaine and I had been together that long—we hadn't—but he was the first boy I could even remotely call a boyfriend. He'd even told me he loved me. I cried so hard I gave myself a headache, even though I'd already taken two pills that day. But if ever a day called for three, this was it, so I pulled the bottle from my nightstand drawer, shocked at how light it felt. I cursed, the panic squeezing my chest until I felt like a beached fish, gasping for breath. But then, Blaine's words echoed again in my head, "I can get you more." And surely he'd tell me how to get my own once he was gone. Oxygen filled my lungs once more, and I opened my bottle, took another pill, and slept through my alarm.

CHAPTER THIRTY-TWO

On Friday, Bardo Academy traveled north and defeated the Tigers of Chipley, improving their season record to a perfect 6-0. Blaine and I had a melancholy date on Saturday night, both of us knowing we didn't have many weekends left, and we spent most of Sunday afternoon at Grayton Beach State Park, making out on the hiking trail and lamenting our togetherless future. I assumed we'd hang out Sunday night too, since we were out of school on Monday for Columbus Day. But his mother wanted him to sort through his room and determine what to trash and what to pack. So, we kissed goodnight as the pink sun dipped into the Gulf, and I went home to what I assumed would be a night spent reading the Nellie Bly biography Bardo Academy's library purchased at my urgent request.

"No date tonight?" my mother asked as I ate a bowl of Lucky Charms for dinner on the couch, the novelty of having different tables for every meal having long since worn off. I shook my head no, and she sat next to me. "Well, I'd hate for you to sit at home by yourself all night. Why don't you come with us?"

"Mom, even if the house was on fire, I wouldn't leave to go on a date with you and Lenny."

"It's not a date," Mom said, sticking her tongue out at me. "We're going to a Columbus Day party for work."

"Yeah, no. I wouldn't know anyone but you, and it would be a bunch of old people getting drunk and dancing awkwardly."

Mom laughed. "Suit yourself. I just thought you'd like to see Dalton Wolfe's house."

"Wait, what?"

Apparently, Dalton Wolfe's enterprises closed every October to celebrate the discovery of the country that would make men like Dalton Wolfe possible. In a rare show of gratitude toward his hired hands, Dalton invited them all to his Bardo mansion for hotdogs and tallboys on Sunday night and gave them Monday off to recover from their hangovers. When Mom informed me of this, I ran upstairs to get dressed.

Dalton Wolfe lived in a ten-thousand-square-foot absurdity perched atop the towering dunes on a half-acre of pristine Bardo coastline. This was not a surprise, considering the man owned most of the Florida Panhandle. What did shock me, especially considering Mr. Wolfe's abhorrence for wasted land—the trailers of Pineview Villas a prime example—was that he also owned the empty half-acre lots on either side of his fortress. Lots valued at several million dollars apiece. On one, he'd installed a large putting green and several bunkers so his short game would never be found lacking. And on the other side was a lush garden oasis, complete with palm trees, a koi pond, several fountains, and commanding views of the white sands below. This is where his Columbus Day parties took place.

White tables and chairs littered the garden lawn, and the catering was served under a long, white tent next to the DJ, who was apparently spinning an album titled "Music Old People Cannot Resist." We'd arrived early, a quarter till seven, and already the awkward adult dancing I'd prophesied had come to pass.

"Mom, I'm begging you, please don't embarrass me," I said under my breath as we stepped into the garden.

"Sorry, girl," Mom said, "I make no promises."

My mother looked so pretty that night. I forgot sometimes she was only thirty-six, much younger than most of my friends' parents. She was even dressed cuter than me, in a yellow babydoll top over tight jeans. I found myself wondering why she'd never found a decent man. Then I remembered she'd been too busy working sixty-hour weeks so Axl and I wouldn't starve, and her options were limited to guys who'd flirt with a waitress at the Dandridge Waffle King.

"Do you want to meet the people I work with?" Mom asked.

"Not particularly," I said, and she rolled her eyes at me.

"Fine. Go get some food and sit by yourself and pout. We'll leave after I've said hello to everyone and sufficiently embarrassed you with my dancing."

Mom began dirty dancing on Lenny right there, and I turned and walked away, her laughter chasing after me.

The Wolfes, who didn't spare any expense on their home, spared several on the catering, and my hotdog bun was so stale I threw it away half-eaten and tried to fill up on sweet tea instead. There was no one at the party I recognized. No one under thirty I could see.

So I found an empty table in the corner of the garden and watched a bunch of strangers drink and dance themselves familiar. Spotting Dalton Wolfe's large silhouette in a second-story window next door, I wondered if he and Ella Kay would even attend their own party or if they'd stay inside, looking down on their serfs.

On the beach below, kids began shooting Roman candles at each other, and on the dance floor, something resembling the Electric Slide broke out. I needed to find Dalton Wolfe, but more pressing, my sweet tea dinner necessitated I find a bathroom. Killing two birds with one stone, I ignored the porta-potties the Wolfes had so germaphobicly brought in for the occasion and walked toward their giant house searching for Dalton and a toilet that wouldn't tip over in a stiff breeze.

I feared Dalton and Ella Kay had barricaded themselves inside, but the door leading out to the garden was unlocked. I slipped inside the kitchen, which undoubtedly was recently featured on the cover of *Ridiculously Gigantic Kitchens Quarterly*. A television flickered in the next room, and as I rounded the corner to investigate, I found myself eye to eye with Ella Kay, a woman who looked like she used the phrase, "You people" a lot.

"May I help you?" she asked, her voice dripping with an odd mixture of fear and disdain. She either thought I was an employee or a burglar and hadn't decided which was worse.

I'm here to confront your murdering husband, I thought. "I'm looking for the restroom," I said.

Ella Kay sighed dramatically. "Did we not bring in portables for you people?"

And there it was.

"Yes, ma'am, but people were in them."

She looked over my shoulder toward the garden like she intended to investigate this claim, but that would require touching a porta-potty door or, even worse, talking to her husband's employees. "Fine," she said, and after a short deliberation in which she appeared to calculate which bathroom my germs would do the least amount of damage to, she pointed down a hallway. "You can use Dalton's. Second door on the left. But please, make it quick."

I thanked her with more grace than she deserved before walking down the hall with Ella Kay's eyes burning holes in my back. Dalton's bathroom, as she called it, had a television mounted on the wall, a stack of *Playboys* in the corner, and a golden toilet. Well, gold-plated, I guess, but honestly, who knew with this guy? I gagged imagining the gross things that took place in this room, and as Ella Kay requested, I made it quick.

Dalton Wolfe's office sat across the hall from his poop and porn cave. I peeked inside at his littered desk and the floor-to-ceiling library shelves before letting myself in. Walking across the room, I quickly began shuffling through the papers on his desk, searching for something incriminating, I guess, but not knowing what that would even look like. Best I could tell, it was all invoices and mortgage deeds and bank statements. I pulled out my phone to take some photographs just in case Elton could spot something fishy in the numbers.

I was snapping away when Dalton Wolfe filled the office doorway and boomed, "What the hell are you doing?"

1983

Dalton Wolfe was relieved.

He'd already blown through a boatload of political capital bringing scholarship football players to Bardo Academy against the wishes of everyone in town. An undefeated regular season and an area championship had silenced even his most vocal critics. Still, this thing with Junior and Ricky could have derailed everything.

Well-respected. That's what people called Dalton Wolfe. Like the old Kinks song, he was a well-respected man about town.

A man of his word.

A man of high morals.

A man beyond reproach.

Born in 1935 in DeFuniak Springs, Dalton Wolfe was a founding member of the Lucky Sperm Club. Too young for World War II and Korea, too old for Vietnam, Dalton's father, Cornelius, was richer than God and Gatsby combined, having made a fortune bottling Pepsi-Cola before buying up half the Panhandle. Dalton enrolled at Florida State University in 1953, made twelve tackles in the 1954 Sun Bowl against Texas Western, and graduated six years later with a GPA hovering just above the academic probation line. He went to work for his father the next day.

Dalton would have married his high school sweetheart, a poor little Walton County girl with the biggest blue eyes you've ever seen, but his parents forbade it. People would talk, they said, and nothing was worse than people talking. So, in 1959, he married Ella Kay, the daughter of a prominent Pensacola family that claimed to have descended straight from Hernando de Soto. Together they lived ever after, happiness be damned.

Now two years shy of half a century, Dalton Wolfe was the past president of a laundry list of civic organizations too long to mention and currently served on the boards of WalCo Bank, C. E. Petroleum, and the Florida Power & Light Company. Plus, rumor had it, Governor Graham was strongly considering Dalton for the open spot on Florida State University's Board of Trustees.

He and Ella Kay gave generously to local and national charities, naming scholarships and buildings after themselves whenever possible. They were social, but not too social. Not since his days living in the Pi Kappa Phi house had anyone apart from Ella Kay seen Dalton Wolfe consume more than two drinks in an evening, and she knew to lock her bedroom door when he did, for they'd slept in separate bedrooms since the late sixties.

No, Dalton Wolfe's life wasn't perfect, but he knew what to keep behind closed doors, unlike his dumbass son. My God, he was lucky the Driscoll boy told him what was going on with Ricky Lee. A scandal like that would unravel decades of hard work and do irreparable damage to his standing in the community. Thank God there were only a couple weeks left in the season. After that, Dalton would send Ricky to a prep school across the state. But until then, order must be restored.

"You wanted to see me?" Junior asked, stepping into his father's office.

"Sit down," Dalton barked, skipping the pleasantries.

My God, the boy looked terrible, with his ripped jeans and his Flock of Seagulls haircut. Dalton felt a strong urge to cancel MTV and drag his son to the barbershop that instant, but he resisted.

Every boy in Bardo Academy had a stupid haircut.

Only his was running around with the starting quarterback.

Dalton knew to choose his battles.

"Junior, we need to discuss the company you're keeping."

"Who, Ricky?" Junior asked, and his father nodded. "If you didn't want me hanging around Ricky, you shouldn't have paid his family to move here."

Dalton Wolfe ignored this and said, "I know about the drugs, son." Drugs, Dalton figured, was the only explanation for what Mason Driscoll told him—the thought his only son might be a degenerate beyond consideration.

"What are you talking about?" Junior asked.

"From now on, you are to stay away from Ricky Lee. You will return home immediately after practice, and you will not leave this house on weekends. Understood?"

"You can't do this!" Junior shouted.

"Oh, I can," Dalton said, rising to his full height and casting a giant shadow over his son.

"Fuck you!" Junior shouted, backing up in case he'd provoked the bear to anger. But Dalton merely pointed to the door, and Junior stomped out.

Dalton poured himself a drink and sighed. That went about as well as he'd expected, but still, he was relieved. Relieved to have nipped this potential scandal in the bud.

Junior would stay away from Ricky Lee.

If not, Dalton Wolfe would have to take matters into his own hands.

CHAPTER THIRTY-THREE

Dalton Wolfe filled his office doorway and boomed, "What the hell are you doing?"

"Looking for a bathroom," I managed, backing away from his desk and quickly pocketing my phone.

"Well, this ain't it," Dalton said with a chuckle, and as he made his way around the left side of his desk, I escaped around the right. "There's a toilet across the hall there," he said, straightening a stack of paper on his desk. "I can't blame you for not wanting to use those port-o-potties. Just don't tell nobody, okay? We can't have the whole party stomping around the house looking for the john." He paused to picture the scene and laughed. "Ella Kay would have a conniption."

Every fiber of my being screamed to turn and run away, but with an easy escape behind me, it was now or never. I summoned my last ounce of courage and cleared my throat. "Mr. Wolfe, we need to talk."

He glanced up from his desk. "You're our quarterback's little sister, right? Lizzy, ain't it?"

"Izzy," I said, realizing Dalton Wolfe thought about me way less than I thought about him.

"That's right," he said, snapping his fingers and seemingly complimenting me on knowing my own name. "What do we need to talk about, Izzy? You want a new car like your brother's? He's playing well, but not that well."

The good and bad thing about extracting information from a near blackout drunk is they never remember the conversation. All three of Mom's boyfriends who admitted to being married while in a sloshed stupor showed up the next day like nothing had happened, only to get tossed from our trailer onto their cheating asses a second time. Dalton Wolfe had promised to ring my skinny little neck and feed me to sharks if I ever mentioned the name Ricky Lee to him again. But his jovial demeanor suggested he had no memory of our conversation two weeks ago or his threat to turn me into fish food. I pressed my luck.

"I know about Junior and Ricky Lee," I said, and Dalton dropped the stack of paper like it was one of the rattlesnakes surrounding Pineview Villas.

"How?" he demanded.

"Ricky's mother let me go through a box of his belongings, and I found their love notes."

"What in God's name were you doing talking to Ruby Lee?"

"I'm investigating Ricky's murder for the *Bardo Breeze*."

Dalton Wolfe cursed and shook his head. "I don't suppose I'd have ever agreed to pay your tuition if I'd known you'd be such troublemaker."

"How come when you start digging for the truth, the only people who call you a troublemaker are the ones hiding it?"

Dalton smirked and asked, "Who else knows about the notes?" He hadn't moved yet, and he didn't seem likely to choke me again, but I took a step back toward the door in case.

"Just me," I lied, hoping to keep Elton out of this.

Dalton Wolfe balled his fists until his knuckles cracked, then, to my surprise, he eased into his desk chair. "Junior was a messed-up kid," he said, shaking his head solemnly. "He drank a lot, smoked pot, and by the time Ricky came to town, he'd moved on to harder stuff. I blame myself. Maybe I worked too hard? Maybe I served on too many boards? If I'd been at home more, maybe I could have helped him?"

"Helped him be straight?" I asked.

"I just told you Junior was on drugs," Dalton Wolfe said, glaring at me across the desk.

"And I'm telling you I know Mason Driscoll told you about Ricky and Junior's relationship, and I've talked to lawyers, sheriffs, and even a judge who heard when you found out, you killed Ricky Lee and paid off Chief Duncan to make it go away." That last part required six-degrees of Tanner Cobb, but Dalton Wolfe didn't need to know that. "You built an entire church so you wouldn't have to worry about worshiping with gay people. You killed Ricky Lee. I'm surprised you didn't kill Junior too."

Dalton Wolfe stood, and I backed up another step closer to the door. "Why don't you take a look at that picture there," he said, pointing to a framed photograph on his bookshelf. I glanced at the photo, not wanting to take my eyes off Dalton for too long. It appeared to show him and three other men at a football game several years ago.

"Used to be, some fraternity brothers and I would make one Dolphins game a season," Dalton said. "I remember that trip in particular for three reasons. First, I'd just bought my Hawker 400. That's a jet airplane, if you don't know. Seats eight, with a range of over two thousand miles. We could fly that plane from Miami to Seattle without stopping once for gas." Dalton looked at the ceiling, reminiscing about his old private jet before turning back to me. "Second, that was Dan Marino's rookie year. He'd taken the league by storm, and we couldn't wait to watch him play. But he sprained his knee against Houston the week before, so we wound up watching his backup—"

"Don Strock," I said.

Dalton Wolfe cocked his head, understandably surprised by my familiarity with the '83 Dolphins depth chart. "Yep, Don Strock. We did beat the Falcons 31-24, but I didn't see Marino play until the next season. Which brings me to the third thing I remember about that trip. We left on Saturday morning, the day after Bardo won their semifinal playoff game. And on Sunday night, after the Dolphins game, we flew from Miami down to the Keys for a couple days of fishing. But we had to cut the trip short, and if you've done your homework, you know why."

"Because Ricky Lee was reported missing," I said in defeat.

"Because Ricky Lee was reported missing," he repeated, clicking his tongue.

Dalton Wolfe smirked, letting it all sink in. He couldn't have killed Ricky Lee. He was hundreds of miles away with witnesses and flight records to prove it.

"Good lord, little girl, what were you planning to do tonight? Get a confession and haul me off to jail?"

I stood there speechless. I knew Dalton Wolfe had killed Ricky, but he hadn't.

Dalton shook his head and coughed. "Sometimes, I don't know why I even bother with folks like y'all. Now listen up, you run along and tell your brother I appreciate all his hard work, but his services are no longer required at Bardo Academy."

"What? No! You can't do that," I stammered, Axl's warning not to upset the Wolfe family roaring in my ears. Why couldn't I mind my own business? Why couldn't I leave well enough alone? For the first time in our family's tragic history, we'd found a modicum of stability. But now ... now I'd gone and blown it all to hell.

"Oh, I think I can," Dalton said. "Look, I've done this long enough to know when a family ain't worth the trouble. Usually, they keep coming back for more and more money, not to accuse me of murder, but whatever. There's a hotshot quarterback in Holmes County I can bring in next season, and everyone will forget your brother ever went to school here. Y'all need to go on back to Dandridge and pretend none of this ever happened. I'm sure some nice junior college will let Axl play football for 'em. Hell, they might even teach him to read. But he ain't playing for Florida State, and y'all best be out of my house by tomorrow night."

Dalton resumed shuffling his stack of paper, and I noticed a photograph on the wall of him and Ella Kay cutting a ribbon to open some hospital they'd given a bazillion dollars to name after themselves. Staring at the photo, Mason Driscoll's words came back to me. *You've been in Bardo long enough to know how much people here care about their image, and no one more than Dalton Wolfe.* I only had one bullet left in my gun, so I fired it.

"My uncle writes for the *Observer*."

Dalton Wolfe didn't look up.

"He's an investigative reporter."

Now he did, dropping the stack of paper once again. "Is he now?"

I nodded with all the conviction I could muster. "I'll give him the notes, and he'll write a story about Ricky and Junior, then everyone will know."

Dalton Wolfe rubbed his chin in thought, picturing his next move and seeing my checkmate. "Now, Izzy," he said, starting to negotiate because negotiating is what he did best, "I know you don't want to go and tarnish the legacy of two boys who are both dead and gone."

I kept eye contact and prayed Dalton Wolfe couldn't hear my heart beating across the room.

"If you'll drop all this nonsense," he said, waving a hand at me, "call off your little investigation, I don't see no reason not to let y'all stay here in Bardo."

It was an uneasy truce, but a truce, nonetheless. "Really?" I asked.

"Sure," he said, "but I'm gonna need every one of them letters Junior sent Ricky."

"No," I said, finding one last reserve of strength, "not until we graduate. Then you can have them."

Dalton Wolfe tried his best to kill me with his glare, but when that didn't work, he said, "Fine. Now you get out of my house and stay the hell out of my business, you hear?"

CHAPTER THIRTY-FOUR

"Explain to me again why you were arguing with Dalton Wolfe about using his golden toilet."

"Keep it down," I told Elton after a kid from my French class caught a snippet of our conversation in the hallway and gave us a funny look.

"Apologies," Elton said, loud enough to wake the dead.

It was the Tuesday after Columbus Day, and we were on our way to the *Bardo Breeze* newsroom for last-period extras. I'd spent the previous two minutes trying to recount my weekend run-in with Dalton Wolfe for Elton, but he'd recently discovered Tap Tap Revenge on his phone and was only half-listening to me while blazing through a Death Cab for Cutie song on the extreme difficulty setting. We took our customary seats in the back cubicle, and I snatched Elton's phone from his hands.

"Izzy, I had not yet completed—"

"You're not listening to me," I said, handing his phone back, and Elton mumbled an apology. "I didn't have an argument with Dalton Wolfe about using his golden toilet. I was just telling you he has one and a stack of porn, which is gross, but beside the point. The point is, I confronted him in his office about killing Ricky Lee, and there's no way he did it."

"How do you know?"

"Because he was in Miami, watching Don Strock play quarterback for the Dolphins, and he's got friends and flight records to prove it."

"Oh," Elton said, not particularly bothered by this information. "I suppose we need a new suspect."

"Like who?" I said, banging my fist on the table so hard that Elton pushed his chair away from me, and Denham Frost and the rest of the newspaper staff stopped what they were doing and looked toward the commotion. "Sorry," I said, waving an apology. "I killed a spider."

"You don't get it," I whispered, turning back to Elton. "We're done. It had to be Dalton Wolfe. He's image-conscious and homophobic and plenty violent after a few drinks. He had the motive and the means, and he's got enough money to buy Miami, let alone pay off a small-town cop to make a murder go away. But it wasn't him, so who else could it be? Not Junior. He loved Ricky."

"Could Ricky have terminated his relationship with Junior?" Elton asked. "I am uncertain how homosexual relationships work."

"Same as straight ones."

"I am uncertain about those likewise."

I smiled at him and said, "Maybe, but Mason Driscoll called things off with Junior, and that didn't send him into a murderous rage. Besides, Ricky and Junior were crazy about each other right up until the end, unless there's some final note we never found. Speaking of Driscoll, did you look into his parents?"

"Affirmative," Elton said. "His father was an orthodontist like he said, and they were poor."

"Bardo by the Sea poor?" I asked with a grin.

"What does that mean?"

"That they drove a Mercedes but couldn't splurge for the moon-roof and heated seats?"

"I will need to confirm," Elton said, not catching the joke.

Elton began working on his state championship team article, and I continued thinking aloud, much to his chagrin. "Tanner Cobb and the Cowden players literally threatened to disembowel Ricky, but every family in that town could pool their money together and still not have enough to pay off the police. And we know it wasn't your father."

"You thought my father killed Ricky Lee?" Elton asked, looking up with wide eyes.

"No, well, yes, but only for a couple weeks. I mean, he benefited the most from Ricky not playing in the championship game, and Dalton Wolfe could have covered it up in exchange for your father's commitment to Florida State."

Elton's jaw dropped ever so slightly, and he said, "My father could have killed Ricky Lee."

"He didn't," I said, putting a hand on Elton's shoulder he was too upset to notice. "Junior Wolfe told me your father was at church all night when Ricky disappeared."

"Oh," Elton said, with something resembling relief in his voice, "I am pleased it was not him."

"We've got to think," I said, tapping out a beat with my pen on the table. "Who had a reason to kill Ricky Lee?"

"Perhaps it was drug dealers," Elton suggested. "Sometimes, the most obvious answer is the correct one."

"No way," I said. "Too many people have told us something fishy went down. For one, we know someone paid off the police chief."

"We suspect," Elton corrected.

"Junior Wolfe told me as much."

"Suicidal Junior Wolfe," Elton reminded me.

"And Driscoll told us they hardly questioned him about Ricky."

"Incompetence and dishonesty are not mutually exclusive."

I frowned at him and said, "Don't forget about the woman on the beach who found Ricky's body. She knew something was up."

"You mean the hundred-year-old woman who refuses to sell her rundown shack for three million dollars?" Elton asked.

"Okay, what about Tanner Cobb? He told us—"

"Are you referring to the shirtless attorney who told us Dalton Wolfe killed Ricky in front of his son?"

This time I laughed and said, "If I didn't know any better, I'd swear you were being sarcastic."

Elton shrugged, and I stuck my tongue out at him. "Well, it wasn't drug dealers. They'd have never gone through all the trouble of stabbing Ricky two dozen times and dumping his body at sea."

"Drug dealers have already made several poor life choices," Elton said, "we cannot speak with any certainty on what they would or would not do to a corpse."

I opened my mouth to argue, but he had a point, so I sat back and sighed in defeat. "When we talk to people outside of Bardo, we just get a bunch of wild rumors that don't lead us anywhere. And no one living in Bardo will even admit to anything scandalous ever happening here, much less talk to us about it because they're afraid it will lower their property values."

"It would," Elton said, but I ignored him.

"The evidence was conveniently destroyed, and the lead

investigator is missing, if not dead himself." I shrugged and said, "I think we're stuck. Whoever killed Ricky was too rich to get caught. Money remains undefeated."

Elton's phone buzzed in his backpack. "Private number," he said, showing me the screen with wide eyes. "It could be President Bush."

"I somehow doubt it. It's probably a telemark—"

"Tuesday greetings, Mr. President. Elton Jones-Davies speaking."

I shook my head, and Elton said, "Yes, hello, Mr. Duncan, I—"

"Wait, Jack Duncan?" I asked, and when Elton nodded, I snatched the phone from his hand and ran into the hallway to avoid stares from Denham Frost and the rest of the newspaper staff.

"Chief Duncan, this is Izzy Brown. We really need to talk to you. There are—"

"Shut up and listen," Jack Duncan barked, so I did. "If you are still snooping around Bardo trying to figure out what happened to Ricky Lee, you are in a world of danger."

"So, you're saying we're on the right track?"

"No, I'm saying you should mind your own business before someone finds you dead in a ditch."

"Where are you? Will you meet us somewhere? We—"

"I'm a long way from Bardo, and I've got the cash and motivation to stay hidden for the rest of my life. You don't have my options."

"You covered up the murder, didn't you?"

There was a long silence on the other end, and I checked the screen to see if he'd hung up, but the call timer was still ticking. "Look, they told me it was an accident, and it probably was. The kids had a bright future. One life had already been ruined. There wasn't much point in ruining more."

"What are you talking about? It wasn't an accident? Someone slit Ricky's throat."

"They knew. They knew I had … "

"Who knew you had what?"

"Debt. They knew. God, and it had been so long, I thought maybe they wouldn't care—I just wanted to live closer to my mother, but—Look, I've got hell to pay. I know that. But you've got to understand, I'm trying to do the right thing now."

"Then tell me who did it."

"That wouldn't, no, that wouldn't help anyone. And I don't need your blood on my hands too. Let it go, girl. I'm begging you."

"Please, Chief Duncan, don't—"

He hung up, and I tried to redial the private number, but the call wouldn't go through. I banged my fist on a locker and cursed, trying to recall the conversation. He said something about the kids having a bright future, so it must have been Bardo Academy students who killed Ricky, and their parents paid to cover it up. Maybe we were closer than I thought. I ran back into the newsroom.

"Hey, I talked to Jack Duncan," I told Elton, who was working on his state championship story again and had seemingly forgotten the police chief who ran away from us on his yacht had just called.

"What did he say?"

I looked at Elton. To be so big and strong, he was as innocent as a child. I didn't want to put him in danger. I promised his mother I wouldn't. But we were so damn close.

"He said we're on the right track."

CHAPTER THIRTY-FIVE

Having never dated the same boy longer than a minute, I wasn't exactly sure how to handle my rapidly ending relationship with Blaine, and I suppose he wasn't either. The Atlantic Ocean and several time zones were scheduled to break us up in a matter of days, and spending time together only left us miserable. Still, it beat being apart, so most evenings, he came over to our place because his house was full of moving boxes and reminders of what was to come.

"I've been thinking," he said, lying next to me on my bed, gazing at the glow-in-the-dark stars I'd stuck to the ceiling, and listening to the gentle Gulf breeze whistle through my open balcony door.

"That's dangerous," I teased.

"I'm serious," he said. "I think we could fly you over to spend a couple of weeks with us this summer."

You'd better fly me in first class if I've got to spend two weeks with your father, I thought. "Yeah, maybe," I said.

"Do you have a passport?" he asked.

"I've only left Florida to visit my cousins in Alabama," I said.

"Besides, even if I had one, it's hard to imagine your father paying for my transatlantic flight."

Blaine conceded my point with a grunt.

"I'm sure we'll come back to Florida to visit," he said later. "My grandmother lives in a nursing home on 98, and Dad has a sister in Watercolor. And then, you know, college is only two years away, so I'll move back to the States."

"Blaine Park, I hope you are not asking me to hold tight for two entire years because twenty of Bardo's most eligible bachelors are currently lined up in my driveway waiting for you to leave."

"Very funny," Blaine said, rolling over to kiss me, and when he pulled back, he added, "I don't expect you to wait for me, but I'm holding out hope we somehow end up together in the end."

"Me too," I said, smiling and kissing him back until my lips were chapped. I sat up and opened my nightstand drawer to get some ChapStick, and when I did, I saw my rapidly emptying bottle of pills. "By the way," I said, shaking the bottle, "if you can get me another bottle of these, that would be amazing."

"What, now?"

"Well, no, not this instant, we're making out. But in the next few days. I'm almost out."

"Holy shit, Izzy," Blaine said, sitting up, "there were fifty pills in that bottle."

"Right, and you gave it to me like six weeks ago, and now I'm almost out."

Blaine looked scared, and that scared me, and a hot flash ran up my back, turning my cheeks sunburn red. "I thought that bottle would last you half a year or more," he said. "I only take one a week."

"But I have migraines all the time and anxiety every day, so I take one before school and sometimes before bed, and I feel normal. It's like you said, they don't get me high or anything. I just feel like everyone else gets to feel without medicine."

"I'm sorry," Blaine said, shaking his head, "but I'm not comfortable getting you more."

"Why the hell not?" I snapped. I hadn't meant to yell at him, but I was suddenly so mad I was shaking.

"Because you're taking way too many."

"Fine, I'll buy my own. At least tell me where to get them."

He shook his head.

"Tell me where I can get them!" I yelled.

Blaine closed his eyes and took a deep breath. "Downstairs."

"What?"

"That guy your mom is dating, Lenny. I've been buying from him since spring. That's why I freaked out the other night when he walked in and introduced himself."

"Hold up," I said, jumping off the bed, "my mother is dating your drug dealer, and you didn't think this was information I needed to know?"

"It's not that, Izzy, I didn't think—"

"Wait, does Axl know?"

Blaine hesitated long enough for me to know the truth.

I stomped down the hall and burst into Axl's room. "Did you know?" I demanded.

"Why so serious?" Axl asked, quoting Heath Ledger's Joker, something he'd done annoyingly often ever since watching *The Dark Knight* four times over the summer.

"Did you know?" I yelled, snatching a Nerf football off his dresser and throwing it at him.

"What are you talking about?"

"Did you know our mother is dating a drug dealer?"

Axl's hesitation said it all.

"You knew, and you didn't tell Mom?"

"Look," Axl said, sitting up in bed, "Lenny isn't some crack dealer. I could walk into a pain clinic tomorrow with a toothache and get the same stuff he sells. He just … cuts out the middleman."

"Oh my God. Do you even hear yourself?"

"What?" Axl asked. "It's not like you had a problem taking his stuff?"

"Wait, you know?"

Axl nodded behind me, and I turned to see Blaine standing in the doorway.

"You told my brother you bought me pills?" I yelled at Blaine, shoving him hard in the chest. "Who else did you tell?"

"No one," Blaine promised, backing up several feet so I couldn't shove him again.

"So what if I know?" Axl asked. "I also know you haven't complained about a headache in weeks, and you've stopped freaking out about everything all the time."

I sat in Axl's desk chair and tried to calm down. "What now?" I asked, looking from my brother to my boyfriend. "We just let Mom date this guy until the police raid our house one morning and kick us out of Bardo forever?"

"Come on, Izzy, think about it," Axl said, throwing a pillow at me, "what's the longest Mom has ever stayed with one dude? Three months? Lenny will be gone soon enough. You've got to let these things run their course."

To have shared a womb, Axl and I are different in so many ways. For instance, when watching an NFL game, my brother will stare at replays of gruesome injuries until the announcers get sick and stop showing them. I, on the other hand, have to leave the room immediately and sometimes go for days trying to forget what I saw. Perhaps his ability to quickly purge unpleasantries from his mind explains where he found the confidence to play quarterback. Axl never worried about failing because he never failed, or at least he forgot his failures so quickly it was as if they never happened. And maybe my inability to push unwanted thoughts away explains why I've gone through life wrapped in a cocoon of anxiety. Because now that I knew about Lenny, I'd worry about him every minute I wasn't asleep.

"So, he's not dangerous?" I asked.

"No," Blaine said, "he's not. I wasn't thrilled running into him here. Didn't particularly want him to know my real name. I figured he'd try and extort me somehow if he found out my parents had money, but he hasn't. He just liked watching me squirm a little. He's cool."

"No shit, he's a step up from most of the dudes Mom brings home," Axl said. "He's even got an associate's degree in marketing or something from a junior college in Tampa."

"You're both sure?" I asked, and Blaine and my brother nodded. "Okay," I said, sweet oxygen returning to my lungs, in part because Lenny probably wasn't going to get my mother killed in a drug shootout, but mostly because I realized more pills would not be hard to come by. I punched Blaine on the arm, then grabbed Axl's old Dandridge letterman's jacket off the floor and threw it at my brother. "But I'm still pissed off at both of you."

"Sorry," they mumbled in unison, and while Blaine rubbed his arm, Axl admired the old letterman's jacket he used to wear like a second skin.

"I haven't worn this since December," Axl said, putting on the jacket and pulling something out of the pocket. "Sweet, a condom. You saved me seventy-five cents. Thanks, sis."

"Gross," I said, rolling my eyes. Then it hit me. "Wait," I said, "that's it!"

"What's it?" Axl and Blaine asked, the condom sending their filthy minds to the same place.

"Oh my God," I said, grabbing my brother's face. "Thank you, thank you, thank you!"

"Izzy, what are you talking about?" Blaine asked, but I was already running to my room to call Elton.

CHAPTER THIRTY-SIX

After four tries, I finally found the right key. I took a breath, opened the door, and flinched, waiting for the ear-piercing alarm that would undoubtedly bring the police and my arrest for trespassing, burglary, theft, and a whole laundry list of crimes and misdemeanors I wasn't even aware I'd committed. But my late-night entry into Bardo Academy was met by a deafening silence, and I exhaled after holding my breath for what felt like the better part of eternity.

Stepping through the door, I noticed the alarm on the wall. We had a similar one at our new house in Tartarus Shores, but we'd never bothered to activate it. The school's alarm wasn't flashing out a warning, and I wouldn't know how to turn it off even if it was. Everything looked normal, but the alarm could have already alerted a technician in a faraway control center, who would in turn alert authorities. I needed to act quickly, just in case.

The keys belonged to Blaine's mother. On Saturday night, he took me to dinner at Délicieux 30A, a restaurant so expensive they even charge you for nasty Florida tap water, then we went to see *High School Musical 3*—Blaine's choice, believe it or not. Afterwards, I asked that we go back to his place, even though most of the furniture was packed for the move. We sat outside on the deck, counting the stars and listening to the waves crash ashore. Like always, we spent the better part of an hour lamenting our fate as star-crossed lovers between intense make-out sessions, and before he drove me home, I excused myself to the bathroom.

Mrs. Park's keys were hanging right where they always were, on the hook in the kitchen next to a family photograph taken on a Colorado ski vacation. I pocketed them quietly, and Blaine took me home. Around one in the morning, I snuck out and drove Mom's car to Bardo Academy. Then it was on.

≈≈≈≈≈≈

"Negative," Elton said when I told him of my plans at school on Friday as we walked to the pep rally.

"What do you mean, negative?"

"Your plan is abhorrent," Elton said. "First, it is illegal, and second, it is …"

"See, you can't even think of two reasons not to do it."

Elton scowled. "It is illegal," he repeated. "I do not need two reasons."

"It's not as illegal as murder," I argued, "or grand theft auto, or stabbing a manatee."

"Illegal is illegal," Elton said.

I rolled my eyes at him. "Right, so when you run a stop sign—"

"I do not run stop signs."

"Fine, when you drive over the speed limit, you don't—"

"I do not drive over the speed limit."

I began to argue, but he was right, at least about his driving. "Okay, when I run a stop sign, surely you don't believe that is the same as murder, right?" Elton thought about this longer than a person should, and I snapped at him. "Holy hell, Elton, what is wrong with you? Of course it's not."

"Two wrongs do not make a right," he said.

"You told me you struggle with idioms."

"That is a proverb," he corrected, and I wanted to punch him.

We'd stopped outside of the gymnasium, and I pulled him a few steps off the sidewalk so no one might overhear. "If I do this and solve a twenty-five-year-old murder case, do you seriously think I'll get into trouble? Of course not. The town will probably throw us a parade. Besides, they can't convict you of a crime if it helps solve a bigger crime. That's double-jeopardy."

Elton huffed. "That is not how—"

"Elton," I said, and with great effort, he looked me in the eyes. "That was a joke."

"Right," he said.

"Hey, but we could get married, then no one could force you to testify against me."

"I'm not allowed to date," Elton said automatically.

"I know," I said, giving him a hug he squirmed out of. "And you're right. It's a bad idea. I won't go through with it."

"Good," he said, and I wondered if he knew I was lying.

Now standing in front of the trophy case, staring at my ski-masked covered reflection in the glass, I realized I had no way of opening it. None of the keys on Mrs. Park's ring were small enough to fit, so some ad-libbing was in order. First, in a move of brilliant improvisation, even if I do say so myself, I took a sheet of paper from the printer, scribbled a note left-handed, and set it on the receptionist's desk. Then I took her sea turtle paperweight, channeled my inner Axl, and threw it into the trophy case with all my might, sending a shower of glass cascading onto the floor.

Like Indiana Jones, I tiptoed across the floor and slowly lifted Ricky Lee's letterman's jacket out from under the 1983 state championship trophy, half-expecting to set off a series of booby traps in the process. But no poison darts shot from the walls, and no giant boulder chased me off campus, so I reached into the left-hand pocket of Ricky's old jacket and pulled out nothing but lint. Not the end of the world, so I tried the other side and came up empty again. Shit.

I dropped the jacket onto the floor and shook my head in disbelief. This had to be it. I just knew it. And now I'd stolen my boyfriend's mom's keys, broken into the school, and smashed up the trophy case for nothing. But bending to pick up the jacket and place it back under the trophy where it belonged, I noticed the inner pocket, and I gasped with hope. I said a silent prayer, reached inside the third pocket, and felt a folded sheet of paper. Bingo. I pulled out the note and slowly opened it, the quarter-century-old paper nearly falling apart at the folds. On one side were the lyrics to "Open Arms" by Journey. The other side said this.

Dear Ricky,

Saturday night at midnight, meet me on the east side of Topsail Hill, two hundred yards past the last house. I'll bring a blanket, you get the beer. You have my heart, so long as air fills my lungs.

Yours forever, with love,

J-Wolfe

"Oh no," I whispered, pocketing the note. I had to tell Elton.

I turned to leave just as the Bardo Police burst into the office with their guns drawn.

1983

Tommy Park was nobody.

As the president of WalCo Bank's only son and one of the wealthiest kids in Bardo, Tommy couldn't understand why he wasn't more popular. He begrudgingly accepted the alpha status of rich, handsome guys like Junior Wolfe. But now that even white-trash Ricky Lee had passed him by, Tommy had grown increasingly incensed. He should date the head cheerleader, or at least a cheerleader. He should be the odds-on favorite for prom king, or at least have a date to the prom. He should rule the school with an iron first, or at least not walk the halls with complete anonymity.

But he wasn't.

And he didn't.

And he probably never would.

Short and slow, Tommy possessed all the athletic prowess of a sea turtle. His father played linebacker at FSU in the late fifties, and at his insistence, Tommy was a member of the Bardo Academy football team. The program listed Tommy as the second-string right guard, though in reality, he only saw the field in the waning minutes of blowout wins or losses and spent most of the time getting knocked on his ass. Tommy did have a letterman's jacket, but he never wore it because it only prompted questions of whether or not he deserved to have one in the first place from the gaggle of dicks that were his teammates. Instead, Tommy usually opted for the red leather Michael Jackson "Thriller" jacket his parents paid a small fortune for. Tommy hoped moonwalking through the halls of Bardo Academy in his zipper-laden jacket might change his luck with the ladies. It did not.

By senior year, Tommy accepted that high school was a lost cause. Perhaps college would be better. He'd join his father's fraternity at Florida State, splash some cash, and make a lot of friends. In the meantime, he'd keep his head down, plug along, and not worry about the parties he wasn't invited to or the dates he didn't have. Tommy spent most weekend nights with his friends in the Bardo Comic Book Club, playing D&D and drinking beer when they could score some. On Saturdays, Tommy took to the water in his daysailer but rarely left Powell Lake. He'd solo sailed forever but was still scared of the open sea and preferred skimming along the smooth surface of the lake. Most days, he'd pack a lunch, land on the shore, and spend a few hours tromping through the woods, pretending he was Indiana Jones. He even wore a fedora. He was that cool. And on one of these adventures, while running from imaginary natives, Tommy stumbled upon a small clearing and—Oh. My. God.

That's Junior Wolfe.

And Ricky Lee.

And they're—

Tommy couldn't breathe. The information he now possessed was more powerful than any of the Russian nuclear missiles the news said could rain down on America at any moment. Tommy's bomb, if he chose to drop it, would obliterate the entire social structure of Bardo Academy, and perhaps, Bardo by the Sea itself. The mighty would fall, and the meek would inherit the school.

He agonized over what to do for days. Starting a rumor wasn't enough. That could backfire and leave him even more of a social pariah than before. No, Tommy needed proof. He returned the next Saturday with the expensive camera his parents bought him for Christmas. Hiding in the bushes like some perverted *National Geographic* photographer, Tommy waited. Two hours passed with nothing to show for his trouble but a blurry photograph of a great blue heron. He almost packed up and went home after convincing himself he'd imagined the whole thing, but then they were back. Junior and Ricky, k-i-s-s-i-n-g.

Tommy snapped away and formulated a plan. He held all the cards now, and if he played them right, high school could still turn out the way he'd always dreamed.

Tommy Park was nobody, but not for long.

CHAPTER THIRTY-SEVEN

Within half an hour of my apprehension by Bardo's finest, I found myself seated on a bench in the office lobby while my mother, Mrs. Park, and Principal Baugh stared down in varying degrees of disappointment. Red and blue police lights still flashed outside, which seemed entirely unnecessary, but at least the cops had holstered their weapons.

Principal Baugh yawned and checked her watch. "Okay, Izzy, I need you to walk us through everything, and then I will decide if you leave here with your mother or the police."

I took a deep breath, rehearsed my story in my head, and spun my web of lies. "It's just, Friday is the big game against Milton, and if we win, we're Area champs. But if we lose, we might not even make the playoffs. And not to put too fine a point on it, but Axl is on scholarship to win football games. I was afraid if we lost ..."

Here I rubbed my eyes and tried in vain to summon even a solitary tear, but I was too scared to cry, so I sniffled loudly instead.

"I was afraid if we lost the game, Mr. Wolfe would send us back to Dandridge."

"Oh, Izzy," Mrs. Park said, playing good cop to Principal Baugh's bad one, "it is an important football game, but that still doesn't explain the destruction of school property or the theft of my keys."

"Elton and I are writing a story about the 1983 state championship team for the *Breeze*," I said, "and before the Baker game that year, someone spray-painted a gator logo on our locker room."

"I remember that," Mrs. Park said, smiling and shaking her head at the memory.

"Our boys were furious," Principal Baugh said, now smiling too.

"If I recall, the referees called the game off in the fourth quarter because Baker didn't have enough healthy players to finish," Mrs. Park said, and both women laughed.

"Right, and I thought, maybe if I ..." I pointed toward the receptionist's desk. "I left a note."

Principal Baugh retrieved the note from the desk and read it aloud. "We're going to smash you worse than we smashed your trophy case. Go Panthers!"

I sat there, waiting for my punishment. Expulsion. Prison. Lethal Injection. Nothing seemed off the table until Mrs. Park laughed and said, "Oh, come on, Selena, it was a harmless prank, and I'm sure Izzy will agree to pay for the damages."

"She will," my mother said, staring daggers through me.

"Fine," Principal Baugh said, pointing a long finger at me, "three-days in-school suspension, and if I so much as remember you exist between now and summer, I'll have no choice but to permanently expel you from Bardo Academy."

"That is more than fair," Mrs. Park said, putting an arm around my shoulder. "Don't you agree, Izzy?"

I nodded, and Principal Baugh said, "I will inform Officer Mielke we will not be pressing charges." Then she glanced at the note in her hand and added, "And I suppose it wouldn't hurt anyone if I passed this along to Coach Martin. His team would want to know what those Milton thugs did to our trophy case."

Mom wanted to kill me, but thankfully the cops were still there, so she growled something about talking to me when I got home and stomped out to Axl's car. Principal Baugh handed me a broom, and I got to work sweeping the glass while Mrs. Park picked Ricky Lee's letterman's jacket up from the floor. She handled it carefully, like a priceless relic, and gently placed it under the state championship trophy before calling me over.

"Thank you," I said, "I'm surprised she didn't give me the death penalty. I think Principal Baugh hates me."

"Oh, she does," Mrs. Park said with a wink. "I can tell because she's always hated me too. In high school, we competed for everything—boys, head cheerleader, homecoming queen. That we can work in the same building without strangling each other is a miracle, but it helps we both think we're the one running things." I smiled, and Mrs. Park added, "Luckily for you, Selena believes a winning football team reflects well on her as principal, so your little story worked."

"What?" I asked, my cheeks suddenly hotter than the sand in August.

"I assume you were here tonight looking for clues, not to inspire the football team. Did you find what you were looking for in Ricky's jacket?"

"No, ma'am," I lied. "We gave that up weeks ago. If the police couldn't solve it, it was dumb to think we could."

She studied my face, understandably not sure if she could believe the girl who'd stolen her keys, broken into the school, and smashed a trophy case.

"A wise decision," she finally said, putting a hand on my shoulder. "Ricky's death devastated this community," she added, running her fingers across the fuzzy '84 stitched onto the faux leather sleeve of his jacket. "Opening old wounds wouldn't help anyone."

She held the dustpan while I swept the glass, then took me by the shoulders and said, "Izzy, I know the last few weeks were difficult for you and Blaine. You're the first girl he's ever been serious about, and he was crushed when I told him we'd have to move." She pointed toward the trophy case I'd destroyed and added, "I know you're hurting too, so it's only natural you'd act out like this."

"Yes, ma'am," I said. "I'm just thankful we have until the end of the month together."

"Well, Blaine doesn't know this yet—I planned to tell him in the morning—but this will be our last week in Bardo. Thomas needs us sooner than expected. We leave on Sunday."

"Oh," I said, fighting back the tears.

"I'm so sorry, Izzy," Mrs. Park said, taking me by the hand. "Let me walk you out to your car."

"Uh, no, it's okay," I said, pulling my hand back and wiping my tears. "I need sit here a minute."

"I understand," Mrs. Park said, and she left me there to cry.

Elton wouldn't answer my calls on Sunday, and I couldn't find him before the bell on Monday morning, so I didn't see him until that afternoon once they'd released me from in-school suspension. "Haven't you heard of returning a phone call?" I asked, putting an arm around him that he shook off more violently than usual.

"I only return the phone calls of people I desire to speak to," Elton said, not slowing his long stride through the school parking lot.

"Wait," I said, hurrying to catch him, "what's that supposed to mean?"

"You promised you would not break into the school."

"I heard Milton students did that," I said, and Elton walked away again. "Hang on," I said, running to stand in front of him so he'd have to stop, "I can see how you might have gotten the impression I wasn't going to go through with that, but—"

"I'm late for Tae Kwon Do," Elton said, walking away for the third time.

"Look," I said, jogging to keep up, "I know you don't agree with my methods, but you haven't even heard what I found."

"I do not care what you found."

"Yes, you do, you donkey."

"You broke the law, Izzy," Elton said, wagging a long finger in my face. "You could have gotten into serious trouble, and I could have gotten into trouble for being associated with you."

"Elton, you won't get in—"

"You lied to me, Izzy," Elton shouted. Several Bardo students stopped and stared at us across the parking lot, but Elton continued shouting. "And that is particularly detestable because you know how difficult it is for me to tell when someone is lying. I am wired to take people at their word, especially people I consider my best friend. But best friends do not lie!"

His words hit me like a Category 5 hurricane, and a lump rose in my throat. "Elton, I'm sorry. I know I shouldn't have lied to you, but you haven't even let me tell you what I found."

"I told you, I do not care what you found."

"Don't say that. We've worked on this for weeks. Of course you care."

"No, Izzy, I do not. I am no longer assisting you with this project, and I hope you will honor my wishes and never speak to me about it again."

He turned to walk away again, but this time I didn't follow.

CHAPTER THIRTY-EIGHT

Clyde, the security guard, was in a lousy mood when I arrived at the gates of Eden Shores on Wednesday after school. Axl once told me Clyde liked to bet on dogs at the greyhound track in Ebro, and I'm guessing he didn't pick many winners the previous weekend.

"State your business," Clyde demanded.

"Hey Clyde, I'm here to see Sophie."

Scowling, he stepped from his little booth, a large golf umbrella protecting him from the deluge, and he copied Mom's license plate number into his little book. After ringing the Wolfes' house for confirmation, he waved me through.

The Wolfes' driveway gate was open, but I stopped at the speaker box and called up anyway. Sophie said she'd be in her room and to let myself in. I parked next to the chromed-out Hummer Junior Wolfe never got around to selling, and entering the house, my eyes instinctively drifted up the spiral stairway to the chandelier, which looked smaller than I'd remembered. After barely two months in Bardo, was I so numb to ostentatious wealth that such things no longer impressed me?

Tiptoeing across the living room, I glimpsed the angry waves crashing outside. An overambitious tropical depression made landfall east of Pensacola that morning. The National Hurricane Center would upgrade it to a tropical storm based on structural damage and data collected from buoys in the Gulf, but not for another week. At the time, none of us knew the storm we were riding out was that bad, but I've learned that's the best way to go through life.

"Are you from the bank?" a woman asked, and I jumped and spun around to see Sophie's mother, Leslie, in a bathrobe, perilously holding a glass of red wine. "Are they now sending skinny little girls to take away my things?"

Mrs. Wolfe crossed the room and carelessly dropped her glass on an end table without somehow spilling a drop. She pointed at the piano and said, "Go ahead, take the Steinway. It's not like anyone ever plays it. All that money for lessons and not one of my children can even play chopsticks."

I deduced she was either coming from or going to one of her rosé and Xanax baths. Still, I didn't know how to respond to anything she'd said, so I stared at my feet and hoped she'd go away.

"Go on, dear," she said, "take the piano. Put it on your back and carry it out the front door."

"Uh … I'm Axl's sister, Izzy," I finally managed. "I'm here to see Sophie."

Mrs. Wolfe appeared disappointed by this information. Seems her heart was set on watching me attempt to move a 900-pound piano by myself. "Fine," she said, fluttering her fingers toward the ceiling, "she's probably in her room."

"Thank you," I mumbled before shuffling past Mrs. Wolfe and quickly running upstairs.

I was grounded, of course. When I got home from Bardo Academy the night of my failed break-in, Mom told me I was to stay in my room, in her words, "Till Gabriel blows his horn." When I told her Blaine was moving on Sunday, she softened slightly and offered a small reprieve, granting me permission to attend the football game and Homecoming dance. She also allowed me to leave the house if schoolwork necessitated it. And it was under the guise of an imaginary assignment I slipped away to visit Sophie Wolfe on Wednesday, even though we didn't have a single class together. For her part, Sophie believed my visit pertained to the color of her homecoming corsage.

"You have to understand," I told Sophie, as we sat on the bed in her pinker than pink room, "homecoming at Dandridge wasn't a big deal like it is here. The dance was right after the game. Girls didn't wear dresses, and the football players walked over to the gym straight from their post-game showers. Axl doesn't even know what a corsage is, and when I told him he needed to buy one to match your dress color, he flipped out. He's got enough stress with the game Friday, so I told him not to worry about it. I'd figure it all out."

"That's so sweet of him to worry," Sophie said, opening her closet to reveal more clothes than I would ever own in several lifetimes. "I'm wearing this old thing," she said, pulling out a pink and black number with a plunging neckline that would assure her greatest assets were the topic of every conversation. I took a photograph of her dress with my phone and vowed to ensure Axl's suit and tie complemented her in every way.

"Just don't tell Axl I came over, okay? He made me promise not to bother you with any of this."

"Who is Axl?" she asked with a sly smile, then, showing a surprising amount of empathy, asked how I was handling Blaine's imminent departure from Bardo.

"It sucks," I said, "but I don't think we would have stayed together that much longer."

"What makes you say that?"

"Oh, just the impassable chasm between the rich and poor."

"You're so weird," Sophie said, rolling her eyes. Then, ignoring what I'd just said, she spent a small eternity detailing several wealthy and eligible Bardo classmates she'd be happy to set me up with once Blaine was safely across the Atlantic. Boys who hadn't bothered to even say hello to me in my two months at Bardo Academy, but who, Sophie assured me, would jump at the chance to ask me out once she put in a good word. I thanked her when she was done, said I'd see myself out, then got down to the real business of my visit.

To my horror, Junior Wolfe's office was protected by a punch code lock. Shit. I tried 1234 with no luck, then 4321 and 1983, but the lock was unmoved. Double shit. What would Junior Wolfe use for a passcode? I was racking my brains when I noticed a framed photograph of the Wolfe family celebrating a Seminole victory. Dalton Wolfe's instructions on the day we moved into Tartarus Shores came back to me. *18-16, in the Orange Bowl. Now don't forget that score. It's the code to get you through.* I typed the old football score into Junior's door lock, and it opened like Ali Baba's cave.

Slipping inside, I flipped on the light and began my search. The floor-to-ceiling shelves were a mess, with books stacked haphazardly and dozens of picture frames still displaying the stock photography they came with. "Where are they?" I mumbled to myself, fearing I wouldn't find what I'd come for. No one could blame Junior if he'd trashed them to rid himself of the painful memories. But to my relief, on a bottom shelf in the back corner of the office, I found his old Bardo Academy yearbooks.

I opened the front cover and began scanning the messages from classmates. And there, among the encouragements to never change, declarations of brotherly love, and claims of first crack signing, was the sweet note and little doodle that all but confirmed my suspicion.

"Holy shit," I whispered, snapping a picture of the message with my phone, just as footsteps echoed in the hallway. A shiver ran up my spine, and I froze, waiting to get busted while trying and failing to think of even a bad excuse for my presence in the deceased developer's office. The footsteps stopped outside, but whoever it was simply kept going. I exhaled in relief, but no sooner had I started for the door, the footsteps returned, and Sophie burst into the office.

"Izzy, what are you doing in here?"

I wanted to lie. I started to lie. But Junior Wolfe was Sophie's father, and she deserved the truth, so I gave it to her.

CHAPTER THIRTY-NINE

Friday morning, I woke with a headache so large I feared its gravitational pull would collapse the known universe in on my skull. When Axl banged on my door to tell me he was leaving for school, I managed to grunt my intentions to stay home, and rolling over, I reached into my nightstand drawer for my bottle, which was now so light it had started contributing to my anxiety instead of relieving it. I swallowed one, leaving three, then went downstairs in hopes of finding Lenny.

"Good morning, sunshine," Lenny said, eating a honeybun on our couch while watching SportsCenter.

"Morning," I mumbled, grabbing a Pop-Tart from the cabinet and microwaving it because I couldn't be bothered to plug in the toaster.

"You okay?" he asked, turning to look at me. "You sound liked warmed over death."

"Thanks," I deadpanned, and Lenny laughed. "It's just a headache," I said.

"Yeah, headaches suck," Lenny offered and turned back to the television.

I sat in the recliner with my nuked Pop-Tart and said, "I had some medicine that helped, but my prescription ran out."

SportsCenter showed highlights of Lenny's Tampa Bay Rays' World Series win over Philadelphia the night before, and he didn't seem to register what I'd said. Or he did and was going to make me ask.

I swallowed my pride. "Do you know where I could get some more? I don't have time to go to the doctor right now."

Lenny cocked his head. "What were you taking?"

I shrugged, realizing I didn't know what I'd been taking the last two months. "They were pink," I said, "with a twenty on one side and 'OC' on the other."

"OxyContin, twenty milligrams," Lenny said automatically. "I bet those did help your headaches."

"They did," I said after Lenny turned back to the television, seemingly forgetting the conversation we were having. "Help my headaches," I added.

"Yeah, I can get you more," he said after a moment, "no problem."

"Oh, thanks," I said, shocked and exhilarated at how easy that was. "How much do I owe you? Mom took most of my savings to pay for the trophy case I broke, so it might be a couple weeks before I can—"

"Get the hell out of here," Lenny said with a dismissive wave. "I ain't charging my girlfriend's daughter. I'll have them for you tonight. Just don't tell your mama, okay?"

"Yeah, of course, thank you," I said, choking on my own hypocrisy, as Lenny snapped his fingers and pointed at me in his super douchey way before turning back to the television.

By midmorning, my headache reluctantly surrendered, but I decided to stay home from school anyway. I spent an hour in my room going over everything I knew about Ricky Lee's murder—the newspaper clippings, the secret letters from Junior Wolfe, the yearbook signatures, and the final note in Ricky's letterman's jacket that lured him to his gruesome death. I'd been overconfident and embarrassingly wrong when I walked into Dalton Wolfe's office and accused him of the crime, and it almost cost us our life in Bardo. But this time … this time I knew. This time I was sure. I grabbed my phone and made the call.

"You listen here," Mason Driscoll said by way of hello, "I've spoken to my attorneys, and if you so much as—"

"Shut up, Driscoll. You haven't spoken to your attorneys about anything."

The politician went quiet, the bluff he'd worked on since our last conversation crumbling the moment it left his lying mouth.

"I know who killed Ricky Lee," I told him, "and if you arrange a meeting tonight at the Bardo game, I'll give you all the notes that mention you."

"A meeting with who?" he asked.

I told him

"My God, are you sure?"

Sixty-five to seventy percent sure, I thought. "One hundred percent sure," I said.

Driscoll was quiet for a moment before asking, "How do you know they'll even agree to a meeting? What do you want me to say?"

"You've seen the news. Just make a bunch of promises you can't keep. That should come naturally enough."

Driscoll considered this. "If I do this for you, how do I know you'll give me the notes? How do I know you won't make copies and keep extorting me over and over again?"

"You won't know," I said. "You're going to have to take my word for it. But you can believe me when I say that when this is over, you are the last person I ever want to talk to again. So make the call."

Axl came home around three after the pep rally and stomped upstairs toward his room. I met him in the hallway, and he asked about my head.

"Fine," I said, though my headache had clawed its way back from whatever abyss the pill sent it to. "How was the pep rally?"

"Lame," he said, shaking his head. "Though three senior guys performed a pretty hilarious rendition of 'Single Ladies'."

"Leotards and everything?" I asked.

"Yep," Axl said, shaking his head trying to clear the mental image. "Oh, and Sophie said you came to her house yesterday."

Dammit, Sophie.

"Yeah, I was …"

The lie wouldn't come quickly enough, and Axl, to his credit, guessed my reason for visiting a girl I couldn't stand.

"Oh my God, Izzy, please tell me you're not still at it with the Ricky Lee shit. I've begged you not to piss off the Wolfe family. Can't you mind your own business?"

"Actually," I said, "you don't have to worry about Dalton Wolfe anymore. He's going to keep paying our tuition whether you win the state championship or never complete another pass."

"What are you talking about?"

"I sort of accused him of murdering Ricky Lee at his Columbus Day party," I said with an innocent shrug.

Axl's eyes widened in a mixture of fear and confusion, and he took an aggressive step toward me. "Tell me you're joking."

"I was wrong," I said, "he didn't murder Ricky. But he is a piece of shit, and I'm blackmailing him into keeping us in Bardo."

I'd thought the assurance Dalton Wolfe would let us stay in Bardo, whether he played well or not, would comfort my brother. I thought wrong.

Axl punched the wall in anger. "Holy shit, Izzy," he said, his muscles contracting so hard he was shaking, "you can't blackmail Dalton Wolfe. He has cops and judges, and God knows who else in his pocket."

"Doesn't matter," I said. "I've got him where I want him."

"Oh, sure, he's just going to sit back and let some stupid high school kid play him for a fool. I bet he can't sleep at night without dreaming of how he's going to get you back. You've fucked us, Izzy. He's taking you down, and we're all going with you. God, how could you be so selfish?"

"Selfish? What are you talking about? A boy was murdered. A poor boy like you."

"Come on, Izzy, you—"

"Dalton Wolfe used him like he's using you, and this awful town chewed him up and spit him out, and they'll do the same thing to us one day if we let them. How can you call me selfish? I'm fighting for Ricky Lee. I'm fighting for justice."

"The hell you are. You're just jealous of me."

"Yeah, right," I said, rolling my eyes.

"But you are," he said. "You've always thought you were so much

smarter than me. Smarter than Mom. You were going to make something of yourself, and then we'd have to crawl on our knees and beg
you to save us from the trailer park. It drove you crazy that you were
on scholarship because of me. That we're living in this house because
of me. You couldn't stand it that I saved our family," he yelled, hitting
himself in the chest, "and you've tried to sabotage everything since the
day you arrived. God, the minute things start going well for us you
alwyays go and screw it up."

He was right, of course. All my fantasies of escaping Pineview
Villas had a scene where I returned to rescue Mom, and sometimes
Axl, but not before letting them grovel. So, yeah, I was jealous of him,
not only that he'd been the one to get us out of Dandridge, but that
Mom had put her faith in him from the beginning, and not me. And I
was bitter they'd both been proven right, but not to the point of sabo-
taging our life in Bardo, at least not consciously.

"Whatever, Axl," I said, not giving him the pleasure of knowing
how close he had me pegged. "I wish you could hear how stupid you
sound,"

"And I wish you were never born," he yelled back before stomping
away, leaving me in tears.

I went downstairs a few minutes before six to wait on the porch for Blaine. I hadn't spoken to Mom much since she'd grounded me until Judgment Day, and I didn't particularly want to talk to her then. But she was on the couch, eating a frozen dinner when I walked through the living room.

"Hey, stranger," she said, toasting me with her Diet Coke.

"Hey, Mom."

She patted the couch for me to sit next to her, so I did. Setting her plate on the coffee table, she turned to me and took a deep breath. "Izzy, I know this is your last weekend with Blaine, but I don't want you doing anything stupid you'll regret."

"Oookay," I said, this conversation going in an entirely different direction than I'd anticipated.

"I'm just saying, I know you've got big plans for your life, and I can tell you from experience, those plans probably ain't gonna happen if you let this boy knock you up with twins."

"Mom, I'm not—"

She held up a finger. "Don't 'Mom' me. Rodney and I were about your age when we made Axl and you in the back of his Buick."

"Gross, Mom. Thanks for that visual."

"That car was gross," Mom said. "I don't think Rodney vacuumed it once in all the time I knew him."

I shook my head at her and laughed despite myself. "You don't have to worry. I'm breaking up with Blaine tonight."

"Before the homecoming dance?"

I shook my head and tried not to cry. All afternoon I'd toyed with the idea but hadn't made my mind up until I heard the words leave my lips. I didn't want to break up with Blaine, but I knew what was coming, and in the end, we'd both need the closure. "It's for the best," I said.

Mom shrugged. "Well, I know you're sad, but think of it this way, some poor girl will end up with his daddy for a father-in-law, but it won't be you."

I smiled, actually comforted by the thought, and Mom said, "Of course, your daddy's momma once told me I wasn't worth the shit on her shoes, so maybe all in-laws are terrible in their own way." Mom chuckled to herself and added, "You don't know how many times I've had to pray for forgiveness for all the diseases I wished on that woman."

I laughed and stood to leave, but Mom said, "Hold on, I've got to tell you something." She put her arm around me and said, "I ain't really mad at you for busting up that trophy case."

"You're not?"

Mom shook her head. "I did worse things than that every week when I was your age."

I laughed. "Anything you'd care to share?"

"Nope. Don't want to give you any ideas."

"So … I'm not grounded?" I asked with a smile.

"Oh, no, you're still grounded forever. But I ain't mad." She squeezed me and said, "Izzy, I don't tell you this enough, but I'm proud of you."

"Thanks," I said, blushing.

"Well, I am. I know how smart you are. I see how hard you work in school. And look, I know you've always wanted more than I could ever provide. You deserve more, and one day you'll get it."

A single tear fell from her cheek, and it took everything I had to keep from bawling.

"It's funny. I don't think I've worried about you once since second grade. Mature. That's what your teachers always called you. They'd say, 'Mrs. Brown, Izzy sure is mature. She's like having a little grown-up in class.' You had to grow up a lot sooner than most children. You took on a lot of responsibility when you probably just wanted to be a kid, and I don't think I'll ever be able to repay you."

"Mom, it's nothing. I did what anyone else would do."

"Oh, you think Axl ever washed a dish or swept a floor. That boy, he's got talent, but he ain't got your work ethic. Your daddy had talent too. Played guitar, and he could sing like an angel. I don't guess I ever told you that."

I shook my head but now knew why Axl and I would occasionally find guitar picks in the couch cushions.

"Rodney was smart as a whip too," Mom said, "but I don't think a lazier man ever existed. Then he got messed up with drinking and pills, and, well, you know the rest of that story. You've got his brains, Izzy, but you've got my drive, and that's why I ain't ever had to worry about you. You're gonna make something of yourself. I just know it. I tried for you kids. I hope you know how hard I tried. And still, I didn't think we'd make it, but I guess we did," she said, gesturing at the living room.

"We did," I said, hugging her one more time as Blaine's headlights shone through our windows.

"Now go on," she said, wiping her eyes and shooing me away. "I'll see you at the game."

<p style="text-align:center">~~~~~~</p>

Blaine was quiet on our drive to the stadium, which gave me time to think, but not enough. Exposing Ricky Lee's killer was absolutely the right thing to do, but it was going to cost us everything. Even if Dalton Wolfe wanted us to stay, the rest of Bardo would chase us out of town with pitchforks after I dug up their skeletons. Why couldn't I mind my own business, I wondered. Life would be so much simpler if I could.

"I've been thinking," Blaine said as we pulled into the stadium parking lot at school and he turned down the Vampire Weekend song he'd been blasting so we wouldn't have to talk.

"Me too," I said, reaching for his hand.

He squeezed my hand and let go. "Izzy, I think we need to break up."

"Wait, what?" I said, blindsided.

"Romantically speaking, we're doomed," he said. "I don't know if this makes sense, but I don't think I could stand going to the dance with you tomorrow night. It will either be awful and depressing, or it will be the best night ever, which would, in turn, make it awful and depressing."

"No, that makes sense," I said. I was relieved I didn't have to break up with him, but getting dumped stung, and I couldn't fight back my tears.

"I'm sorry," he said, now crying too. "I'm sorry for everything."

I grabbed him by the face and kissed him hard, our tears mixing together and falling as one before we pulled away at the same time.

"I'm going to—"

"I think I'll just—"

"You first."

"I don't think I'm going to stay for the game," Blaine said. "Can you get a ride home?"

I nodded, my lips quivering as I fought back a fresh round of tears. We kissed goodbye, making promises about emails and texts from Montenegro, then I was standing in the parking lot, talking to him through his open window.

"Whatever happens," he said, "know I love you, okay?"

"I love you too," I said before kissing him one last time and watching him drive away

The teams were on the field warming up when I entered the stadium in a daze, marching band drums and the smell of concession stand popcorn filling the air. Blaine and I had done the right thing, but the end was a gut punch, and I wasn't taking it well. Stumbling through the crowd, I made my way up to the press box to find Elton. The door was open, so I stepped inside and saw him and Archie sitting in front of a bank of computer monitors operating the video board.

"Elton," I said from the doorway, and he turned to me wide-eyed.

"You cannot be in here!" Elton shouted.

"I just need to give you—"

"She cannot be in here," Elton shouted at Archie.

"Greetings, Izzy," Archie said, waving.

"Hey, Archie," I said back.

"You cannot be in here. She cannot be in here," Elton continued, growing more agitated by the moment.

Archie tried to reason with him, but he'd lost it, so I stepped out of the press box to keep the scene from escalating.

"Apologies, fair Izzy," Archie said, following me outside and bowing for some reason. "I do not have an issue with visitors, but technically, you are not allowed in the press box, and Elton Jones-Davies—"

"Follows the rules," I said, and Archie nodded.

"It's okay," I said, handing him the note I'd written. "But will you please give this to him and make sure he reads it? He's mad at me, and he'll probably fight you on it, so tell him it's been notarized, and he's legally required to open it."

"Yes, ma'am," Archie said with a dramatic salute. "I will insist he reads it forthwith."

I hoped so. My life might depend on it.

1983

Her Majesty was well aware.

Well aware, if word got out that her boyfriend had cheated on her with another boy, she'd be ruined forever. Uncharacteristically, her first inclination was to run. She called her father, Conrad, and begged him to let her move to Texas and live with him and his skank of a third wife. He said no.

"Katydid, there's not the first thing for you out here," Conrad told her. "Just because you watch *Dallas* don't mean you'd like living in Bumfuck, Texas."

Her Majesty's father was right. She spent two weeks with him every summer but always at his condo in Houston. He'd take her to baseball games in the Astrodome, movies, concerts, and shows. It was non-stop stimulation provided by a man who confused this with parenting. Odessa wasn't Houston, but still, Her Majesty was willing to risk it.

Her life in Bardo was over if people found out.

And Bardo was small.

People always found out.

"Katydid, I send more money than y'all can spend, and I bought y'all that big-ass house on the prettiest stretch of white sand in Florida. If you can't be happy there, I'm worried about you."

"I guess Mom is easier to please than I am," Her Majesty replied.

"I seriously doubt it," her father mumbled.

After five rocky years of marriage, Her Majesty's parents divorced when she was two. She could not remember when they lived under the same roof, so she could not say for sure which party shouldered most of the blame for their failed marriage. But she could make an educated guess.

"Marry the richest and most powerful man you can," Her Majesty's mother told her weekly. "If you're happy together, great. If not, you'll leave with half his money, and then you'll be happy."

"But you're miserable," Her Majesty would argue.

"No, I'm not," her mother would say, finishing her Chardonnay breakfast.

Whatever.

Her father tried to convince her of the bright side. "Listen, Katydid, I know your mama is hard to live with. But you graduate in May, then you'll go off to college."

But not far off. Preston, Her Majesty's older brother, had gone to Duke, went buck wild, and was expelled his first semester for sexually assaulting a gargoyle. Now, both parents, in an unprecedented show of solidarity, agreed Her Majesty shouldn't go off too far for college, lest she also tarnish the family name. Thanks to that idiot Preston, Her Majesty would attend Florida State with the rest of the mouth breathers from Bardo Academy.

"Just for a semester or two," her father promised, "until we know we can trust you."

"Can't you look at me and know I wouldn't molest a gargoyle?" Her Majesty argued, and her father stifled a laugh, but he wouldn't relent.

"Now shoot straight with me, Katydid. Why the sudden interest in living in west Texas? Boy trouble?"

"You could say that," she said.

Her Majesty had no clue what Tommy Park wanted the day he showed up at her house in his ridiculous Michael Jackson jacket. He stuttered and stammered through several minutes of small talk, and for a moment, she thought he was there to ask her out. He'd had a painfully obvious crush on her since kindergarten. Tommy was the wealthiest kid in Bardo, so her mother would approve, but gross, no thanks. He was working up to something, though, and when Her Majesty tried to cut their conversation short, he got to the point and handed her a photograph.

"Is this a joke?"

"Where did you get this?"

"Who knows about it?"

"No. I took it. Just us," Tommy answered. "I thought … I thought you'd want to know."

Her Majesty snatched the photograph and retreated into her castle. And now that her father had nixed her escape plan, she fumed. That Ricky Lee would cheat on her was infuriating enough, but cheating on her with Junior Wolfe, my God, she'd never felt rage like this. She'd done that poor Cowden trailer trash a favor by dating him, and this is how he repaid her? Her Majesty began ripping up photographs of Ricky and notes he'd written her, just the thought of his stupid face flushing her skin to the brink of combustion. She didn't even like him, to be honest. He was painfully dull, and the sex was like something out of a health class film.

The French had a term for insulting the monarch, lèse-majesté, and those who committed it soon found themselves headless.

Katherine Ewing knew classmates referred to her as Her Majesty, but she didn't mind. She didn't mind because she *was* the Queen.

And no one insulted the queen and lived to tell.

CHAPTER FORTY-ONE

As Milton kicked off to start the game, I slipped across campus, entered Bardo Academy, and tiptoed through the empty hallways. I felt oddly at ease alone in the school, perhaps because I'd felt alone there even surrounded by classmates. It seemed strange to me now that Blaine never bothered to introduce me to his other friends, and I began to formulate a theory that he was embarrassed by me. I didn't exactly believe my theory, but I wanted to be angry at him and this was the best I could come up with on short notice.

The *Bardo Breeze* newsroom was dark, and I flipped on the lights, but no one was waiting. Shit. Had Driscoll even made the call? Had my trap been too obvious? I walked to the back of the room and sat in the cubicle where Elton and I worked. On the desk was the final draft of his state championship story. I smiled when I saw he'd added my name to the byline, even though I'd hindered his work more than I'd helped. I knew then he'd forgiven me. I just prayed he'd read my note.

"Izzy, what aren't you at the game?"

Startled, I almost fell from my chair when Katherine Park entered the room.

She smiled and added, "You, of all people, should know better than to sneak around school after hours."

"But I didn't want to miss our meeting," I said, and her eyes narrowed. "Out of curiosity, what did Driscoll say to lure you here?"

"That he could persuade the feds to unfreeze some assets I'd like to withdraw before we move," Katherine Park said, shaking her head in disbelief. "So, you told him?"

I nodded.

Mrs. Park spit out a swear. "Who else knows?"

"Sophie Wolfe, and all Bardo soon enough."

Katherine Park stepped further into the room, and I cursed myself. I'd planned to have my back to the door, but already things weren't going as planned.

"You found something in Ricky's jacket that night, didn't you?" Mrs. Park asked.

I nodded. "I found the note you sent him. The note that lured him out to Topsail Hill after midnight so you could slit his throat."

Mrs. Park smiled. "I'm afraid you're mistaken, Izzy. Junior Wolfe sent that note."

"Someone signed it from Junior Wolfe. Well, from J-Wolfe, which is how Junior signed your yearbook. And it was nauseatingly romantic, the way Junior wrote to you. But Junior and Ricky didn't use their real names in notes, and they'd never, ever send each other lyrics to a Journey song. Ricky must have thought it was a joke, because they hated Journey almost as much as they hated you."

Katherine Park's face twitched, and I knew that last line hit close to home.

"I didn't know you dated Ricky Lee for a long time," I said, standing and facing her down the aisle of cubicles. "There were no photographs of you together in the yearbook, which makes sense. You were the editor. And not a soul in town wanted to talk to me about Ricky Lee. It's like they were afraid the killer would come for them next. But I read the notes you sent Ricky, signed with your cute little cat drawing. And when I saw how you signed Junior's yearbook the same way, I knew. You caught Ricky cheating on you with Junior, killed him in cold blood, and dumped his body in the Gulf."

Katherine Park clapped slowly, her confident smirk leaving me uneasy. "Well done, Izzy Brown. The next Nellie Bly, indeed. You got one out of three correct—33 percent. Right on par with your standardized test scores, as I recall. It was Thomas who caught Junior and Ricky together in the woods."

"Off Powell Lake," I said.

"That's right," Mrs. Park said, with a point and a nod. "Thomas used to run around those woods pretending he was an ugly Indiana Jones. One day he stumbled upon my boyfriend making out with my ex-boyfriend. He snapped some photographs and brought them to me, probably hoping I'd dump Ricky and start dating him out of gratitude." Mrs. Park shivered at the thought of dating her husband.

"So Mr. Park caught Ricky and Junior," I said to myself, "and he told you?"

Mrs. Park nodded. "He handed me the photographs, and I ran to my room and pitched a holy fit. I broke mirrors and windows and my television. Believe it or not, it was the first time I'd ever felt the betrayal of something not going my way." She shook her head and smiled. "Izzy, I'm self-aware enough now to admit my parents spoiled me to the point of abuse. My classmates called me Her Majesty because I always got my way. Always. All these years later, I've learned to deal with life's disappointment better. But when I found out Ricky cheated on me, I don't believe I've ever been so angry."

"So angry you killed him and dumped his body in the Gulf."

"So angry I killed him, yes. But Thomas dumped the body. He'd have done anything I asked. Of course, that fool didn't sail out far enough. He was always scared of the open water, even more so at night." She rolled her eyes. "If he'd sailed out a little farther, no one would have ever found Ricky, but he didn't, and his body washed up a week later."

I blinked in disbelief. I'd done it. I'd solved Ricky Lee's murder. Found the killer and got her to confess and everything. But my elation was short-lived because there was no way Katherine Park would admit this to me and let me live. She planned to kill me too.

"Oh, Izzy," she said, "I'm afraid your inquisitiveness has crossed into the realm of meddlesome."

"You sent the note," I said.

"I did," Mrs. Park said, reaching into her purse. "I only wish you'd have taken my words to heart. Then perhaps we could have avoided all this unpleasantness." I watched in horror as she pulled a small pistol from her purse, just as Denham Frost picked a most inopportune time to drop by the newsroom in search of extra copies of the homecoming edition of the *Breeze*.

"Mrs. Park? Izzy? What are you—"

With gunslinger speed, Katherine Park spun and fired. I screamed as Denham Frost fell in a heap.

"Dammit, Izzy, now look what you've made me do," Mrs. Park said, looking down on my fallen classmate.

There was a moment's hesitation here, as if Mrs. Park had woken from a trance and now stared in regret at the carnage she'd wrought. I thought she might give herself up, I thought she might run, but instead, she smiled and turned her gun on me as her son's words rang in my ears.

I think you don't know my mother.

CHAPTER FORTY-TWO

My ears rang from the gunshot, but no one in the stadium could have heard it over the roar of the game. I was trapped, and no one was coming to my rescue.

"Two more days," Katherine Park said, slowly walking toward me with her weapon raised. "If you'd have waited two more days, I'd be gone, and you'd still be alive."

"Look," I said, with my hands in the air, "just because you're going to prison forever doesn't mean you have to kill me. I'll write. We could be pen pals."

"Oh, Izzy, you think I'm going to prison for killing Ricky Lee? That's cute. Jack Duncan thought the same thing. For such a dumb-looking man, he was a sharp knife. He interviewed me with my parents, Thomas with his, and then brought us all together and pointed out the several discrepancies in our stories. That's when our fathers took over. As you know, Thomas's father ran the bank, so he was well aware of the crushing debt Chief Duncan had accumulated through the years. My father, Conrad, owned half the oil fields in Texas, and he—"

"Conrad Ewing," I said. "C. E. Petroleum."

"Smart girl," Mrs. Park said, her pistol still leveled at my chest. "Our fathers made Jack Duncan a millionaire, and all he had to do was chalk up Ricky's murder to a drug deal gone wrong and stay the hell out of Florida. I didn't realize the fool had moved back until you told me that day in my office, so I had to reach out and gently remind him of our deal and what I'm capable of." She smiled, relishing whatever threat she'd made to Jack Duncan, then asked, "Are you familiar with Montenegro?"

I nodded.

"Little Montenegro, down on the Adriatic Sea," she said. "Amazing weather, a beautiful coastline, and the only European country without an extradition treaty with the United States. You see, Izzy, I didn't get in trouble then, and I won't get in trouble now. Blaine and I will leave tonight, but no one will find your skinny little body until first period Monday morning."

"Alternative plan," I said, "you tie me up, and no one finds me until Monday, but I'm just hungry, not dead.

Mrs. Park seemed to remember she held a gun and looked annoyed she'd have to use it again. "Izzy, why in God's name couldn't you mind your own business? Why did you even care what happened to Ricky Lee?"

"Because righting wrongs is what separates us from the animals."

"Wrong answer," Katherine Park said, aiming slightly higher.

"Because I saw the way this town treats poor kids like Axl and me. Poor kids like Ricky Lee. You use us and toss us out like trash."

"What about your friend Elton's father? Did Bardo toss him out like trash? Or the dozens of scholarship recipients who've gone on to earn master's degrees and doctorates? Did Bardo chew them up too? You see, Izzy, unlike Thomas, I can differentiate between poor people and trash. Most poor people, when presented with an opportunity, will flourish. But trash, like your family, will throw away every chance they get. Not all poor people are trash, but all trash end up poor. Morally, if not financially. Just look at you and your brother, rewarded scholarships to the finest high school on the Gulf Coast, and within three months, you're both hooked on drugs. Yes, Izzy, I know about the drugs. So, let's stop pretending you were on some gallant crusade. You don't care about Ricky Lee. You don't care about anyone but yourself. You wanted to become a famous journalist and never look back, but you're trash, Izzy, and trash always returns to the dump. Now, if you'll excuse me, my son and I have a plane to catch."

"Oh my God, you're literally insane," I yelled. "You honestly think Blaine will want to live with you and his dad when he finds out what you did?"

"First of all, neither Blaine nor I will ever have to put up with his father again. That's one body they'll never find, because, unlike Thomas, I'm not scared to sail on the open sea."

"You killed Mr. Park?"

"Free at last," Mrs. Park said, taking a deep, triumphant breath. "Of course, America looks poised to elect a Black man president in a couple weeks, which would have surely sent my husband to an early grave had I not."

I shook my head in disbelief while Mrs. Park cackled at her own joke.

"It was our fathers' idea for us to marry so young," Mrs. Park said. "We knew each other's secrets, and no one could force us to testify against one another. It wasn't, as you witnessed, a fairytale marriage. But I was rich. I was Queen of Bardo, and Thomas never minded sharing his bed with a pool boy or two."

My face scrunched in disgust, but Mrs. Park just laughed. "Thomas," she said, looking skyward as if trying to recall her late husband. "Thomas had a conscience. He never got over what we did to Ricky, and he tried to make up for it by never saying no to Junior Wolfe." She shook her head. "The loans he gave that man. Thomas might as well have given him the key to the safe. Not to mention the reckless expansion and no-bid contracts Thomas approved just to put money in Junior's pocket. But, perhaps there was a method to my late husband's madness. Even if Junior suspected something, he wouldn't have risked outing us and cutting off his access to endless cash."

I recalled my late-night conversation with Junior Wolfe on Bardo Beach. He had suspicions but admitted he'd been too much of a coward to do anything about it. *It would have cost me too much.* It would have cost him, but his silence cost him so much more.

"Still," Katherine Park continued, "in less than a decade, my husband ran a seventy-five-year-old financial institution into the ground. And now, with the feds looking into every corner of our lives, I knew Thomas would crack. So, he had to go."

"And you don't think Blaine will care when he learns—"

"I'll tell you what my son cares about. Money. He wanted to be an elementary school teacher, but he was going to go into medicine.

Why? Because Thomas threatened to cut him off if he didn't. Izzy, I knew this day would come. I've stashed away money in Europe for years. We'll be rich, and Blaine will love me just like he always has."

"You're wrong. Blaine isn't—" I couldn't even finish my thought because I knew she was right about Blaine. He'd told me as much, but I'd always chosen to ignore it.

"Enough of this," Katherine Park said. "You don't have to worry about Blaine anymore." She closed one eye and aimed her pistol. "In fact, you don't have to worry about anything ever again."

I suspect there was some battle going on between the angel and demon residing on Elton's shoulders after he opened the note I'd sent him. Since being entrusted with Bardo Academy's high-definition video scoreboard, he and Archie had gone seven straight games without the slightest hiccup. The score, down and distance, and timeouts remaining were always correct, and the slow-motion replays were perfectly timed, never to interfere with the live action. I imagine he pulled up the security camera feed from the *Breeze* newsroom and watched it on one of his monitors, the argument in his head driving him mad. What I'd asked him to do wasn't a crime, but it had cost his predecessor his job and would likely cost Elton his. But then he watched in horror as Mrs. Park shot Denham Frost, and he sprang to action. With the press of a button, Mrs. Park and I appeared on the scoreboard, and the football game ground to a halt as fans, players, and referees stopped to watch.

"Oh, Izzy, you think I'm going to prison for killing Ricky Lee?"

Mrs. Park said. "That's cute. Jack Duncan thought I'd go to prison too. For such a dumb-looking man, he was a sharp knife."

"Is that Katherine Park?"

"Oh my God, she's got a gun!"

"What room are they in?"

"That's the *Breeze* newsroom!"

Policemen, teachers, and parents ran toward the school, but Elton was ahead of them. He'd taken off the moment he realized I was in trouble.

"In fact, you don't have to worry about anything ever again."

I found a strange comfort in Katherine Park's words. The last words I'd ever hear. She was right, I hoped. Wherever I was about to go, at least I'd have no worries.

Instinctively, I shielded my face with my hands and closed my eyes tight, so I didn't see what happened next, but News Channel 7 showed the security camera footage so often the following weeks, I felt like I'd watched the whole thing.

Elton, racing through Bardo Academy's halls at speeds not seen since his father ran wild in the 1983 state championship game. He slides into the newsroom, takes two giant steps, and leaps into a textbook perfect flying twin foot side kick. Katherine Park spins around just in time to see the soles of two size sixteen sneakers as they leave Nike logos imprinted on her face, knocking her out stone cold. It's funny, Elton told me he took Tae Kwon Do a dozen times, but until he went all Bruce Lee on Mrs. Park, I never truly believed him.

I open my eyes to see Elton, his mouth agape, staring down at Mrs. Park in disbelief.

"The student handbook classifies fighting as a type II infraction, punishable by up to three days' suspension," he said, looking at me with genuine fear in his eyes. "Izzy, will they suspend me for this?"

I burst into tears and ran across the room, wrapping my arms around him tight.

"No, you donkey. They're going to throw you a parade."

Elton smiled, and for once, he hugged me back.

CHAPTER FORTY-THREE

Naturally, officials postponed Bardo Academy's game against Milton until Saturday. Dazed by what they'd just witnessed, players, parents, and students milled about the stadium for the next couple of hours while police cars and ambulances came and went. Denham Frost was okay. Well, she still sucked, but she didn't die. The bullet entered just below her collar bone and passed through without nicking any vital organs. Mrs. Park was transported by ambulance to Sacred Heart Hospital with a severe concussion and a broken nose. Doctors released her later that evening into police custody, and she was charged with the murders of Ricky Lee and Thomas B. Park III. Murders she'd unknowingly already confessed to on the high-definition scoreboard.

After Elton and I spoke at length to several Walton County sheriff's deputies about all we'd been up to that fall, his mother asked my mother if she could take us for ice cream. I was still pretty shaken up, but being with Elton helped, and Mom waived my eternal grounding for the night. Around ten, they drove me home, only to find several Bardo police cars waiting in my driveway.

"Mom," I shouted, bursting through the front door. "Mom, are you okay?"

As always, I feared things had gone south with Lenny. But I found her sitting at our breakfast table, talking to an officer, and looking okay but exhausted. When she glanced up and saw me, she closed her eyes and shook her head.

Another cop was going through our kitchen cabinets, and I heard more footsteps upstairs. "Mom," I asked across the room, "what is going on?" But she just burst into tears and dropped her head into her hands.

Just then, another Bardo policeman stomped down the steps holding a clear bag containing the bottle of pills Blaine gave me. Realizing what was happening, I turned in a panic. I think I planned to jump into the Gulf and swim to Cuba, but several more cops blocked my way. "Izzy Brown," a big fat one with crumbs in his bushy mustache said, "you are under arrest for unlawful possession of a controlled substance."

He slapped his handcuffs on me tight, explained my rights, and with a heavy hand, led me out of the house to the backseat of a patrol car parked in the driveway. I burst into tears before he even slammed the door, and I was still crying five minutes later when Dalton Wolfe slipped into the back seat next to me.

"Well, I'll be damned," Dalton Wolfe drawled, his giant presence in the car making me claustrophobic. "Remind me, girl, weren't you in my office a few weeks ago talking a whole lot of shit? Now look at you, under arrest."

I kept staring out the window, praying he'd leave, but he didn't.

"Yes, ma'am. You were gonna tell your uncle at the *Observer* all about Junior and Ricky if I didn't keep paying your tuition. You do know I own the *Observer*, don't you?" He laughed. "You think you're the first person to ever try and blackmail me? Good God, somebody tries it once a month. You don't get as rich as me without stepping on some toes."

"What do you want?" I snarled, but I couldn't face him.

"To gloat, mostly. I'll admit it, you had me over a barrel with those notes you found. Last thing I wanted was for folks to find out about Junior and Ricky. But after thinking about it a little, I came to the conclusion that folks already knew Junior was messed up in the head. He killed himself, for crying out loud. Years ago, it might have mattered to me more, but now I'm seventy-three and richer than Croesus. What the hell should I care what anybody thinks anyhow? That's when I turned my attention to revenge. I needed the goods on you, and, as luck would have it, I got a call from a classmate of yours just this morning letting me know all about your little pill problem."

"Who?"

"Just think a minute. Who do you know that's had money all their life but was about to lose it?"

"Sophie?" God, I never should have told her.

Dalton Wolfe shook his head. "No, not Sophie. What do you think I am, an animal? I'm gonna take care of my own granddaughter, even if her daddy was garbage. Now keep thinking, you'll get there soon enough, and it's gonna sting."

Who could actually live on a teacher's salary anyway?

Run away? And just be poor?

I'll tell you what my son cares about. Money.

"Blaine," I said, closing my eyes and thinking back to the last thing he ever said to me. *Whatever happens, know I love you.* The bastard, he'd already set it all in motion.

"Yes, ma'am. Good old Blaine Park called me this morning, and we cut ourselves a little deal. Pretty sorry of him, turning on his girl-friend like that, but folks do get desperate when they're about to lose it all. That's when those of us who don't panic reap the rewards."

Junior Wolfe once told my brother anyone can make money during a real estate boom, but only the best of the best can do it when the market is down. "It only hurts people who panic," he'd said. He was right, of course, apart from the insinuation he was the best of the best. But his father was. A quick search of Florida public records shows just how many properties Dalton Wolfe snatched up in the fall of 2008 and beyond. When the sky starts to fall, the rich go outside with buckets.

A policeman walked by and tapped on the window, and Dalton gave him a thumbs-up while Axl's lecture about Mr. Wolfe having cops and judges in his pocket echoed in my brain. "All right, girl," he said, slapping the seat between us, "you have yourself a nice life."

"I'll tell," I said as he opened the door to climb out. "I'll tell every newspaper in Florida you gave Axl that car and his phone, and you put us up in the house." Threatening to get Florida State into trouble wasn't much, but it was all I had left.

"Knock yourself out," Dalton Wolfe said. "You're a felon and drug-gie. Ain't nobody gonna believe a word you say anyhow." He turned to leave but couldn't resist one more jab, so he leaned back inside the patrol car and added, "And so you know, I fired your momma's ass and told her and your brother they can take their white trash selves on back to Washington County where they belong."

"Fuck you."

"Now, that ain't no way for a lady to talk," Dalton Wolfe said, slapping a cop on the back as he walked by. "You enjoy prison, you hear. I hope you get yourself clean in there."

Then he slammed the door and stomped away.

CHAPTER FORTY-FOUR

I didn't go to prison. Dalton Wolfe was powerful, but even he couldn't have a sixteen-year-old girl locked away just for possessing three little pills. However, I did spend a couple of the most humiliating nights of my life in the Okaloosa Juvenile Detention Center, complete with a strip-search conducted by a woman named Marge, who still haunts my dreams. On Monday, deputies transported me back to Walton County to appear before a judge. As I waited in the holding area for my court-appointed attorney, a familiar face waddled in.

"You sure pissed off the wrong folks," Tanner Cobb said by way of hello.

I blinked at him and quickly shook my head. The man was typically underdressed for a luau, but today he wore a dark gray suit and had somehow wrangled his unmanageable hair into a respectable pompadour.

"What?" he asked, popping his jacket lapels. "Didn't think I could clean up when I have to?"

"What are you doing here?" I asked.

"You put me on retainer," he said, and I smiled weakly. "I heard what went down Friday night at the game. So, it was the oil baron's daughter all along?"

I nodded. "Also known as my boyfriend's mother."

"Ouch," he said, making a pained face. "Well, that's some damn fine investigative work by you and Stretch, and it's bullshit they've kept you this long. When we get in there with the judge, you let me do the talking, and I'll have you out of here in no time." And he did, without a blemish on my record, after agreeing to six weeks of after-school drug counseling.

Mom met us in the parking lot and thanked Tanner for his help.

"Mr. Cobb, what do we owe you?"

He waved my mother off. "Pro bono," he said, then winked at me and added, "that's Latin for free."

Mom thanked him again, flashed me the same disappointed look she'd give me every day for the next several weeks, and went to wait in the car.

"Thank you, again," I said, bumping fists with Tanner Cobb, who'd already taken off his coat and looked itching to lose his shirt.

"My pleasure," he said. "So, are we even now? Or do you plan to keep me on retainer ad infinitum? That's Latin for a long-ass time."

"I release you from my service," I said, grinning.

"And that note we sent Ricky?"

"It's gone. I burned it the day we left your office. You were a stupid kid, but you're a good man, and wherever Ricky is now, he knows you helped set things right in the end."

Tanner Cobb bit his lip and rubbed away a tear. "Alright, Pippi Longstocking," he said, "you come by and say hello next time you're in

Cowden." Then he waddled across the parking lot to his truck, unbuttoning his shirt as he went.

After barely two months in Bardo by the Sea, we were back in Dandridge, naturally. Mom found a three-bedroom apartment at a complex called, get this, Pineview Château, and Axl and I re-enrolled at our old school, but he wasn't eligible to play football and lost the remainder of his sophomore season, something he angrily reminded me of whenever he talked to me at all. Several private schools had already reached out with scholarship offers for his junior year, but there wasn't much chance they'd take me too. I couldn't blame them.

I never heard from Blaine again. Of course, the Bardo police kept my phone and probably gave it back to Dalton Wolfe, so he had no way of calling, even if he wanted to, which he wouldn't, and I wouldn't answer if he did. There are bad breakups, and there are breakups where you get your boyfriend's mother arrested, and he gets you arrested in turn. I suspect he learned from Sophie that I was blackmailing Dalton Wolfe, presenting him with the opportunity to sell out his girlfriend in exchange for the one thing he cared about. I hope he at least struggled with the decision. As for me, I still have sweet memories of the boy but can only view them through the prism of our Shakespearean breakup. Still, I cried when the passport Blaine talked me into applying for arrived in the mail, overcome by what could have been.

The rest of the fall, Axl, Mom, and I co-existed more than lived together. We were no more than roommates brought together by a shared need for shelter. Apart from general banalities about the quality of each other's days, we hardly spoke to one another, which at least kept us from fighting over who bore the lion's share of responsibility for our unceremonious exit from Bardo, something they both agreed on. I missed them both, but particularly Axl. I missed aggravating him as my sisterly duties required. I missed him teasing me about my love life, or lack thereof. I even missed fighting with him, because at least then he acknowledged my existence. I wondered if he was still taking pills, or if he'd quit them as easily as he'd started. Everything else came easy to him, so I hoped so. But he never wanted to talk about it, or anything else. Soon, I went back to work at Stanton's, partly for the money, but mostly for an excuse to leave that unbearably quiet apartment. I spent the rest of my free time at the Dandridge library, prepping for the damned ACT.

Like a stray dog, Lenny Roach wandered back up in mid-November after making sure my legal troubles would not somehow become his legal troubles. Soon he was once again a permanent fixture on our couch, and one night he knocked on my bedroom door.

"You could have sold me out to the cops that night," Lenny said, standing next to my bed while I did homework.

It crossed my mind, I thought. "The cops were there for me," I said.

"Sure, but in my line of work, when people go down, sometimes they try and take everyone else with them. But you didn't, and I appreciate that."

"Yeah, no problem, Lenny."

"For those headaches," he said, handing me a bottle twice as heavy as the one Blaine gave me.

My short time in juvie was awful. Without my daily jolt of oxycodone, I spent what should have been the night of my homecoming date night with Blaine sweating and crying in the fetal position. But weeks after taking my last pill, my body had adjusted to life without opioids, and I was back to normal. Of course, normal for me meant a couple debilitating migraines a week coupled with the occasional sense of impending doom. I should have tossed the pills in the garbage. I should have driven them to the shore and thrown them in the ocean. But I thanked Lenny and put them in my nightstand drawer instead.

I hadn't spoken to Elton since the night he saved my life, and without his number, I had no way of reaching him either. I suspected his mother was understandably concerned that her son was running around with a pill head and that she'd forbade him from ever contacting me again. But one day, over Christmas break, the two of them showed up at our apartment.

"Holiday Greetings," Elton said when I answered the door.

"Elton!" I squealed, giving him a bear hug he stoically tolerated, then I tried to shake his mother's hand, but she hugged me too. "I've missed you so much," I said, punching Elton's arm. "How's school? You dating anyone?"

"I'm not allowed to—" He stopped mid-sentence and smiled at me.

"I pulled Elton from Bardo Academy soon after you left," Holly Jones-Davies said. "Seems most of the parents did not appreciate the poor publicity Bardo received, and their children began taking it out on Elton."

"Oh, Elton," I said, covering my mouth, "I'm so sorry."

"Don't be," his mother said. "You two did the right thing. I was proud of you both."

"So, are y'all moving to Dandridge?" I asked with a smile, just as a neighbor drove by in his bullet-riddled truck blasting Lynyrd Skynyrd.

Elton shook his head violently, and his mother smiled and said, "No, but I've spoken to Terrance, and we're moving back to England. Elton doesn't have many mates at school, and I cannot live in that town a minute longer."

"Mother has enrolled me in St. Beckham's School for Boys. Girls attend there too. They just never changed the name."

I laughed to keep from crying and gave Elton another hug. "I'm going to miss you so much."

"Actually, Izzy, that's why we're here," Elton's mother said. "You were a good friend to my son—the best friend he's ever had. I know how bright you are, but I'm worried about the path you're on. That's why Elton and I both thought it would be great if you'd consider coming with us."

"To England?"

They both nodded, and I laughed out loud. "Mrs. Jones-Davies, we could never afford to—"

"Izzy, I'm married to Mustang Jones. You wouldn't have to pay for anything."

I shook with excitement. "I don't … I don't know what my mother would say."

"That's what we're here to find out," Elton's mother said, walking past me into our apartment. Elton and I followed, my traitorous mind already flooded with false hopes of rainy walks down cobblestone streets, foggy rides on double-decker buses, and marrying Prince Harry. It was silly, getting my hopes up and planning for such an unlikely future. But what are plans if not wishful thinking?

EPILOGUE

Ricky Lee is immortal.

Today, a larger-than-life statue of the quarterback stands outside Dalton C. Wolfe Stadium. A plaque at the statue's base lists Ricky's gridiron accomplishments and records but makes no mention of his life or death. Nevertheless, a Bardo Academy student wrapped a rainbow scarf around Ricky's neck in 2015, the day same-sex marriage became legal in Florida. Yes, Bardo by the Sea has changed some since I left. But not that much.

Driscoll for Senate signs sprout like weeds every six years.

Minorities at Bardo Academy are still rarer than unbroken sand dollars.

And Saint Anastasia continues to pack its homophobic pews every Sunday.

But even so, the rainbow scarf remains around Ricky's neck to this day.

Of course, Dalton Wolfe would have vehemently objected to the statue and the scarf had he not died of a massive heart attack during half-time of Florida State's 2013 national championship game. Tanner Cobb emailed me to say he heard Ella Kay found Dalton slumped over on his golden toilet with a *Playboy* still in his hand. I should know better than to trust Tanner's courthouse rumors, but this one carries a whiff of truth.

Katherine Park is currently serving a life sentence at the Lowell Correctional Institution north of Ocala. In a 2018 episode of *Snapped*, fellow inmates revealed she runs the prison library with an iron fist, and they refer to her as Her Majesty behind her back.

In 2017, a wealthy animal lover from California purchased Mulligan Shores, also known as Nowhere, and turned the property into a wildlife preserve. Now twenty-seven descendants of the Florida black bear that ate Perry Harkins roam the woods where Blaine and I once made out. Down on the coast, two dozen three-story pastel homes now fill the once empty lots of Tartarus Shores. Happy families live there or pay a small fortune to rent them for a week at a time in the summer. The for sale signs featuring Junior Wolfe's smiling face, like Junior himself, are long gone, and most residents don't even know about the murdered boy who washed up near their beach all those years ago. Occasionally, a concerned buyer will broach the sensitive subject with their realtor after learning about Ricky through a Google search, only to have their fears relieved in the hushest of tones.

That was decades ago, the realtor will say.

Nothing like that could happen around here now.

We've got a gate to keep that stuff out.

Buddhists believe between death and rebirth, a person spends forty-nine days in the bardo. That I attended Bardo Academy for forty-nine days was just a coincidence, probably. Even so, I left Bardo a new person. Sure, I still had migraines and anxiety. I was painfully single again, and thanks to my arrest, I was somehow even further away from a college scholarship than when I arrived. But I now had a purpose—a reason to wake up in the morning. Bringing Katherine Park to justice sparked a fire in me, and I vowed to keep sticking my freckled little nose where it didn't belong. I would keep crossing that line from inquisitive to meddlesome and be a general pain in the ass to anyone hiding the truth. I couldn't wait for the next case.

Ricky Lee could rest in peace, but my work had just begun.

THE END

Izzy and Elton will return in
GRAVES UPON BONES
Fall 2022

For updates visit www.chadalangibbs.com

ACKNOWLEDGEMENTS

One night while reading an early draft of this book, my wife, Tricia, burst out laughing so hard I had no choice but to conclude that I was a comic genius. Turns out she was laughing at a typo. However, I still must thank Tricia first for her endless encouragement, both deliberate and unintentional.

Thanks to my sons, Linus and Oliver, for insisting I put down my laptop from time to time for a quick game of soccer or a Beyblade battle.

Thanks to my editor, Becky Philpott, who for fifteen years has kept my readers blissfully unaware of my grammatical and spelling insufficiencies.

Thanks to my sensitivity reader, Hannah Givens, and to everyone who read early drafts of this book, including my amazing niece Ava Dorminey, my Disney World panic attack pal Shay Baugh, my mother-in-law Karen Day, and my sister-in-law and brother-in-law Lori and Johnny Dorminey. Also, thanks to my friend Philip Justiss for his insights into the insanity that was the 2008 Florida real estate scene.

And finally, thank you to my readers. I hope you enjoy reading about Izzy and Elton as much as I enjoy writing them and that you're excited to go on this journey together.